Driving Nowhere

By

Craig McCabe

First published by Authorhouse UK 2007

2nd Edition published by Trend 2008

Authors note:-

Before Driving Nowhere came about, I did not actually intend on writing a novel. It all started as a bit of fun by my retelling of certain happenings of what various customers had said or did each night that I was working in the taxi. To make sure that I did not forget a certain conversation, I decided to write it down. One night after my shift, I let someone read it. They laughed, and could not believe that what I had written had really happened. I then asked them, 'Now, if I had told you about this, instead of you reading it, would it still have been as funny?' To which they replied 'No, probably not.' Soon after, I had a small collection of scrap paper containing stories from my shifts on the taxi, to which I pieced together and added to the plot of Driving Nowhere.

Three novels later, I still did not see my-self as an author. To me an author was someone that had studied for his or her masters in English, or who worked for years on their novel to perfect it. Me, I wrote Driving Nowhere as a bit of fun and my second novel 'Youngsters' was written in six months. A year later, I started writing 'The Roadie' without even having a plot.

During my time (Five years, on and off) writing my forth novel 'A Sense of Loyalty' my head was slowly being filled with ideas for other plots, possibly enough to keep me writing for the next twenty to thirty years.

Although 'A Sense of Loyalty' is not a direct sequel to Driving Nowhere, there is a crossover with certain characters, which made me decide to go back and revise the story to make subtle changes so that there was more of a connection between them. The story is a little rough around the edges but I am still proud of it as this was my first piece of writing.

Thanks for reading and your continued support is very much appreciated

Craig Xx

Chapter 1

Shane

I have been on all day and this miserable looking bastard, who happens to be my next customer, is actually struggling to get his fat arse into the car. It is not that I have anything against fat people but if I was finding it hard to get in or out of a car I am quite sure I would do something about it. I can smell his foul body odour before he even shuts the door, a swift movement of the trigger finger on the window button should help. I have a strong air freshener, my window is open and yet stinky man here is still over-powering the smell. This is definitely my last fare of the day, I have had a text from Gaz saying that everyone is in the East View bar and that is more than enough encouragement for me to finish. As soon as I drop off stinky man here, I will be heading there for a well-deserved drink.

"Sorry eh have chest problems, gives me trouble breathing and that" He says once he is in and his breathing eventually settles down.

Yeah you are too fat. Lose some fucking weight. He now comes out with the classic line that I hear several times a day.

"So huv ye been busy then"

I do not want to answer him, as I am afraid if I open my mouth I will inhale his bad odour.

"It's not been too bad" I say as I veer my head towards the window.

I have a slight grin every time I answer this as I know this is everyone's ice breaker to let me know they want to talk but don't know what to talk to me about.

"So do ye like driving the taxis then?"

"It's like any job really. It gets to you after a while."

The bad part is having to picking up people like you, you smelly fucker.

"I don't like it because you have got to work all the unsociable hours, you know, the ones when everybody's out on the piss."

Total lies, I work whenever I feel like it, but I will go along with it and tell him what he wants to hear.

"You see that's the busy time when you make your money. Then there are the arsehole drunks that you have to put up with, also the junkies and the general moaning bastards" ...and the nosey fuckers like you fatso.

"Also if you don't work you don't get paid, as there's no holiday pay in this job, apart from all that it's okay, I mean it's better than signing on as a jobs a job, as long as it pays your bills right."

This must be too much information for him as he is not answering to that, or maybe he is searching his tiny mind for something else to ask me. When I first started on working the taxis, I would have said that this was the greatest fucking job in the world because all you do is sit on your arse and drive around all day. You work when you feel like it and there is no boss on your back all day telling you what to do. My job before this was in a factory, which was that bad the bastards timed me when I went to the toilet. The place had no windows so when it came to the winter; it was dark when I went in and dark when I came out. I only ever saw daylight at the weekends, and even then, I would be lucky to catch a few hours after being out most of the night.

"You're a bit young ta be on the taxis are ye no?"

And there it is, over two years on the taxis and at least once a week without fail somebody will ask me that, he must have thought long and hard to come up with that one. It is not so bad when it is a decent looking girl asking, but when it is someone like this, I feel that it is a bit patronizing. I remember one of my first fares on the taxi, a customer refused to get in the car as he thought I was a joy rider. I suppose it is a bit unusual to see such a young person driving a taxi, as most of them are usually fat, old baldy men. Most of the other drivers that I have come across are arrogant, moaning, two faced bastards. When they first started in this line of work they probably loved it just as I did, but over the years it has slowly but surely worn them down, due to my daily gripes I now feel as though I am morphing into them, minus the expanding waistline and bald head obviously. Sometimes if I am sitting behind another taxi on the rank, the customer will see me and walk past the car in front to get into mine. The other drivers hate this but there is nothing they can do about it. Don't get me wrong, they do get out of their car and shout to the customer that they are first in line for a pick up, but the customer usually just tells them to 'fuck off'. The other drivers act as if it is my fault and give the usual abusive hand signals, there is the occasional argument but nothing ever comes of it though as most of them are all mouth.

"Eh'll bet ye dae a lot oh shagging in this joab? All those young girls pretending that they don't have enough money for the fare."

He now starts to tell me some random story that another driver told him about a customer who offered him a blowjob instead of paying the fare. What the fuck is he all about? I usually get these questions from young people and have a laugh about it because they know the score but this smelly fucker must be at least in his fifties the dirty old bastard. He must be waiting on me telling him some filthy story so that he can go home and have a good wank about it. The thought makes me sick, or maybe it is just his body odour that is now starting to turn my stomach.

"Do you know what? The people that tell those stories are full of shit. If they are true, you can imagine what those fucking women look like if they are willing to lower themselves to do something like that."

He appears to be a bit disappointed at my answer, of course I do a lot of shagging, but I'll be fucked If I'm going to let this old pervert know the perks of my job. I arrive at his destination and I cannot get away quick enough and get to the pub, so that I can forget about all these sad depressing customers lives that I have had to endure today. As I speed off along the road, I forget to log my computer off and it beeps to give me another job. Out of habit, I press the button and accept the job. It is the train station. I tell myself that this is definitely the last one and drive off towards the centre of town. I have all the windows down to release the foul stench that the smelly fucker left behind but it appears to be lingering around. I get a little paranoid when I have another fare after someone like that has been in my car as I feel that the next customer thinks that the smell is coming from me. As I pull up at the train station there are several people waiting in the taxi queue but I notice a girl standing back from them with a holdall. She is small with dark hair and even from a distance I can tell she is pretty. I get out the car to shout the name while looking at the queue for confirmation from my customer and the dark haired girl acknowledges that she is my fare. I smile back but feel that this is not my usual fake smile that I reserve for all my other customers. She takes her holdall in the back with her and tells me her destination. I drive off but cannot help looking in the mirror at her. I am not usually one to be stuck for words but this girl is stunning, in a natural way.

"By the way if there's a horrible smell in the car it's not me, my last customer was a big fat smelly man."

She looks at me and smirks.

"Do you say that to everybody who gets into your car?" She says cheekily as I catch her smiling at me in the mirror.

"I can only smell your air freshener."

"Lucky you, I can still smell him."

"That's because the particles will still be up your nose. In-stead of trying to smell other things to get it away you'll have to blow your nose first."

"You are full of useful information aren't you?"

"I love that song, is that a C.D. or the radio?"

"C.D"

"Are you into Indie music?"

"I like a bit of everything really."

"Do you ever go to live gigs?"

"I go to T in the park."

"No I mean to see local bands."

"Not really, no."

"Here." She says handing me a flyer with a list of bands on it.

"What is this?"

"My friend organises bands to play at this pub. They are really good, you should come along."

"Thanks, maybe I will."

I look at the flyer. 'The Doghouse' and the first thing I think of is how am I ever going to persuade the guys to go there. Just as the conversation gets going I arrive at her destination. She hands me the fare with a few quid extra and tells me to keep it.

"Thanks."

"Hopefully I'll see you at the gig. Oh, if you do go and you are there early enough to catch the first band. Be prepared."

"Prepared for what?"

"The View, their fans could be a bit wild."

As she walks away I smile but think to myself that I don't know what the hell she is talking about. I turn to drive off and see a car full of evil looking wide-o's drive past and stare at me. I look back around to see the girl but she's gone. I switch off the computer and drive away in the direction of the pub. On the way I can't get the picture of the girl out of my head and feel quite stupid as I didn't even ask her name. I look in my mirror and she soon disappears from my mind as I see that the car of Wide-o's has doubled back and is now following me. I arrive at the East View and park the car a few streets away. It should be safe enough until the morning. As I walk towards the front of the pub the same car passes and slows down. I keep looking ahead and walk through the door without turning around.

Chapter 2

I don't know why this pub is called The East View as it doesn't actually have a view except to look onto an old derelict building and it isn't even in the East of the city. It is more in the middle. As soon as I walk through the doors I spy Gaz in the corner drooling in some girl's ear. Gaz is one of my closest friends and I have known him for most of my life. Sitting not too far from Gaz is Jamie, Kyle, Joey and Mickey. Jamie is my younger half-brother; he is only nineteen but has been hanging around with us for a few years now. He walks about thinking he's some sort of gangster and is constantly being put in his place by me or Gaz. Kyle is a mate whom I've got to know in recent years. He is very laid back and hates any sort of confrontation. Mickey is a funny guy who can handle himself but knows his limits. He is quite forward and not afraid to let you know what's on his mind. Joey is the tallest and looks as though he can handle himself but is more like a cuddly teddy bear. He is a student who works in the gym and gets us in for free. Since working there, we have all notice that he is bulking up and there is a constant piss take that he is on steroids, which he constantly denies. This is not an introduction to the company I keep, more of a subconscious way of me figuring out who will have my back after witnessing the Wide-o's that were following me in the car, enter the pub. I sit down next to Gaz and give him a nod in the direction of the doors at the far end of the pub. He leans in closer to me.

"What's going on?"

"I think something is about to kick off. Those guys who have just walked in, they've been following me since I dropped off my last fare."

Gaz looks over at the group. There is one who has his stare fixed on me and he seems very familiar. He has the stereo typical hard man features with the shaved head, the stocky build where it looks like he has no neck and the deep slanted eyes with not much going on behind them.

"That's Murdo. He'll no dae anything if he kens yer we me."

The thing about Gaz, and this is something that the rest of the group here do not know, is that Gaz is drug dealer, and due to the amount of dodgy acquaintances in his circle, I can always count on him to know someone that knows someone to sort shit out. Gaz is a couple of years older than me and very wise for his age, he lived across the road from me with his Gran and Grandad, Kate and Big Danny when we were growing up and for someone who was thrown out of school at an early age with no qualifications, he is one of the most intelligent people I know…well except from Big Danny. Gaz is the type of person who watches Countdown and does better than the contestants. It is really funny when he watches it with Big Danny as they continue to rattle out these unusually long words that nobody in their right mind would think of. One of Gaz's favourite saying's is that you can get by with a little knowledge as long as you have a lot of common sense as common sense can be disguised as knowledge and someone with common sense can always gain knowledge. But having a lot of knowledge is nothing without common sense. He is the type of person who will do anything for you and wouldn't expect anything in return. He's also a chancer with girls and will tell them anything to get in their knickers… I guess we are very alike in one sense.

"What do you mean if he knows I'm with you?"

"Watch this… Awright Dek" Gaz shouts across the pub.

Murdo gives him a lift of the head in acknowledgment before turning to his group and signalling them to head back out the door.

"How do you know him?"

"E've had a few dealings we him in the past. He's an acquaintance oh an acquaintance, if ye ken what I mean."

"Well, if he starts he'll get it the same as any other wide-o would."

"Calm doon and keep yer voice doon tae. Do ye ken what he's just done time for?"

I am about to tell him that I couldn't care less but Kyle interrupts.

"He stabbed some poor guy for shagging his missus."

Suddenly, my aggressive manner appears to fade, a lot.

Dek Murdo was one of those guys when you were growing up that had the reputation of being 'hard as fuck.' He was a lot older than all of us and we heard stories for years about him being 'off his head' and a 'fuckin nut job.' As we grew up we all learned that he was just a bullying bastard who picked on the younger ones. Anyway as things go, some people that he bullied over the years grew up to be a lot harder than him and stopped taking any of his shit, that's when the knives started to get pulled. This all went hand in hand with his reputation and also his nickname 'Mad Dog' which he evidently gave himself.

As more drinks are passed over from the bar, Gaz gives me the full story of his most recent incarceration. The evil bastard was working as a bouncer on a club and his missus was talking to some guy, so Dek starts on him. The poor guy was actually giving Dek a good go until he, surprise surprise, pulled out a blade and stuck it in him. With his previous record and loads of other charges he was due up for, all he served was four years."

"I fucking hate people that use blades, they usually tend to be the ones who act all tough but can't fight sleep."

"Do ye want ta find oot?" Gaz says with a big grin on his face.

"Maybe later"

The both of us have a little snigger then I down my drink and get up to order another round. While at the bar I receive a text from Lisa, a girl that I have been seeing recently.

'I FINISH IN AN HOUR IF U WANT 2 POP UP L8R 4 A DRINK XXX'

I have tried to end it a few times but whenever I am out on the piss and taken a few drugs, I seem to find myself knocking on her door. She works the phones and computers in the same taxi office that I work from. She is the typical Barbie Doll, blonde, slim and tanned. Since I started shagging her I seem to be getting loads more work sent my way. If she's working during the night and a big out of town job comes off, she phones me and gets me out of bed to go and do it. We were only friends at first and I would see her out at the weekends but I never tried it on, although she did flirt with me a bit. I think I was really pissed one night when I ended up back at her flat. It was all a bit of fun and I thought she knew the crack but after a few weeks, she changed. She became very clingy, well actually, it was more like possessive. Whenever I was out, she would turn up and get jealous if I was talking to other girls. If I was having people back to mine she would go crazy because I invited other girls up. I had to make excuses so that she wouldn't come up to mine because once she was in, she wouldn't leave. All my mates hate her and all she does is bitch about her own mates. When I don't want to see her, I can't use the excuse that I am working because she knows whether I am or not. If my computer is on in the car this registers with the main computer in the office. There is also a tracking device connected to this, which means she knows exactly where I am. This was designed to determine which car is the closest to whatever jobs come in. I think the other drivers are starting to get suspicious though, as it's always my car that gets the call to the office at the end of her shift to pick her up, but she is great in bed.

After several more rounds of drinks and a few more desperate texts from Lisa, I tell Gaz that I am leaving and he starts moaning that I just got here.

"We're ah heading in the toon later, eh though ye were up for it. Whar are ye sneaking off ta anywey? Oh shit, it isna her fae the office again is it? That fuckin Lisa, yer wee spunk bucket."

I look at him with the schoolboy grin like I'm trying to hide something and then the both of us just snigger.

"It's getting a bit regular again mate? You canna stand her, and we canna stand her, so how do ye no just tell her ta fuck off?"

"What do you mean 'we' can't stand her? If she walked in here right now and asked you to shag her, you would have you dick out before she even finished her sentence."

"Nah Jamie would hae his oot well before me."

"That's true."

Gaz hates me seeing Lisa, well he actually hates me seeing any girl regularly because after a club I always end up going back to hers and he has nowhere to go when he's pulled. He still lives at his Grans house and she doesn't like him taking girls back there. She doesn't mind him walking about her house with a joint hanging out his mouth but bringing a girl back is not on. I will have to ditch Lisa though, as I miss shagging the girls that Gaz brings up to the flat. When he pulls a bird he always makes sure she has a friend for you and they are usually the type of girls that when they walk in your flat their knickers just fall off. If he can't find one for you he'll pull one that will be up for it from both of us. The downside to this is that sometimes these girls are big, fat and ugly, but most of all, they usually stink. The worst part is that I get left with them in the morning as Gaz always sneaks off home after shooting his load to take his fucking dog out. He has one of those Staffordshire Terriers which he calls 'Biscuit' I mean, what sort of name is Biscuit. He takes it everywhere and treats it like a fucking baby, even letting it sleep in his bed. If we are going to a party after a club, no matter where it is, he'll get a taxi home and bring it back with him. Don't get me wrong, Biscuit is a great dog, all black and very cute, not like some of the ugly cross breeds that you see being dragged around. Although most around our end of town have probably come from Biscuit due to the amount humping it does. When Gaz doesn't have him on his lead, which is quite often and it sees another dog. It bounds over and tries to ride it, male or female. Gaz gets the piss ripped out of him for this as we all blame it on the dog sleeping in his bed.

Gaz had dabbled in recreational drugs like most of us since we were young teenagers and after being asked to leave school he started work on the government's Youth Training Scheme, which was basically a fancy name for slave labour jobs. This was a scheme where employers took on sixteen or seventeen year olds and their wages were paid by the government. This was supposedly an incentive for the employer to take them on after a two year period. This system was abused by employers who took on these people and used them for free labour with a promise that they would be offered a full apprenticeship after their two years training. They had no intention of offering them full employment and they would be terminated before the two years were up. The employers would make a phone call and within the week they would receive another young naïve school leaver. Gaz had went through several of these jobs as he had the employers figured out within a week and would either be sacked or had walked out for refusing to do their meaningless errands of making them tea or cleaning the toilets. During this time Gaz used to supply cannabis between our close friends. He never made any money out of it as he only sold enough to get his own for free. The circle of friends gradually grew bigger and they all ended up coming to Gaz. When other drugs appeared on our scene like speed and ecstasy, Gaz saw an opportunity. Several years down the line he was the main man in the area and had three to four people selling it for him. There was never any trouble and the people who sold for him only sold to trusted buyers. He never touched smack and coke wasn't around in those days like it is now. This went on for years until Gaz's supplier got busted. He was sent down for several years, which gave Gaz an opportunity. His supplier's supplier was a big shot from Glasgow and he asked Gaz if he wanted to take over. Gaz agreed, but being the paranoid guy that he is he told him that it was under his conditions and had a system set up where there was no contact between either of them. The introduction of mobile phones was the key to this whole system working between them. Gaz had a local contact and told him that a supplier from Glasgow was looking for a dealer. He did not mention names but told his contact that he would get a phone call to where and when the drop off would be. A mule from Glasgow would travel through to Dundee either by train or bus. They would receive instructions by text to go to a pub in the centre. It was a different pub each time. Gaz would be close by, driving a taxi. He would wait until he was next in line to get a job and then phone a taxi to the pub that the guy was in. Gaz would then pull up outside the pub, he would shout in the door a pre-arranged name and the guy would get in the taxi. The package would be left in the back and Gaz would drop the guy off at another pub in the town. The guy would have a quick drink in the pub and then make his way back to Glasgow. Gaz would then text his contact in Dundee and arrange for his guy to phone a taxi and coincidently, it would be Gaz's taxi that would get the job. If the dealer in Dundee ever happened to get busted they would not know who Gaz was or who the main supplier was. Before this arrangement with the big shot, Gaz did plan on calling it a day at one point. This was at a time he met Debbie, a nice girl who didn't appreciate her partner being a drug dealer, although she never complained when he was spending all his cash on expensive gifts for her. Within a few months of meeting her they had moved into a flat and had taken on Biscuit, who was only six weeks old. Gaz was still handling the drugs himself and he had people knocking on his door at all hours of the day and night looking for gear. It got too much for Debbie and she gave him an ultimatum, stop dealing or she was leaving. Obviously Gaz didn't stop dealing as the money was too easy and it paid for the lifestyle he wanted, the furnished flat, the expensive clothes and nights out on the town four or five times a week, the typical drug dealer's lifestyle. Although it has to be said, it didn't matter how much he would spend on clothes, he still looked like a down and out. Gaz is the type of person that if you placed him in a designer made to measure suit he would still look scruffy. Debbie couldn't live with the threat of the flat being busted by the police so she left. Personally I think she was seeing someone else but I've never said that to Gaz. It lasted six months before she packed her bags and took off leaving him with Biscuit. It was actually her idea to get the dog and walked away without a second thought. Gaz couldn't give him up as he had become attached to it. After his supplier got busted it turned Gaz into a paranoid wreck. He had to ditch the flat and move back with Kate and Big Danny. If the drug squad were onto his supplier at the time, then they were onto him. If they had looked at his lifestyle, he was fucked. Now he just keeps enough to keep him going and the rest he gives to me to put away. He has no bank account, no credit cards or anything that can be attached to his name. Most drug busts come from tip offs or grassers wanting a reduced sentence. He knows the only way he can ever get caught is if word of his arrangement ever got out, but as far as I know the only people that know about it are me and the big shot. If nobody else knows about it, then nobody can grass. The only way he can get busted is if the police did a random check on the taxi when he was doing a drop.

I go to sneak out the door before anyone notices as Gaz is keeping everyone amused by ripping the piss out of Jamie, who just so happens to spy me sneaking away and tries to divert the attention onto me.

"Whar are you going?"

"Lisa's"

"You lucky bastard eh'd love ta shag her."

"I'll be sure to mention that when I see her then."

We both laugh as I go out the door but at the back of my mind I'm thinking, brother or no brother, I'll bet if that cunt got half a chance he would shag her while I was seeing her. I walk off leaving them listen to Gaz telling them everyone that when Jamie was younger he used to hide his skiddy undies under the bed.

Chapter 3

It's only a short walk to Lisa's block from the East View, which in one way is a good thing as I don't have too far to walk, but in another way it's too convenient at closing time when I am fuelled up looking for my hole. When she first started at the taxi office I didn't take much notice of her until one night when I was out on the town a bit worse for wear I seemingly made a pass at her. She came up the road with me and I have regretted it ever since. She told me her friends knew me and to stay away as I was a bit of player. I didn't argue, I just told her straight that I only wanted my hole. She joked that once I had been with her, I wouldn't want anybody else. I didn't know that in her mind she actually meant it. She started turning up everywhere I went and flirting with me. I thought she knew the score but it's like she thinks that the more we have sex the more I'll want to be with her. She hates all of my mates as they apparently stop us from having a proper relationship, that may be true but being their company sometimes drives me to go and see her. Although If I wasn't getting sex handed on a plate I wouldn't even bother. I feel really confused when I think about all this as when I am with my mates all I want to do is be with a girl and when I'm with a girl and just shot my load I can't wait to get back to my mates. There is the odd occasion where I've met a girl at the weekend and agreed to go to the pictures or go for a quiet drink during the week with them and the whole time all I am thinking is that I can't wait to get her back to my flat and give her one. As soon as this happens I can't get her out of my flat quick enough. I hear people tell me that they would love my lifestyle and they are resentful that I have no kids, no ties, I go out when I want, do what I want and I have no woman nagging at me to do this or that, all the while I feel envious of their relationship. These thoughts are getting way too deep. I maybe shouldn't have taken that coke Gaz laid out for me in the toilet. He put out two monster lines on the cistern for me and Joey and I thought I was being the smart arse by taking them both to piss Joey off, but, now look where the fuck I am. I press the intercom and she lets me in. The landings have the usual stench of alcohol and piss, which I don't understand as the security door is supposed to stop the fucking minks getting in, unless it's one of her neighbours, or even worse, Lisa herself. I get to the top floor and press the buzzer

"Hi come in, would you like a drink?"

"I wouldn't mind."

"Vodka and coke"

I nod and she gives me a cheeky smile before heading through to the kitchen. I make my way to the living room and sit on the couch. For how much of a state this block is in, Lisa's flat is very nice. She has her Robbie DVD on, great, it looks like I'm going to be shagging while listening to this shite again. It's like she has everything set up for me coming up here, she's obviously after her hole as well. This is so fucked up. Both of us have sex on our minds but for two totally different reasons. Mine is because I am coked up and need to release my urges and hers is to please me so that I'll stay with her.

"Were you in the East view?" She shouts from the kitchen.

"Yeah I only had a few. I finished work later than I planned."

"I know. I saw that you had logged off and I couldn't wait to finish so I could see you."

Fuck, this has got to stop she's getting way to into this, well after tonight obviously.

She hands me the vodka, which I quickly devour, then she squeezes in behind me on the couch and starts rubbing my neck and shoulders.

"Would you like to lie on the floor and I'll give you a mas-sage."

"Okay, but could you get me another Vodka first, large one this time."

As she goes to the kitchen, I take off my top and lie on her large fluffy rug. She brings me the drink and I sit up and take a large gulp. She sits on my lower back and pours a little oil on my shoulders then starts to rub. The shivers tingle down my spine as she continues rubbing down my back to the top of my arse.

"Turn over." She rises up so that I can move.

As I turn over I reach for my drink and take another large gulp. I put down the glass and she pours oil over my chest and starts rubbing it all over. When she reaches the top of my jeans she strokes across my stomach and then up my sides, this goes on for a while as I think she is enjoying teasing me. Eventually she starts kissing my chest and working her way down with her tongue. She opens my buttons and pulls down my jeans and boxers. She keeps stroking my balls while kissing my dick, teasing me. I lean over for my drink and she takes it from me, she takes a little sip and hands it back to me. As I'm swallowing another large gulp she puts my dick in her mouth but she hasn't swallowed the vodka.

"Ahhhhh"

This is fucking heaven, the vodka is really cold but her tongue is hot. She works me up until I nearly come and then lets it go. I pull her up to me and we start kissing. I start to undress her slowly, stroking her lovely toned body. She picks up the remote from the television, turns up the volume and then grabs my hand leading me to the bedroom. I walk back and pick up my jeans, take out my wallet and slide out a condom from behind my credit card.

"It's okay, just leave it."

"Yeah right" I mumble as I walk back into the bedroom. The last thing I need is for her to get pregnant.

We move onto the bed and try out a few positions. The sweat is dripping down my head so I stop and go to the bath-room to wipe it, on the way back I go to the kitchen for more vodka. As I'm pouring a drink I realise that I am humming along to a fucking Robbie song, I suddenly stop. I take my drink through to the bedroom and lie on the bed. Lisa starts playing with my semi to get it hard again and as I look down at her, I get a reality check of where I am and I suddenly realise that this was a big mistake. I guess the coke is wearing off.

"What's wrong?"

"Nothing's wrong. Why?"

"This is not like you."

"What?"

"Well it doesn't normally take you that long to get hard."

I don't answer but reach up and take a large gulp from the glass. I look at Lisa but I am thinking about someone else, if she knew she would probably kill me. I have to put her out of my mind just now and finish what I started here. I pull her close to me and put in a little effort of foreplay until I am eventually hard again. I sit on the edge of the bed with her legs rapped around me. I slide forward while holding her up with my hands on her arse. She puts her arms around my neck as I thrust faster and get into a rhythm. Her groaning gets very loud then she shouts in a very shaky voice.

"I'm away to come"

"Ahhhhh"

The both of us let out similar noises as we lie back on the bed. Lisa feeling fucked and me feeling fucked up. I role over, drink the rest of the vodka and curl up with Lisa's arms around me and go to sleep. I wake up in the morning feeling rough as fuck and still have that Robbie song going through my head. I go to the toilet and as I pee it comes out in every fucking direction, all over the seat, the floor and the wall.

"Oh fuck." Why does that always happen after I've shot my load?

I quickly grab a load of toilet roll and give it a wipe.

"Would you like a cup of coffee?"

"No I'd better go, I have to go to work soon."

I can't get out of here quick enough. I would usually tell myself that this was worthwhile and that I had great sex, but not this time. This time I just feel guilty and stupid, guilty for coming up here in the first place and stupid for taking that fucking coke. I put the rest of my clothes on and head to the door. She follows me and tries to kiss me. I give her a quick peck and tell her I'll phone her.

"I don't want you to go, please stay."

"I can't. I have to go to work."

"No you don't. You work when you want. Take the day off and stay with me."

"Don't do this again Lisa."

"What? I just want to see you. Can we meet up again tonight then?"

"I don't know. I'll see"

I walk to the door and try to get out before she turns nasty

"Fuck" She's locked the door. Here we go.

"Open the door Lisa."

"Just stay a while longer Shane, please." She says opening her bathrobe revealing her naked body.

"I can't Lisa, please, open the door."

"Oh so now you've got what you want, that's it."

I knew this would happen, why did I take that fucking coke?

"Lisa, give me the key."

"No you're staying here."

"Lisa I have to go to work." I say a bit louder as I start to get angry.

"No you don't. You just want away from me."

She leans forward and puts her arms around me but I don't return the hug. She starts crying as she knows the waterworks get to me as I fell for her act before. I put my arms around her and she hugs me tighter. I reach into her robe pocket and gently take out the front door key. I release my arms and walk quickly putting the key into the lock. I hear a scream and feel my hair being pulled from behind. I grab her wrist tightly to stop her and she lets go. I release my grip and then she attacks me with her fists and feet, punching, kicking and screaming all at the same time. Nothing lands on me as I block most of it with my elbows and knees. She screams again louder and runs off into the bathroom locking the door. I stand for a few seconds and listen to her crying. The last time she done this I ended up staying for hours to make sure she was okay. I put my head to the door and contemplate whether to knock and ask if she is alright but I know this is what she wants. This is like a fucking déjà vu. I'm not falling for it this time. I walk to the door and unlock it. I look back one last time and then head off down the stairs. I hold my breath so that I don't breathe in the smell as it's a bit much when you are hung over. I walk back towards the East view and get my car. I know I shouldn't be driving as I still feel half pissed but fuck it. As I'm driving I feel my phone vibrating all the way home. I know it's Lisa so I don't even bother to look at it. I walk into my flat, which is in an overpriced building just off the Perth Road. There are several snotty nosed neighbours in my block and although they don't say anything to me, I know they look me up and down wondering how the fuck I can afford a flat like this, especially when they see people like Gaz walking in and out of their building. They probably think I just rent it but little do they know I own the flat outright with no mortgage. If it wasn't for that pathetic piece of shit who calls himself my stepfather throwing me out at eighteen, I wouldn't be in this position and I know he hates the amount of money I have made buying and selling flats. This one is the business though, with the huge living room and balcony that gives views of Dundee which is amazing at night. The master bedroom has views across the River Tay and over to Fife, which at times is just as good. As soon as I get in, I go straight to the stereo and blast out some Oasis to get that fucking Robbie tune out of my head. I strip off and go in the shower ..."I'm a rock 'n' roll star..."

Chapter 4

Customer No. 2704

I know this address, great, fucking junkies. This is Broughty Ferry, the so called posh end of Dundee. Some of the residents I pick up talk to you like you are a piece of shit and they think because of where they live they are better than you. In reality they live in a scheme that is full of junkies just like everyone else. They probably don't know that their original neighbour is renting out their house to someone who has been evicted from a council house and is now renting privately. What they don't know is that the rent money is actually paid through housing benefit and their high council tax payments are going towards keeping these junkies' as their new unsociable neighbours. The guy swaggers out of his house and gets in the front seat. Before he tells me where he's going he slides and tilts the seat back. This is not because he needs more leg room as the cunt is smaller than me. He sits in a way that he has his elbow up on the side panel and has his row of sovereigns on show. They blend in well with his new tracksuit that is accompanied by the newly added hash burns along with his hundred pound trainers, the stereotypical Chav.

"Eh'm going ta Maryfield Medical Centre. Eh'll no be a minute, and then onta the Hulltoon ta the chemist, then hame"

"Why do you not use one of the chemists in Maryfield?"

"Cause eh'm banned fae the three oh them. Eh'm banned fae the ain at the Hulltoon tae, but they let is in though."

I drive to the medical centre where he's out the car and back in a couple of minutes after picking up his prescription. Next is the chemist, where I wait a little bit longer. On the journey back he tries to make conversation with me but my answers are very blunt as I can't stand this guy and what he is all about. His whole way of life revolves around the world owing him something. This parasite sits on his arse all day and claims every benefit possible. He has a house with a large front and back garden which is rent free, no council tax, free drugs and to top it all, he has told me in the past that he receives extra money because he has kids, which opens a whole new list of benefits for him compared to the average junkie. I have several junkies in my taxi a week and as they go for their daily dose of free methadone all they ever talk about is how to claim for this or that so that they'll get extra money. They know everyone's business and what they are all claiming for. I agree there are some unfortunate people who end up with a drug habit and with the correct help and change of attitude, they beat it. The average person who pays their taxes would agree that the money put aside to help these people is not grudged if it was going to be used correctly but it is being abused by the same people that it was designed to help. These junkies are not mugs. Some of them are very intelligent people and have learned over the years how to screw the system. If they put as much effort into cleaning themselves up and getting a job instead of scamming everyone and everything they would probably be quite successful. Judging by the amount of junkies I have encountered over the years I would say that nine out of ten don't actually want to come off drugs. I arrive back at this guy's house and stop outside his long drive-way. He pulls a huge wad of notes from his pocket and hands me a tenner.

"Just keep it mate." He says as he winks at me before swaggering back to his plush house.

I can't tell if it's all in the mind with some of these junkies as when they get in your car and they are strung out, they are quite nasty, rude, sometimes aggressive and dangerous. They go from house to house trying to get drugs and they get more abusive if they are unsuccessful. The minute they score and get back in the taxi their attitude totally changes. They give you all the 'hey man' and call you 'Mate' when only minutes before they were ready to start on you because they couldn't get a hold of some drugs. I would hate to think what would happen if they didn't get them as who knows what these people are capable of when they are strung out.

Customer No. 510

I pull into the social workers in Douglas and my customer is a woman waiting outside with her three young boys. She gets in the front and her three young boys climb over each other to dive in the back

"Eh'm going ta Dunmore Street in Kirtin."

Before I even drive off, one of the boys dives up onto the parcel shelf at the back window. I turn around to tell him to get down and see the other two with chocolate on their fingers and wiping them all over the windows and down the back seat

"Right the three of you, sit on your arses and get your seat belts on or you're going nowhere."

I shout quite angrily but feel more contempt for their mother who sits in the front and doesn't even turn to see why I am getting onto her kids. During the journey I hear the seat belts clicking open and the boys start laying into each other on the back seat. One of them has squeezed into the space between the front and back seat while one of the other boys is on top punching his lights out. The swearing and filthy language from these boys would put Gaz to shame. Their mother sitting in the front has her mobile phone out and is happily chatting away to someone. She has the latest flip model phone definitely worth a few hundred at least and her kids look and smell like they haven't seen a bar of soap in weeks, easy to see where her priorities lie. I'm nearly in Kirkton and I try to switch off to the noise from them as I speed up to get to their destination as fast as I can. My mother would have booted my arse if I behaved like that when I was younger, well actually Jamie's father would have kicked the shit out of me more like. I feel sorry for these kids as they have a mother who obviously doesn't give a fuck about them and can't teach them how to behave or even a simple right from wrong. She would have known all about it if I had thrown the little fuckers out. What kind of start in life have these boys got? They are going to grow up hassled by social workers and they have a mother who thinks that going around stinking of shit is okay. I can only wonder why there isn't a father around.

Customer No. 2012

"Where are you off to then?"

"Hulltoon please"

"Oh I'm getting a please this time."

I have picked up these two before, they are mother and daughter. I would definitely do them both. The mother is at an age where she's still considered young, and the daughter is working so she must be old enough for me to pump her. Gaz would probably say they were mingers as he likes to pretend he has standards, but I have witnessed some of the girls he pulls due to him turning up at my door with them. They are both talking about going out tonight so I will have to make sure I give them my number so that I can pick them up later.

"Oh fuck, what the hell do they want?" I say as I clock a blue light flashing in my mirror.

"Oh yeah, what have you been up ta?" The daughter smirks.

I watch PC Plod in my mirror get out of his car so I do the same.

"Do you know you have a break light out?" He says with a face of stone.

"No. No I didn't."

"Where's your badge?"

"What? My taxi badge"

"YES. Your taxi badge" He snaps.

"It's in the car."

"You're supposed to wear your badge at all times when you are plying for hire. NOW GET IT ON."

I want to shout, yes sir and do the Hitler salute but I don't think that would go down too well. This arrogant prick is on his own so I could probably just tell him to fuck off but then he would just make a call and have about five cars here in minutes the fascist cunt. He starts ranting and raving about how I should check the car before every shift. Does he think I have a bionic fucking eye that can see the back of the car while I have my foot on the brake, the fucking idiot? What is his problem anyway? He's pulled me over because I have a brake light out, which is fair enough but he's going a bit over the top. I see those boy racers ripping about the streets every night and not once do they get pulled.

"Have you Polis no got anything better ta dae?" The young girl in the back shouts out of the window.

"How many hooses have been screwed in the time you've been standing there?" The mother adds.

"When you've dropped off your passenger, go and get the light fixed and if I see you driving later on and it's not fixed I'm going to put you off the road."

"No problem." I say through gritted teeth.

I give him a look up and down before getting back in the car and my head is filled with thoughts of different ways of torturing him. The woman and daughter are still shouting abuse at him out the window.

"What the fuck did he get oot oh that? Fuckin nothing better ta dae, that's what their problem is. They want ta go and catch some real bloody criminals."

The woman in the back is right thought, I wonder what was on his mind when he decided to pull me over. Somehow I don't think he stops every car in front of him that has a brake light not working. What's bothering me more is not what he stopped me for but the way he was talking to me. Young taxi driver in a flashy car maybe? I would say that most of the time I am an easy going guy but when someone with a bit of authority becomes a bullying bastard it really gets me worked up and makes me hate them even more. The banter during the rest of the journey with my fare was a bit of a downer so I never got the chance to pass on my number. All because that fascist prick was having a bad day, he had to go and ruin mine.

Customer No. 410

I sit for a while waiting on my next job, which is a good thing as I'm still feeling quite rough from last night. The sore head kicked in around an hour ago and that's after taking a few pain killers. I never thought I had that much to drink last night. It's a good job I didn't get breathalysed earlier because there was a good chance I was slightly over the limit. Eventually my computer beeps with a job, it's Asda for Milne. As I approach the entrance I can see there is already a taxi with the boot open and the driver is loading the bags of shopping. I hope that's not my fucking fare. I drive into a space on the rank as the other taxi is about to drive off.

"Taxi for Milne"

The old lady in the back hears me as her window is open and says "Oh that's me"

I recognise the driver's face but it's not until I read the name on the side of the car that I recognise him, Macintosh. This happens to be the same loud mouth that I had to endure abuse from in my first week on the taxis. I pulled up on the rank one day and this wide cunt started shouting his mouth off at me to fuck off and find some other place to sit. If there wasn't two other taxis on the rank and a load of other witnesses that day I would have got out and smashed him. I told him to piss off and that I'll sit wherever I fucking want. I've seen him a few times over the years while I've waited on jobs but he hasn't said a word. He's a big guy with one of those hard looking faces and a large Desperate Dan chin. I've witnessed him mouth off at other drivers and they've all put their heads down and turned away from him. I could have said something then but I know none of those driver would stick up for me if it was the other way around so fuck them, they all deserve each other.

"She was waiting for ages, ye should have got here quicker."

Macintosh shouts out his window and looks at me with a large smug grin, which makes his chin appear even bigger.

"Is that right?" I say while getting out my car as fast as I can and storming over to him. He drives off before I get near him and he keeps the same smug look on his ugly face before giving me the finger out of the window. I don't know what I would have done if he hadn't drove off as I couldn't exactly do anything with about fifty shoppers walking past me. As I watch him drive off I feel a slight anger rush through my body. This is mixed with adrenaline as I can feel my heart beating faster and my fingertips stating to tingle. I get violent thoughts through my mind of what I'll do to him the next time I see him. I knew he would eventually get wide with me again. I know his type, they can't help themselves. It's like they have something to prove by bullying a weaker or smaller person. Well it's about time he got his comeuppance. When I've seen him mouth off to other people it's never directly affected me so I've never got involved, but not this time. The only thing I know about him is that he's from Lochee and drinks in the Ivanhoe, which to me means a double chip on his shoulder. Every time I have a customer going to or from the Hoe I seem to get shit off them. It doesn't matter if it is young guys or old men with walking sticks or even women; they all have the same arrogant attitude. I've seen me drive not fifty yards from the pub and having to stop and drag some drunken prick out of my car for being wide. On the odd occasion when I have had to go into the pub to shout on a fare, Macintosh has been there, surrounded by his mates being loud and aggressive. He always looks over and gives me a sneer.

I have to wait for quite a while until my next job but this is a good thing as it gives me some time to calm down. All the other taxi drivers see is this young guy with the flashy car moving in on their job and they don't like it. If I was driving for one of them and making them money there wouldn't be a problem. But as I have my own car, in which customers prefer to get in rather than their buckets of shite, they don't like it so they think they can bully and take the piss. Well one of them has done it to the wrong fucking person and he's soon going to know about it. They say what goes around comes around. Well I've waited a long time on this coming around. My customer gets in and they start blabbing on and on all the way through their journey and I don't know what the fuck they are talking about. I am agreeing with everything they say by nodding now and again but the whole time all I am thinking about is Macintosh.

Chapter 5

Text from Joey "ARE YOU STILL UP FOR IT MATE, TIME YOU PICKIN ME UP?"

Oh shit I must have mentioned to him last night in the pub that I would go to the gym with him today. I really can't be bothered but after all that shit with Lisa this morning and then that cunt Macintosh being wide, I think maybe a break from the taxi would be a good idea. I'll head home for my gear and pick him up. Joey is a mate from school who was always big for his age. He was a bit of a wimp and this resulted in him being bullied constantly. He always hung around me and Gaz but we both know this was so that nobody went near him. He started college a few years ago after many dead end jobs and he ended up working in a gym. Since then we have notice him put on a lot of weight and he now has the bulging biceps and six pack, which he tries to say is down to his training program and a good diet. I wouldn't' trust Joey as far as I could throw him, but when we go out it's good to have him hanging around as his size intimidates people and they think twice before starting any shit. We all know he can't fight sleep but other people don't. When he started at the gym and building himself up we noticed his swagger got bigger and he had a bit of an attitude. Around this time I once heard him getting a bit wide with Kyle, but he was soon put in his place. Kyle is the type of person who doesn't bother anybody and along with Gaz they are the only people I really trust. Joey works at the gym part-time and gets us in free. He's always complaining about money, a typical student. He explained to me once about the student loan he gets, which is to pay for his rent and is also meant to feed and clothe him during term time, how students manage this without any extra income is fucking beyond me. The worse part about it is that once he finishes studying and gets a job, he has to pay it all back.

I always wondered why Joey kept asking me to go to the gym and not Gaz or Mickey. At first I thought it was because I had transport to pick him up and then I thought the cunt was a poofter, well I still do, but I later found out it was because when he takes Gaz or Mickey they just muck about or sit in the saunas and shout rude comments to all the females. From our point of view this is not really a bad thing but Joey's boss gave him loads of shit as he was the one who signed them in. There is one thing I hate about going to these gyms is those bodybuilders with their stripy pants. They do a set and then stand and look at themselves in the mirror while chatting for about ten minutes before their next one. The typical bodybuilder scenario, jab some steroids in their arse, lift a few weights, take a job as doorman and then walk about thinking they can fight the fucking world. I have no time for them whatsoever.

I go to sound the horn but see him standing waiting by his door.

"Ahright mate. Are ye ready for a hard work oot?"

"Not really, I'm a bit hung over."

"Whar did you sneak aff ta last night?"

"Where do you think?"

"Ah nah, ye werena shagging ta Robbie again were ye?"

I give him a funny look as I can't remember telling him about Lisa's Robbie obsession.

"Eh just dinna get you Shane. Ah ye dae is moan aboot her. Yet ye still go up ta her flat for a shag. You winna let her in your flat because once she is in, she winna leave, which eh really dinna understand as anybody else wouldna want somebody as stunning as that ta leave. Personally eh would want her tied up in meh fucking bed so she couldna fucking leave. Eh would love ta ken how ye manage ta pull ah these good looking women. Ye blatantly tell them you are only efter yer hole and yet they still keep coming back, well most oh them. Eh think you've found oot we Lisa that no ah burds want the same thing though eh. Do ye ken what? See when eh'm oot in a club it feels like there are burds hanging aboot you just waiting ta be asked up the road. Eh sometimes wonder aboot the burds that eh pull, if they are just we me ta get near you."

"Joey, you don't half talk some shite mate" I say as we ar-rive at the gym.

We get changed and as soon as we walk in I see them, the all grunting, all swaggering, poofy bodybuilders, with their muscle vests and stripy baggy pants. They stare over with their heads back making their necks swell out but I don't even look over as they would just get me worked up. I start stretching off and when I look around Joey has fucked off to talk to them. I just carry on doing my own thing but I glance over catching Joey comparing his biceps with one of them, what a fucking nonce.

"Oh you're back. I thought I was training on my own."

"Eh only went over ta say hi."

"More like bend over" I mumble.

"What?"

"Nothing"

"You're set."

As Joey gets himself into position to lift, I watch one of his friends walk over to use the punch bag. He puts on his gloves and starts hitting the bag. I immediately feel embarrassed for him. He throws several pathetic punches and stops for a breath. I watch as he swings one arm from behind his body towards the bag and it hardly moves. I smile to myself and look away.

"These are the guys who are supposed to protect the public from drunken louts who are out to start trouble. If I was one of them what the fuck would he do if he came up against someone like me?"

"Go and show him how it's done then Shane." Joey nods to-wards the bag.

"Not just now. I wouldn't want to put all your real friends to shame."

As we finish our sets I think to myself that we must have lifted more weights in ten minutes than those bodybuilders did in the whole hour that they have been here. I walk over to the punch bag and Joey tells me he is off to work on his six-pack. I take it easy by throwing a few jabs and hooks. I work around the bag and start to pick up the pace. I throw a few big hooks but keep on the move. Each time I look up I catch one of the bodybuilders glancing over and it makes me think of Macintosh which makes me hit the bag harder. I try to put them all out of my mind and keep working the bag and before I now it, Joey is tapping me on the shoulder.

"Ye had enough yet Rocky."

I look up and some of the bodybuilders are still glancing over, I'm surprised they can stop looking at themselves in the mirror long enough to bother. I take off my gloves and follow Joey to the changing rooms. While driving home we are having a laugh about the posers in the gym when my face drops and I turn the car around.

"Whar are ye going? Are ye no dropping me aff first?"

"Yeah, I'm just checking something out, that's all."

I thought it was him. Macintosh is sitting at the front of a rank on his own. I stop on the opposite side of the road and roll down my window.

"Oi MACINTOSH. Who the fuck do you think you are stealing my job this morning?"

Joey is unaware as to what is going on and sits next to me smiling as if I know the guy.

"Piss off ye wee prick. What the fuck are you gonna dae aboot it anywey?"

I turn to see Joey's face drop as he realises it is not a joke. I step out of the car and hear Joey shouting 'leave it' but I am off in a rage marching across the road. Macintosh gets out of his car and squares up to me.

"Wha the fuck dae ye think are, ye wee p..."

I jump up and smack him in the side of the head with everything I have. He falls across the front of his car but comes back with a big hook scuffing the top of my head. I lean in with a punch to his stomach which makes him bent slightly. His face is more in my reach now and I throw punch after punch until he crumbles to the ground. I feel my arms being pulled from behind. It's Joey who is using his weight to drag me back across the road.

"Eh'll fucking kill you, ye wee prick" Macintosh shouts as he picks himself up.

I struggle free from Joey and run back over the road. We trade a few blows until I land one on his chin putting him on down again.

"Think you're a hard man? You're not that fucking hard are you? You fucking mouthy cunt."

I go to walk away but he still mouths off. I lose it and lay into him with both fists and feet until I am pulled off once again by Joey. I look down to see Macintosh's face covered in blood and his body lies still as Joey pushes me towards my car. He opens my car door and shouts at me to get in then runs back towards Macintosh. At first I think he's about to hit him but he crouches down and puts him into the recovery position.

"What the fuck did you do that for?" I say as we speed off.

"Because if he chokes on his own blood, you will be up for murder"

I don't say anything until we arrive at Joey's flat and the whole time I can feel my hands and legs shaking with adrenaline. I tell Joey to put the kettle on as I go to skin up.

"Give it here. You make the tea." He says as he sees me struggling to put the skins together with my shaky hands. I come through with the tea and Joey passes me the joint. I can tell that Joey is not happy with me and even after a smoke I can feel the tension from him. I finish my cup of tea and get up to leave.

"Let is ken if ye hear anything?" He says. But what he really means is, let me know if I have to watch my back from now on because of you. But it's a different story when someone is giving him shit and he turns to me to help him out.

"No probs" I say as I head off out the door.

I have always thought that if someone like Macintosh goes about like he does he must have something to back it up. It's on my mind that I could have hurt him bad as Joey said he was out cold but fuck him he was a bullying bastard and given half the chance he would have done the same to me. I check my phone before going back to work and have about five messages from Lisa, I don't even read them I just press delete all.

Customer No. 1612

The Claverhouse pub, this is possibly one of the roughest pubs in Dundee where every would-be hard-cunt in the area gathers to talk about who they have smashed or who they are about to smash, women included. The good thing about this pub is that it keeps all these nut jobs in one place. I enter the front door and shout the customer's name.

"TAXI FOR WALSH"

This scrawny rough looking man pipes up from a stool at the bar.

"Eh that's me."

Before I walk back out I notice a bit of a scuffle near the pool table and I recognise a few of their faces but I can't put a name to them. I get back in the car and the scrawny little man is not far behind me.

"Right driver, eh'm going in ta the toon."

"Where about in the town are you going?"

"Anywhar, stop at the bank on the way though will ye?"

"What about the bank in the town around from Commercial Street?"

"Eh that'll dae. Eh hae enough for the taxi but eh still need mare money. Eh mind when money was money."

"What do you mean? When money was money, what is it now?"

"IT'S WORTH FUCK ALL" He shouts.

"Eh got mare for a pound in the seventies than eh would the day."

"Obviously, that's called inflation mate."

"What's that?" He asks.

"What?"

"Inflation" He says.

I can't tell if this guy is really pissed and talking shit or if he's some sort of idiot and talking shit.

"Well you obviously earn more now than you did in the seventies, so the more your wages go up the more everything else goes up."

"Do ye ken what? Yer fucking right" He says. He hears a familiar song on the radio and starts singing out loud. This carries on for a while as he makes up his own words and starts to get louder.

"Those guys back in the pub arguing over the pool, what are their names again? I think I know them" I say making conversation to get him to stop singing.

"Wha Buster, he's a fucking bam."

"Buster, that rings a bell"

"He's just a fucking bam."

What the fuck is this guy on? I really hope this guy is just pissed. I'd hate to think he was like this all the time.

"Eh'll bang yer puss" he shouts looking straight at me.

"You'll what?" I say smile nervously as I am now under the impression that he has a few screws loose.

"Eh'll boot yer bahs ye prick."

"Are you speaking to me?"

"Me, eh, eh'm fine, how's yersel?"

"I'm alright, but I seriously think there's something not right with you though mate"

I can't tell if this guy is taking the piss or what.

"Dinna worry aboot me."

I reach the bank in the town without having to stop and give this guy a slap.

"Right you, ootside, square go."

I start laughing at him.

"Do ye see me laughing, no, now get ootside and we'll hae a square go."

"Look mate I suggest you pay this fare then you can go and have a square go with anybody you want. It's five fifty."

He pulls out his wallet and opens it to find that it's empty. He then puts his hand down his sock and pulls out a roll of money. He hands me a twenty.

"The things ye hae ta dae when ye drink in yer local. Just keep the change ya bam." He says as he gets out of the taxi.

I go to drive off and he stands at my car window.

"Come on then ya bam. Come ahead." He shouts.

I put the twenty in my pocket and laugh as I watch him swagger down the street shouting abuse at random people to 'Come ahead.'

Chapter 6

Customer No. 1608

My next customer appears from her tenement door with two large bags. She is a stunning blonde and looks totally out of place living in a junkie infested block on Park Avenue in Stobswell. I get out of the car to open the boot but she informs me that she will take them into the back with her. I clock the cowboy hat on top of one of the bags as she gets in.

"So where are you off to them?"

"The fantasy bar please."

It now registers that she is a stripper, I was a bit slow there, I should have realised when I saw the hat.

"Is that you away to start?"

"Well, I was supposed to start at nine but I'm a bit late. What about you? Is that you on all night?"

"Me, no, I'm actually away to finish. Have you worked at that place long?"

"No it's only my second night, I usually work in Edinburgh but I thought I would give this one a go."

"So what is it like?"

"I hate it. Some of the other girls are really bitchy towards me. The customers are much sleazier and the money is not that great."

Just by looking at this girl I can see why the other strippers are bitchy towards her. Although she has jeans on I can tell she has a great body. I have picked up strippers in the past and not one of them has ever looked like her.

"Do you ever go to the fantasy bar?"

"I have been in them but they are not really my thing"

"What do you mean?"

"Well when you have nightclubs in Dundee where the girls get their tits out after a few vodka and cokes. There's not really much chance of getting me to pay for someone to get them out, at least I would have more chance of shagging one of the birds' from the nightclub."

"Yeah, you're probably right" She says as she looks at me in the mirror and smiles.

"So what nightclub do you go to them?"

"Fat Sam's"

"Oh I don't like that place now, I go there when I'm not working but it's only because there's nowhere else to go."

"What about the Mardi?"

"Yeah right, that's like an underage disco."

We arrive at the Fantasy bar and she says "Will you be back working again later on tonight? It's just that you could pick me up when I finish, if you happen to be in the area."

"Oh I don't know about that, working late would cost extra."

"I'm sure we could negotiate a price."

I dive straight in "Like a free dance?"

This makes her smile again and I feel a tingle in my balls without her even touching me. We exchange numbers and I tell her if she's stuck for a lift just to give me a call

"My names Shona by the way"

"I'm Shane."

"I'll maybe see you later then Shane."

As soon as I drive off I realise I have all the lads coming up to my flat tonight for a smoke. Not to worry, most of them head off about two. She won't finish until half two so that should work out fine.

I'm glad I didn't have too much to smoke tonight as there is no way I would have been capable of driving. Everybody left except Gaz. He crashed out on the couch so I just threw a cover over him and sneaked out. Shona text me earlier to make sure I was still available to pick her up. I was going to let the others know what was going on but fuck them. If this turns out to be a no show I would never hear the end of it. I park outside and watch as other taxi's pull up and some proper mingers come out. They have probably got great body's and are good at what they do but from where I am sitting they need to take a long look in the mirror. Shona appears with her bags and puts them in the back but this time she gets in the front.

"What do you think you're doing?"

"What do you mean?"

"Why are you not dressed to give me a free dance?"

"Maybe later"

"So where are we going?"

"You know where I live, unless you have somewhere better to go?"

"We could go to mine."

"Okay."

I drive off felling quite excited but trying hard not to show it. I pull up outside my block.

"You live here?" She looks up at the building.

I don't answer and just give her a smile and help her with her bags as she follows me upstairs. When we get in the flat Gaz is still asleep.

"Don't mind him, that's my mate. Come through to the kitchen I'll make you drink, vodka okay?"

"Vodka would be great. Is this really your flat?" She says peering through the curtains that lead onto the balcony.

"Uh huh"

"This must cost you a bomb."

"Not really, I own it."

"What did you win the lottery or something?"

"I wish it was that easy. I used to buy and sell flats. I bought them really cheap and sold them at a profit. Don't worry. I'm not a drug dealer or anything like that. I can't speak for the grubby individual crashed on my sofa but that is a different story."

"Speaking about drugs, I have some coke if you want a line?" She says as she pulls a wrap out from her purse.

"Yeah, cool."

"It fell out of someone's pocket when they were getting their wallet out to pay me, so I sneakily crouched down and put it in my boot."

When she says this I suddenly get a mental picture in my head of this lovely girl dancing for a bunch of sleazy men while they pay good money for her to get her kit off and using their latest cheesy chat up lines to meet her later. Every one of them dying to touch her and here she is in my kitchen. She opens the wrap and I can tell someone is going to be really pissed off tonight at losing this as it's a lot of coke. She cuts up several lines on my bunker and takes a crisp new tenner from her purse.

This has no doubt come from someone's wallet after departed with it to see her flash her fanny at them. She rolls it tightly and hands it to me.

"You first" She says.

I lean forward and snort a line up each nostril. Shona leans forward and does the same. There is still enough left for several more lines which I am sure will not last long. We stand chatting for a while in the kitchen until the coke fully kicks in. she leans forward and kisses me and before I know it she has her hands down opening my jeans.

"Wait a minute. What happened to the dance I was get-ting?"

"Oh yeah, I forgot about that. Go and put some music on and wait through there. What about your friend?"

"I'm sure he won't mind."

I walk through with my vodka and put the stereo on. Gaz's rap music starts to blast out of the speakers and he wakens up. I put my finger to my lips and nod towards the kitchen. He puts his head back down as if he is still sleeping. A few minutes later Shona appears wearing her sexy cowboy outfit. She climbs onto the coffee table and touching herself as she does a sexy dance. I have a fly look at Gaz who is making faces at me wondering what the fuck is going on. Shona climbs down off the table and sits on my knee while slowly taking off her clothes. She starts to rub me through my jeans and it is only a matter of seconds before she has me hard. Shona gets naked and throws a cushion down at my feet for her knees. She opens my buttons and starts licking all around my balls. I lean forward and take off my shirt as Shona pulls my jeans and boxers down to my ankles. She leans over to the skirt she had on and pulls out a condom, opening it and carefully sliding it on me. She sits on top of my thighs and wraps her legs around me. I look over to Gaz and at first I think I'm tripping or something but he has his jeans open and is having a wank. He looks up at me and I burst out laughing.

"What? What are you laughing at?"

I nod in the direction of Gaz

"Was it getting too much for you, was it?"

Gaz gets up and hobbles over with his jeans falling to his knees, while still wanking. He stands in front of Shona and I think he was hoping she would suck it, but she puts her hands on top of his and helps him along.

"You had better not come on me." She says.

He turns away disappointed and hobbles back to the sofa to carry on his thrashing. I stand up lifting Shona in the process and kick my jeans and boxers off my ankles. I put Shona down and lead her by the hand to the bedroom and leave Gaz by himself to finish off. I wake up in the morning with Shona still lying next to me. I offer to get her some coffee but after some fondling and a little foreplay we end up having sex again before we both get up and I give her a lift home.

The weekend can't come quick enough for Gaz who has been doing my head in about going to the Fantasy bar since bringing Shona back to the flat. I kept in touch with her but it was a one off and I don't really want to make it a regular thing with her, although she would be good for the odd occasion. I told him most of them are ugly and nothing like Shona but he still insists that we all go and check it out. Kyle and Mickey are up for it too and after a few drinks up the west end, I now find myself in a taxi on the way to the Fantasy bar. Gaz told me he has a few grams of coke on him and when I told him I didn't want any he snapped at me.

"It's not for you, it's for the strippers."

We go in and Shona comes straight over and introduces us to another couple of girls. They are not too pretty but they do have great bodies. Gaz hands me the wrap with the coke and Shona leads me to a small room and closes the curtain. I pull out the coke and we both take a line. We have a quick hug and a kiss before heading back to the bar. I hand the wrap back to Gaz and in a spit second he is off to another small room with one of the ugly girls he was introduced to. Kyle and Mickey are like kids in a sweet shop as they pay for dance after dance with all these ugly strippers. Gaz pays for a few more dances but chooses the same girls every time.

"They strippers are coming back ta yours for a perty" Gaz says.

"So you've invited them back to mine without even asking me?"

"Well they've been charging me ta go in the wee rooms and snort meh coke. So eh think they're due me."

"What, you've been paying for a dance but actually just going in there to take coke?"

He nods with a big smile on his face.

"What are you up to?"

"Nothing" His grin appears to have gotten wider.

The night goes in quick as the bouncers shout that it is about to close. We have a taxi waiting on us outside but we physically have to drag Gaz away from the place. We head up to mine where we tuck into the crate of beer that we left earlier. Shona and the other two girls come up about half an hour after us and are welcomed into the kitchen by Gaz who has been waiting impatiently on them. He has several lines of coke all laid out for them. Gaz offers them a drink and they all say vodka which is a relief for me as we are currently running low on beer. Shortly after the girls comment on how good the coke is, they ask for another line.

"That's meh mates gear, eh always get good stuff fae him. There's no much left but eh could phone him and get him ta drap some mare aff. The only problem is that eh'm running oot oh cash as eh used it ta pay for ah they dances we you strippers"

"We are not strippers. We are exotic dancers" One of the girls abruptly says to Gaz.

"Oh sorry, meh bad" He turns and gives me a look.

The girls all chip in to buy some more coke and Gaz nips out to meet his 'friend'. While he's out the music is turned up and the girls all have a laugh by taking turns to dance on my coffee table.

"This is what eh call a perty" Gaz says as he bounces back in the flat with another wrap of coke. He cuts them up a few more lines and rushes about topping up their drinks.

"Gaz what are you up to? I had a line of that coke and it's nothing special."

"Yeah but that's only because you never had a vodka we it, it is magic coke. Ye only get an effect when ye follow up the line we a vodka. Here, drink this" He says handing me a small glass with, what looks like vodka and orange juice.

"Hey your right enough, that does make a difference. But maybe that's down to the fucking G.H.B. that you've been putting in it"

"Shhh" He winks.

Several lines and drinks later with my head feeling a little fuzzy, I eventually end up in my bedroom with Shona. I lie back as Shona goes down on me but I start to get bored and my mind starts to wander. The next thing I know she is on top of me and I am inside her without a condom. I can't believe I'm doing this, those idiots next door are swapping around without condoms and they are the ones that will go through life not giving a fuck and never catch a thing. Where I will be the one that will not use one just the once on some spunk bucket and end up with the fucking virus. I don't last long as I feel I am about to shoot my load and whisper it in her ear that I will have to stop as I am about to come.

"No, keep going" She shouts.

"I don't have a condom on."

"It's okay, keep going."

I shoot my load up her and Shona slides down and starts sucking me off again.

"Does that not taste horrible?"

"Not really, just a bit salty"

She comes back up to give me a kiss but I pull back as I feel her tongue.

"I don't want to taste it."

"Why?" She says as she puts her hand down and scoops up some of my sperm from her onto her fingers and starts licking them. For all those nice thoughts I had about this girl, they virtually vanished in the split second that I witnessed her doing this. I get up and walk through to the living room naked and am surprised to see that everyone else is naked or near enough. If anyone walked into my flat they would think there was a full scale orgy going on. After all the coke has been consumed and the alcohol level is at a minimum the girls decide to leave. They get a taxi together and I have to lend them money after they spent it on the so called 'best coke ever.' I really thought these girls had been around and seen it all but I was obviously mistaken as they were so naive not to notice they were being spiked with G.H.B.

"You're a cunt Gaz. We could have been onto a good thing with them, and you're due me the money I had to give them for the taxi"

Mickey and Kyle are looking confused as to what's going on.

"You guys didn't think that was just coke making them feel like that did you?"

"Gaz, ye never, did you crush up E's and mix it with the coke?" Kyle asks.

"No, it was G.H.B. in the vodka" I announce.

We all laugh as Gaz pulls a wad of notes out of his pocket.

"The strippers charged me a tenner a dance and eh basically charged them a tenner a line of the finest Coke a Cola around." He says as he pulls out the empty bottle of G.H.B.

"You're forgetting one thing."

"What's that?"

"They're not strippers. They're exotic dancers."

"Woooooh"

Chapter 7

Text from Jamie...WE ARE IN LAINGS, TIME U CUMIN DOON?
I text back...HALF AN HOUR

I'll do another job, go home to drop off the car and walk to Laing's. I hope I don't see Lisa tonight. She has been texting and phoning all day. She was actually in the office and called me through the car radio while I was working just to talk to me. I said I would call her later as I was busy but fuck that, I can't be bothered with her. I get calls from withheld numbers as if I don't know it's her. She actually phoned from a phone box and I thought it was a number I knew so I answered it. It was her and all she did was cry, she was trying to talk but I couldn't make out what she was saying so I hung up.

Customer No. 11099

Another smelly fucker, I can tell this even before he even gets into the car

"Mate is it ahright if eh smoke?"

On every window of the taxi there is a no smoking sticker and everybody knows that you're not allowed to smoke in taxis. Actually, you're lucky if you're allowed to smoke anywhere nowadays.

"No sorry mate."

"Fuck, eh'v just lit up tae"

Just lit it up, it's a fucking nipper. The smelly fucker looks at me as if it's my fault as he pinches the top of it to nip it again. It's actually not worth fucking nipping as there's less than an inch left to smoke. Why do people light up if they've just phone for a taxi? The journey is less than five minutes but they can't wait that long to have their nicotine rush. He gets in the car and sure as fuck he is a stinker. His clothes smell like they have not been washed in weeks.

"Eh'm only going ta Asda, but will ye wait for is? Eh'll only be fev minutes and then eh'm coming back."

"Yeah sure, no problem"

On the way to Asda, he informs me that he is only going for tins of beer.

"There is a shop across the road from your house. Why do you not get them out of there?"

"Cause eh grudge giving that Paki shop the extra twenty pence he puts on each tin."

I pull up outside Asda and wait impatiently as the smelly man saunters in for his cheap beer. I watch the front door and expect him to come out with several crates which would justify the fare but no, he slowly walks out with a twelve pack. If you compare the prices he has saved himself two pound forty by purchasing the cans from the supermarket but when I return back to where I picked him up, his taxi fare comes to four pound sixty. Due to his refusal to line the pockets of his local ethnic minority shop his crate of beer has now cost him an extra two pound twenty. He reaches into his filthy jacket pocket and hands me a fiver from his yellow nicotine stained fingers and his long dirty fingernails. I go to hand him the change.

"Nah just keep it mate."

"Cheers."

Before he walks off, the cigarette he nipped before the journey is quickly pulled back out of his pocket and lit up. He swaggers off towards his house with his tins of beer and leaves behind his disgusting smell still lingering in the car.

***

I arrive at the pub after a short walk along the Perth road. I forgot how close the pub actually was. As I go through the large glass doors I see Jamie by the bar, I go to shout over the music but decide to walk around and give him a friendly little slap in the head and tell him to get me a pint.

Jamie is my younger half-brother, well I used to say little but he is actually bigger than me now. Jamie is only nineteen but looks and acts much older, this could be due to him hanging around with Gaz as they still live a few doors from one another. When Jamie is with Gaz the two of them can sit wasted for days on end, a real couple of stoners. We have the same mother but although I have never met my dad, Jamie's dad has been with my mother since I was a toddler but I still don't think of him as my dad. I have had a lot of problems with him when I was growing up and I still can't stand the cunt. I was about sixteen when I first knocked him out for his constant bullying. There were a few more knockouts after that until he learned to back off. He was always on my case. He was worse when Gaz was around, like he was trying to show off that he was in charge or something. He used to do the same with Jamie when he was growing up but that started to fade not long after I hit him, I guess he must have realised that if I was capable of growing up and doing that to him then here's to what Jamie would fucking do to him.

Jamie is served the drinks and I help him carry the round over to the table where Gaz, Kyle, Joey and Mickey are sitting. As I go over to the table Gaz shouts "Guys, watch what ye say it's the psycho coming over."

They all laugh except Joey who looks at me all serious, I smile back but he knows I'm pissed off because his version of what happened will obviously be exaggerated and make me out to be some sort of thug who beat up a guy for mouthing off, when he knows it wasn't like that. We only have one drink in Laing's and Gaz has us moving onto the next pub down, Brae's. During this time I am continually receiving texts from Lisa asking where I am. I show them to Gaz who gives me a smug look as if to say I told you so.

On the way to Brae's Gaz pulls me up about Macintosh.

"So what's the crack aboot the guy ye smashed?"

"He an areshole, he's been on my case for years and he pushed it too far this time"

"Wah is he?"

"He's another taxi driver, Macintosh. He drinks in the Ivanhoe."

"The Hoe, so he's a Lochee boy? Are ye aff yer fucking head?"

"Why?"

"He'll hae a team oot looking for ye."

I just shrug my shoulders at him.

"Eh'm no joking mate. You better watch oot. They'll be looking for ye."

I don't take much notice as Gaz is totally flying out of his head. He's had a few E's and is blabbing on and on about a load of shit and no one is really listening to him. We get into Brae's and he starts pawing at me to get my attention and puts his hand to my ear like he's away to tell me a big secret. I don't think he realizes that no matter what it is, I'm going to tell everybody anyway.

"Shane do ye see that girl at the bar?"

There is a tall girl with a short skirt, long hair and a very pretty face but you can tell she is the type who knows it, a real 'look at me.'

"I see her. What about her?"

"Eh had meh tongue in her knickers last week."

"Fuck off."

"Honestly."

"There's no way she would let you shag her."

"Eh never said eh shagged her. Eh said eh had meh tongue in her knickers."

There is a long silence then I eventually ask him.

"Come on then spill the fuckin beans, tell is how you man-aged to get your tongue in her knickers."

With both of us staring at this girl, Gaz goes on to explains to me that one day last week while working on the taxis he gets a job into the town. It was the girl behind the bar. She had been shopping and had a lot of bags. Gaz starts putting them into the boot when he notices in one of the bags some new lingerie that she had been treating herself to. Gaz says to her

"Dinna worry hen, eh'll put them awa." And she stupidly leaves Gaz alone with her shopping. As the girl is getting in the car, Gaz reaches into the bag and pulls out a kinky pair of red lace knickers. He leans forward with his head nearly in the boot, gathers a load of saliva in his mouth and proceeds to lick the crotch of these knickers. He places them back into the bag shuts the boot then drive the girl home, so technically, he has had his tongue in her knickers.

"You're fucking sick, do you know that?"

"That's good coming fae you. Psycho-boy"

I laugh this off as I know if I try to explain myself when Gaz is in this state it will just go in one ear and out the other. We have another drink in Brae's then head down the road to Nero's bar. As we walk in, Dek 'Mad Dog' Murdo is standing by the bar with a few of his mates. He looks up and gives Gaz a nod of the head but when he sees me he puts on the usual hard man 'Eh want ta fight the world' stare. I don't know what they're up this end of the town for and I really don't want to know. We walk past and find an empty table in the corner. I watch as Murdo says something to his mates and they all turn and stare over at me. I mention it to Gaz but he tells me to ignore it.

"Dinna lower yersel ta that shite mate. Eh'v telt ye before, he's a blade man and there's only one way that a fight we him will turn oot. Take one oh these and forget aboot it." Gaz says handing me a couple of E's.

"Honestly mate, eh havna had a hit like this in a lang time. Eh'm totally wasted. They're the business. They're like the E's we used ta take years ago."

That's enough encouragement for me. I take the two of them and pop one in my mouth and put one in my pocket. After a few drinks I start to mellow out a little even though I keep catching Murdo looking over at me. If he wanted to do anything I'm sure he would have started by now. I pop the other 'e' and get up to go to the toilet as I have a sudden desire to pee. On the way I notice Murdo in deep conversation with the bouncer, he's probably taking about who has the biggest blade on them. I stand at the urinal and unzip waiting on this rush of pee to come out but although my bladder detects that something wants to come out, it just doesn't happen. I stand for about five minutes and still nothing.

"Fuck" This is getting annoying.

I go back upstairs and who has decided to show up, none other than Lisa, my little stalker.

"Shane, I want to talk to you."

"I've nothing to say."

"Please Shane" She says grabbing my shirt to stop me from walking away.

"What are you doing? Leave me alone."

She starts to get louder now and her eyes fill up with tears. People have started looking over and wondering what is going on. I look over to the guys and nod in the direction of the door. Gaz nods back and then shakes his head at me. They all stand up to walk out and I go to follow them with Lisa pulling on my shirt. As I walk past the bar she tugs on my arm quite hard and in frustration I turn a little to tell her to let go, but as I turn, who does my arm catch on the way round? None other than Dek 'Mad Dog' Murdo.

"Hoi, do ye want a fucking bang in the puss?"

I don't even look up but apologise anyway. I go to keep walking towards the door but feel myself being thrown forward.

"Eh'm talking ta you, ye fucking wee wanker."

I have never had a drug drain from my body so quickly in all my life. I turn to see Murdo standing with his face like thunder.

"Come on then" He demands.

Even with the adrenaline shooting through me, I am still cautious enough not to step towards him and Gaz suddenly steps in front of me.

"Leave it Dek. He's we me" Gaz says as the bouncer steps in front of Murdo.

"Eh couldna give a fuck. You keep him oot meh fucking road" He shouts as I am ushered out of the door.

"Why did you do that Gaz? I'm not scared of him."

"Dinna be so fucking stupid, if ye start we him you'll never hear the end oh it."

"What do you mean?"

"Look, one on one, yeah maybe ye could smash him. But you ken he is the type who would come back again and again. He's just come oot oh jail for stabbing some poor cunt, does that no tell ye something. Like he's capable oh doing it again, and remember he'll no just go for you, wha ever you are we will get it tae."

We walk a bit further down the road and Gaz lights up a joint, which I feel is badly needed. He passes it to me to calm me down. He's known me all my life and he knows that it's on my mind to go back there.

"What was ah that aboot?" Jamie enquires "But mare important wha was the wee stunner that ye were chatting up?"

"Eh hope your no referring ta Shane's spunk bucket."

"That wasna that Lisa that you've been trying ta get rid oh was it?"

I give Jamie a nod.

"I ken you're meh brother but fucking hell, you're an idiot. She looks even more of a wee pumper than the last time eh saw hor."

"Why don't you go and get her, it will maybe stop her from coming near me."

"Eh would, but she was standing we that fucking Murdo when we left."

"Good, they fucking deserve each other."

We get to the Nether Inn and I feel quite calm after what happened with Murdo but this is obviously due to the joint that Gaz lit up on the way here. Gaz hands around more E's but I don't take any. I don't want to be too wasted in case I run into Murdo again or worse, end up shagging Lisa again. We have another couple of drinks and then head off to Fatties.

Chapter 8

Fat Sam's is now just another commercialised night club, but a few years ago to us regulars it was just Fatties, our little heaven. This was definitely the place to be on a Saturday night, although we were actually here sometimes Friday, Saturday and Sunday. It used to be the kind of place where if your face didn't fit you didn't get in. It was always full of friendly people. Girls that wanted to talk to you and get to know you and guys who weren't out to start a fight or cause bother. I was always invited back to parties afterwards not that I always went as I usually had my own party to go to. It didn't matter how fucked you were someone always made sure you were alright. Fatties' door policy must have been very good as there was never much trouble in the club. I have lost count of the number of times people were in front of me in the queue and the doorman would say 'Sorry, regulars only.' There would be a bit of mouthing and occasionally a bit of trouble but to me it was as if the doormen could tell who the trouble makers were by their appearance. This was a good thing as it meant they didn't have the aggravation of having to throw them out later. This has all changed now as new owners have extended the club by renovating the space under and above the original building. This extra space is a considerable size, which means the owners have to let in anybody to fill it. All the idiots that wouldn't normally get past the front door are now swaggering about like they own the place. They can now wander through from the extension to the original Fatties where they bang into people purposefully to start trouble and slavering over girls who wouldn't look twice at them. In the past I have heard people comment that Fatties was full of posers and the girls were all stuck up bitches who don't even talk to you. I look at them and think, no fucking wonder they don't talk to you. These girls want their hole as much as any other girls but maybe they just don't want to go up the road with some arsehole, who can't handle their drink, shout abuse at people and swagger about wanting to fight the world.

When we get to Fatties, the queue is very long. Gaz is totally flying and has a word with the doorman that he knows from years back.

"Any chance oh letting a few old regulars ta the front."

"No probs Gaz, is it just the six of you." Gaz gives him a nod and the doorman points to the other side of the entrance.

As we wait on the bouncer to let us pass, Jamie walks off "E'll catch up we you lads later."

Kyle shouts after him "Whar are ye going?"

He doesn't answer but turns, gives a sly grin and keeps walking in the direction of the nightclub next door. We all know he is off to the Mardi to chat up some under agers. Gaz has a word with the doorman about Murdo, just in case he comes in and starts his shit. The doorman tells Gaz not to worry about it as he's banned from Fatties for years anyway. We go straight upstairs to our usual bar to get the drinks in. Kyle follows me and Gaz heads to the toilet but Mickey and Joey are on the dance floor with their hands in the air, bouncing from the e's that they took earlier. Kyle has also had a couple of E's but he doesn't dance, he's one of those people that stands at the bar and gibbers a load of shit to everyone. The place starts to fill up and after several bottles poured down my neck I'm starting to feel more relaxed and put all that shit earlier with Murdo out of my head. As I walk around the club nodding to some familiar faces accompanied with a few random handshakes, I know what I am looking for, the little honey from my taxi. I walk through the three levels of the club with no one coming even close to looking like her. I notice Emma standing at the bar, well it's actually her legs that I notice first, she has on a very short skirt and is leaning over the bar trying to get served. I go over and rub my hand up her leg, I see the expression from the side of her face ready to give a me a mouthful but that soon changes that to a smile when she realises it is me.

"Oh it's you Shane, I thought it was some sleazy bastard, they were away to get a good slap."

Straight away I can see that Emma is wasted as her eyes are popping out of her head and she is chewing her gum at about 100mph. While talking to her I'm really quite jealous of the state that she is in. I have had a few e's from Gaz but I'm not getting anywhere near the hit she's having. I decide to wait with Emma until she gets served but the DJ plays an old tune, which makes Emma grab my hand and pulls me to the dance floor near her friends. The tune has everyone on their feet with their hands in the air. The club is jumping and I can't believe how good I feel after such a shit start to my night. As I'm dancing, Emma's friend Stacey is close by. She leans into my ear so that I can hear her and out the corner of my eye I can see Emma staring.

"Hi Shane, what happened to my phone call, I'm still waiting." She says in her sexy polite voice, I look at her next to Emma and wonder how they ended up as friends because Emma is a 'look at me' blonde bimbo type girl and Stacey is more of a quiet reserved student type.

"Sorry I have had a few things to sort out..." I don't get a chance to say anymore as Emma puts her arm around my neck and pulls me gently saying to Stacey in a friendly tone

"You're not getting him. He's with me."

Stacey smiles at me and says "Good luck."

I have thoughts going through my mind of how much of a good night this is turning out to be, until I hear a voice behind me shout in a very aggressive tone.

"Get your fucking hands off him. He's with me."

I turn to see Lisa standing with a look of pure anger. She then shouts at Emma

"You fucking slapper, get your hands off him."

"Lisa what are you doing? These are friends of mine. Why don't you fuck and off leave me alone?"

As soon as the last part comes out of my mouth I regret it as I know it's enough to get her started. I see the rage in her as she goes for Emma and grabs her by the hair pulling her to the ground. The bouncer sees it all and steps forward grabbing Lisa and throwing her out. I turn to the girls and apologise for what happened but Stacey takes my hand and says "Don't be daft Shane it's not your fault."

"If you follow me to the bar I'll get you all a drink."

I head off the dance floor with Stacey and Emma and the rest of her friends walking swiftly behind. I get to the bar and shout up a round of drinks for them and I can hear Emma behind me asking all the questions

"Shane, who the fuck was that, what was that all about?"

I turn to hand out the drinks "Look, it was someone I was seeing. I'm really sorry about that, I hope these drinks make up for it."

"No they won't, but if you invite us back to yours after here I'm sure that would make up for it" Emma says as she strokes my arm.

"Yeah sure, I'll meet you all outside at the end" I go to walk away but Emma pulls me close so that she can talk in my ear.

"Just thought I'd let you know. I don't have any knickers on."

I move in close to her ear "Durty girl."

"DUURTY, I like that."

I smile and walk away as I have to find the others to tell them to go back to mine. As I'm walking around the club looking for them, at the back of my mind I am still hoping to bump into the girl from my taxi. Although at the same time I can't stop thinking about Emma with her short skirt and no knickers. I know I feel as though I made a connection with her in the short time she was in my car I don't even know her. She could be married with kids for all I know. I eventually find Kyle at the top bar, still wasted and talking shit to some girl who looks under age and who is also wasted. How she managed to get past the doorman I don't know, but I guess if she has I.D. then there's nothing they can do. I pull him aside to tell him to come up to mine but if he is he'd better not fucking bring her with him.

"What's wrong we her?"

"How wasted are you Kyle? She looks about fifteen. Anyway Emma and her friends are coming up so if you see any of the others tell them"

"No problem."

I wander around the club but I don't see any of the others and once I am satisfied that the girl I'm looking for is not here my attention is soon directed to Emma whom I see coming out the toilet. She comes over and asks me to go to the bar with her to find Stacey. I let her lead the way so that I can look at her arse as she walks. We get to the bar and it's very crowded but we find Stacey who is waiting to get served. As I am waiting with her I have my hand on Emma's arse and as her skirt is so short my fingers slip under easily. I work my way through until they slide inside her. She turns around and wraps one of her legs around me and I can feel her getting turned on. While this is happening Stacey is chatting away to which I am nodding in agreement but do not have the faintest ideal as to what she is talking about. Emma is now rubbing my semi through my jeans and I feel like shagging her at the bar in front of everyone, knowing Emma she would probably let me. Before it gets out of hand Stacey passes the drinks. Before Fatties finishes I ask Emma if she wants to leave early so that we could get a taxi easier. We both know it's to get to mine and shag before anyone else gets there. We sneak away without telling anyone. They all know where I live so they will all get there eventually.

Chapter 9

We get to the flat and I go straight into the bedroom and take off my top as it stinks of smoke and it's a bit sweaty from being on the crowded dance floor in Fatties. Emma follows me and goes to the window.

"I love your view."

My bedroom window looks over the Tay and onto Fife. It looks good if you're trying to impress people, but tonight, it's not needed. While Emma continues to look out the window I put my hands on her hips and slide up her skirt revealing her lovely tight arse.

"Hey calm down."

"What do you mean? You're the one that was teasing me by telling me you had no knickers on."

She turns around and starts kissing me. I pull her close to me and can feel myself getting turned on. She slides her hand down and rubs my semi through my jeans. She has me unbuttoned in seconds and is sliding down both my jeans and boxers. I put on a condom and before I know it I am banging her from behind. As soon as I start to get into a rhythm my mind starts to wander. This seems to happen quite a lot when I have taken an e. I start to think that I have no connection with Emma except pure lust. I don't know anything about this girl. I don't even know her last name. She starts to groan a little louder and this puts my mind back on track again but just as I feel I am about to build up the buzzer goes on the intercom.

Emma groans "Don't stop."

I have to make a quick decision. If I don't let them in I will keep shagging Emma for about another ten minutes maybe come, and then I will be stuck with her for the rest of the night, fuck that. I pull out and start taking off the condom, Emma sits down on the leather sofa opposite the bed and spreads her legs while gliding her fingers up to her crotch.

"Do you really want to answer that?"

"I am very tempted not to."

I grab a t-shirt and go to answer the buzzer. When I come back Emma is fixing herself.

"I think you should maybe try out for porn Emma."

She thrusts her arse towards me and puts her finger in her mouth

"Really"

We both smile before a go to unlock the door

"Thanks for waiting on us" Stacey says sarcastically.

I don't answer. I go straight to the stereo and put some music on. It doesn't matter what music it is, as I know when Gaz steps in the door the first thing he will do is change it to his rap shite.

"If anyone wants a drink, just help yourself."

Kyle, Mickey and Joey turn up and say that Gaz has met up with Jamie and are away to pick up more alcohol. Joey shouts me through to the balcony for a smoke, if it is only hash I don't mind but its grass and that stinks out the whole house. Stacey follows me out and Joey leaves once he passes the joint. I only have a few puffs when the phone rings.

"That'll be Gaz" I say as I walk back into the kitchen putting on a silly voice as if to imitate him ..."Ahright Shane eh'm awa ta pick up Biscuit."

But voice on the other end is not Gaz and my smile drops when I hear them talk.

"Who is that you're with?"

"Lisa. What the fuck do you want?"

"Is that why you don't want to see me, to be with her?"

"With who, what are you talking about?"

"The girl who was with you on your balcony"

"What, are you fucking watching me?" I shout.

"I wanted to see you." She says through her tears.

"Lisa. Go away."

"Please don't hang up."

"I have nothing to say to you."

"Please Shane, don't hang up, I just want to see you." She is sounding really desperate now.

"Can I come up and see you."

"I don't think that would be a good idea do you?"

"Tell her to come up." Stacey says, trying to be funny and I give her a sarcastic smile.

"If you had any chance of ever seeing me again, you blew it by what you did earlier."

Through the noise of her crying I make out the words 'Sorry.'

"Look, all this phoning and following me is not helping. It is pushing me further away. Why don't you go home and we can talk about this tomorrow?"

"What do you mean? Will you come up and see me?"

"Look I have to go. I have people here. Go home and I will talk to you tomorrow."

I have no intension of talking to her tomorrow but I just want her to go home before she does something stupid. Before I hang up, Gaz walks in the door with Jamie. He puts a crate of lager on the kitchen table along with a bottle of vodka and he immediately notices the tension in the house as everyone is sitting quietly.

"Wha's on the phone?"

"The stalker" Stacey blurts out before I get a chance to answer.

Gaz walks over to me and grabs the phone.

"Fuck off ye psycho bitch" He says angrily down the phone before hanging up and handing it back to me.

He then takes what is left of the joint and walks out onto the balcony. I look at Stacey and we both laugh. He walks back in through a cloud of smoke and pulls a disc out of his pocket, seconds later, the music is turned off.

"Sorry people, eh'm just putting some decent tunes on ken."

With the atmosphere in the house immediately livening up, I put the phone call to the back of my mind and as I take one Gaz's beers and find a seat in the living room. Stacey follows me through and sits close by. As we are all being entertained by one of Gaz's bizarre stories I happen to catch Stacey looking over at me. I finish my beer and head back to the kitchen for another when Stacey follows me through. She puts her hand on my hip and leans in to kiss me.

"Where's your bedroom?" She says with a cheeky grin.

"What about Emma?"

"What about her? She would do the same to me."

Another of Stacey's friends comes into the kitchen and we discreetly make some distance between us. The two of them start chatting which gives me an excuse to walk away. I go back into the living room with my beer and the only empty seat is next to Emma. Stacey comes through and gives me a look. She comes straight over and kneels down next to Emma and starts chatting. Occasionally she looks in my direction and nods towards the living room door. I know an opportunity like this doesn't happen every day and if I mention this situation to any of the lads they would wonder what the fuck I was waiting on, I am now starting to wonder why I am still sitting here thinking about it. Oh man, these drugs make me think way too much. I finish my drink and go to the toilet. When I come out Stacey is standing waiting on me. She leans into to kiss me once again.

"Which one is your bedroom?"

I nod behind her and she takes my hand to lead the way. We lie on the bed and she cuddles into me. We start fondling each other but somehow I hold back.

"What's wrong?"

"Nothing"

She can obviously tell something else is on my mind, or someone. What's wrong with me? I have this girl lying next to me wanting me to shag her and I'm hesitating because I don't feel a connection with her, because it doesn't feel right.

"Is it because of Emma?"

"Eh, hmm, well she is in the next room."

"Look, don't worry about it. As I said, she would do it to me."

Stacey puts her hand down to my groin and starts rubbing me. This sends tingles through my balls and all the negative thoughts suddenly disappear. My lustful thoughts are soon back and I am hard again. I start to take off Stacey's clothes but she stands up and takes them off herself. As she walks back to my bed I smile but am really checking out her body. I am lying on my bed with a raging hard on, a naked girl is climbing on top of me and I am thinking that her breasts are too saggy and her arse is too fat. I come to the conclusion that I just don't fancy her. I can tell she is trying to be dominant by telling me to do this or try that, like I have never done this before and it starts to annoy me a little. I feel that I just want to shoot my load and get it over with. I sit up with her legs wrapped around me and her arms around my neck. I move to the edge of the bed and tilt forward until she is about to fall back but I have my hands on her wobbly arse lifting her up and down. She starts groaning louder and this gets me into it, then she whispers through deep breaths that she is about to come...thank fuck. She pulls on my neck tightly and I keep going until she tells me to stop. She lies back on the bed and I get on top of her, but after a few minutes she tells me to stop as she can't go on anymore. I still have a raging hard on and am now dying to come myself.

"You don't half know how to fuck me do you?" She says.

These words sound really strange coming from a girl who talks very polite. If she said them to me while we were fucking I maybe would have helped me come. We lie back on the bed and she cuddles up to me again. I am about to dose off when there is a light knock on the bedroom door. I open it to see Joey standing with half a joint.

"Thought you might want this"

"Yeah, cheers mate."

I go to offer Stacey a smoke but she is out like a light. I stub out the joint and turn around to face Stacey. I start wanking as I touch her naked body and it gives me more of a thrill that she could wake up any minute and catch me. My thoughts keep drifting away so I give up and fall asleep. Several hours later I am vaguely woken by the bedroom door opening and I find myself curled up with Stacey's arm wrapped around me. My comfortable position is soon disturbed by Biscuit jumping up on the bed which makes Stacey scream. Biscuit attempts to lick me while nudging his way under the covers.

"Fuck off" I shout, feeling more pissed off that I was woken up rather than him trying to get in the bed. Stacey and I both get up and get dressed. When we go through to the living room we find that everyone is still here except Emma, who apparently stormed off after she found out I was in bed with Stacey. I ask what happened to Jamie as I head to the kitchen for a drink and someone shouts through that he went for a sleep in the spare room. While in the kitchen I am passed a joint so I stay there chatting to Mickey as we pass it between us, then a random thought comes over me. Jamie on an e, going for a sleep, somehow that just would not happen. I walk through to the spare bedroom and glance around the door. I walk back and signal with my hand for everyone to follow me but I also put my finger over my lips for them to be quiet. They all follow me to the spare room to find Jamie lying on the bed naked with his arm under Emma, who is fast asleep. He obviously couldn't move without waking her. We start laughing and Emma wakes up.

"What the...Fuck off." She says and pulls the cover over her head.

A few hours later after everyone has went home except Gaz and Jamie. I tell them what happened with Emma before they came up. Jamie thinks it's funny and starts all the little wisecracks while Gaz just shakes his head calling us a couple of 'sick bastards.' I think he's just pissed off that he never got his hole last night.

Customer No. 1911

I am feeling rougher than usual today so it looks like this is going to be a short shift. My next fare is from the Dundee Sports Centre where a very butch looking girl is waiting with her large sports bag. She gets in and starts chatting away about her football team who were very close to winning some sort of tournament. As she blabs on and on and eventually stops for a breath, I comment with the usual 'Uh Huh' hoping not to sound too uninterested. I hardly make out a word she says as I am too busy clocking the traffic police following me. I start to get a little paranoid as every turn I make they are right behind me. I make a detour down a few narrow back streets and sure enough, there they are, Tayside's finest right up my arse. What the fuck do they want? I approach a mini roundabout, which is more like a speed bump in the road. As the area around this is so small it is very difficult to manoeuvre. As I drive around it my rear wheels go over the edge of it. Within seconds the blue lights are flashing behind me so I pull over.

"What's wrong, why are they stopping you?"

"I don't know" I shrug.

I step out of the car to see what the fuck they want. The officer who was in the passenger seat is out of the police car and marches over to me.

"Is this your car?" He asks aggressively.

"Yeah"

"Is it a taxi?"

Well that's a bit of a stupid fucking question. He has been following me for several miles now, I have a sign on the back of my car which says 'Licensed Cab' and he asks me if it is a taxi. I don't want to be a smart arse here as I know he will take great pleasure in lifting me so I give him a nod.

"Why didn't you go around the roundabout?"

"I did."

"No you never" He snaps his head towards me. "You drove over the top of it." He says keeping his aggressive tone.

His face is only inches from mine and I get the impression that he is taunting me. I feel the rage in me building up but I somehow manage to keep it in check so as not to give him the satisfaction of lifting me.

"If I did it was only my back wheels."

He now has his finger out and pointing it in my face, belittling me in his animated state as he rants and raves about accident statistics. Fucking hell, anyone would think I had caused a major pile up on the motorway the way this prick is acting.

"Put your meter on hold and follow me" He demands

I walk back to my car smirking in disbelief at this whole scenario.

What's the matter, why have they stopped you?" My customer asks.

"Apparently I didn't drive around the mini roundabout properly."

"What, that's what they are pulling you for?"

I give my shoulders a shrug and make a face before reaching in and placing my meter on hold. I walk back to the police car and the officer is standing waiting by the door. I sit in the back and the big fat fucker that is in the driver's seat turns to face me, in a similar manner to his partner, he has adopted the same aggressive attitude.

"Do you see that sign back there?"

How can I see it if it's back there? You fat cunt.

"Uh Huh"

"That is a mini roundabout. You approach it like you would any other roundabout. It's not a road bump that you drive over." He stares at me with his wide eyes.

It is times like this I wish I had a secret camera to video these cunts attitude towards people. I would sell it to some dodgy cable channel just like they do with us. The only difference is that their side wouldn't be edited to make them look good. If these two fuckers weren't in the police and they went about the streets with that attitude they wouldn't last a day. Its double standards all day long with all these cunts, they can talk to you whatever way they want and if you talk back to them in the same manner, you get done for it. It is the same with bouncers, they act all tough while standing on the door with their bullying biddies to back them up but when do you ever see them on a night out in a pub? Never, that's because they would be looking over their shoulder the whole night, waiting on someone they have been wide with to smash them.

"It is a bad habit and it is one that has now cost you thirty pounds." The big fat fucker says as he hands me over a ticket.

He then looks smugly at his partner. It seems like he has been waiting to use that line all day and is now chuffed with himself that he got a chance to use it. Now he can go home and get out his vast supply of kiddie porn like all those other sick coppers and wank himself to death. I am still in shock that they actually pulled me for something as petty as this. These cunts can sit here all day long and nine out of ten cars will go over the top of this fucking bump. The other officer leans over and tells me to blow in the tube. He waits a few seconds before showing the result to his partner. All clear, you couple of pricks, now open my door and let me on my fucking way. I smile at them as they let me out of the patrol car, satisfied that I managed to keep my anger in check and not give them the satisfaction of ruining my day. I get back in the taxi and drive off but they still follow me. I explain the fine to my customer and this sets them off on a little rant.

"They want to go and catch some real bloody criminals. The streets are empty, what harm did it do if you did go over the bump in the road?"

I nod my head in agreement and smile at her but I am watching these cunts in my mirror as they are still driving up my arse. I signal to go into the cul-de-sac where my customer lives and they have the cheek to put the foot down as they pass me. With an attitude like that, it is little wonder that no one has any respect for them.

Customer No. 5715

Fintry Crescent for Munro, I wait for a while at the bottom of the flats and as I am about to drive off, I see the main door open and two girls come out. They are in their late twenty's and look as rough as they come. They have obviously been up since last night. The one that gets in the front is a bit on the obese side. She has one of those tops on that doesn't cover her waist and her stretch marked spare tyre is hanging over my handbrake. I can smell the B.O. wafting from her and as she sits down the car sinks an inch or two due to her weight.

"Hi girls, where are you going?"

"Eh dinna ken. Hey Linda whar are we going?"

Hopefully back in the sea you fucking smelly whale.

"Go ta yours if ye want."

"Going ta Stoby mate, aye"

On the way the fat girl in the front is taking about the guy whose house they have just left. She is ripping into him but I think this is for the girl in the back's benefit as it sounds like she was the one who was supposedly getting it on with him.

"He was trying ta neck we me when you were in the kitchen."

"Was he?"

"Eh, his hands were ah over is."

"What a prick, how did ye no say something ta is?"

"Eh dinna ken. Eh think eh was just shocked."

If some guy was coming on to this girl I can only imagine what he must look like if this is his taste in women. She is absolutely horrible, her teeth are yellow and for someone to want to try and kiss her, they must have some serious issues.

"Here, are ya up for going oot the night?"

"Too right, eh'm aff work the morn. Eh will huv ta change meh clothes though, eh'v had these on since last night."

A shower wouldn't go a miss either, you smell like a cundie. Here's to what that guy would have encountered if she had let him put his hand down her knickers. She pulls down the sun visor to look in the mirror

"Oh meh god, check the state oh meh hair."

I glance slightly over while driving and think to myself, her fat layers are hanging over my handbrake, her B.O. is stinking out my car even though my windows are down, her clothes are filthy, her teeth are yellow and she is worried about her fucking hair.

Chapter 10

Gaz

Eh hae a delivery later so eh'v got Auld Wullies' car for the night. He kens he always gets a good wee bundle at the end oh meh shift, whether eh'm busy or no. He likes the grass so eh always leave him enough for a wee smoke as well.

Customer No. 3004

Pitkerro Road for Stewart, eh'v picked up this couple a few times before and they are a couple oh junkies and a pain in the arse. They hae their bairn we them the day and as soon as they get in the car they start arguing aboot whar ta go first.

"Kirtin post office, but we need ta get there before it shuts." The smelly ginger cow in the back says ta is. It's nearly closing time but eh'm no awa ta speed for them. It would be just meh luck that the Traffic Polis would clock is, and that is the last thing eh need. Eh manage ta get them there on time and eh havena even stopped the car but she's opened the door and trying ta get oot.

"Hud on missis" Eh say, but she just ignores me and storms awa inta the shop. She's back in the car within a few minutes, but her man has been sitting fidgeting and looking really agitated. He tried ta talk ta me but eh cut him aff we blunt answers. Eh think he kens that eh dinna like him.

"Aboot fucking time" He says as she gets in the car.

"Shut your puss you Right, go along this street and eh'll tell ye when ta stop" She points ahead.

She hands him money, obviously from their family allowance she's just cashed. She tells me ta park ootside a hoose on the end oh a row.

"What ye getting him to stop here for?"

"You ken they dinna like taxis stopping ootside their hoose."

He gets oot and runs aroond the corner ta another hoose. He's back a few minutes later and starts whispering ta her. She's pulls oot her phone...

"Go ta the Hulltoon driver" She snaps.

Ah the way ta the Hulltoon eh can feel the tension building up between them as they start getting louder.

"What if he's no got any?"

"Then we'll have ta try...?" Her voice lowers so that eh canna hear what name it is.

"Eh hate going there."

"Eh'm no giving a fuck. If it comes ta it, yer fucking going" She shouts.

We stop at a tenement block in Dundonald Street and the guy bolts oot the car and up the stairs. He's back doon and inta the car within a couple oh minutes looking even more distressed. Eh canna tell if this is because he husna been fixed up or that he has ta face his angry ginger missus. The meter is ticking up and ah that is on meh mind is if they're gonna pay this fucking fare. Eh dinna give a shit if they get their drugs and it turns oot ta be a bad batch and they overdose, eh honestly couldna give a fuck. That's the life they chose and that's the way they want ta live it, but if they are planning on bumping this fare, that fat ginger cow's man will be feeling meh fist in his fucking puss. At the back oh meh mind eh'm actually hoping that they dinna hae enough money for the taxi just so that eh hae an excuse ta hit the cunt. Then eh'll tak their smack off them and chuck it in the fucking bin. Eh'm directed ta a another dodgy hoose near the Hulltoon area and during this time the ginger cow in the back is phoning aroond ta try and find somebody that'll sort them oot. Both oh them are starting ta get a bit aggressive. Eh feel for the bairn that is sitting in the back keeping his puss shut. She eventually finds somebody wah has what they want but the person isna gonna be hame for another twenty minutes.

"Right driver, on ta Lochee"

Lochee, now there's a fucking surprise.

"Eh telt ye, ye should have phoned him first."

"Ah shut yer puss."

This arguing goes on ah the way ta Lochee and at one point eh'm close ta throwing them oot. Eh look at the bairn in the back and eh feel really sorry on him so eh continue the journey.

"That'll be sixteen eighty please."

"Nah, were going back again."

"No in this fucking taxi yer no. This is as far as eh'm going we you."

She hands me seventeen pound and eh dig oot the twenty pence change. As eh hand it ta her she grabs it oot meh hand and storms oot the car slamming the door. It wouldna be the first time that eh'v gave they junkies the benefit oh the doubt and after they've paid for their drugs and drove them hame, they suddenly they dinna hae enough ta pay for the taxi. Eh find it really sad that their lives revolve aroond this shite. Eh understand there is genuine hard luck stories oh how people have ended up as junkies but they are in the minority. Eh feel sorry on their bairn growing up and seeing ah this going on. It makes me wonder what sort oh upbringing that bairn has, if he wakes up in the morning ta clean clothes to wear ta skale or if they even hae anything in their cupboards for his breakfast. To me it seems like he is just an inconvenience to them, I'll bet he's convenient enough when they want the extra benefits they get handed for keeping him though. Eh'm only working the night because eh hae a drap aff later and seeing that makes me want ta walk away fae it. But when eh think aboot it, eh'm no dealing in smack and nobody telt them ta stick a needle in them.

Customer No. 2368

Eh have been dragged aboot a mile and a half to pick up this fat lazy cow and she's only going to the fucking bingo at the end oh the street. The grumpy bitch is only just in the car and she's ranting because her seat belt winna go aroond her. Eh'm no awa to help her because there's a good chance eh'll wrap it aroond her fucking neck. Eh drive to the main door oh the bingo and there is a large queue.

"Looks busy the day, eh" Eh say trying ta make conversation.

The ignorant cow doesna even answer, she looks up and grunts.

"That will be two pound twenty please."

She hands me the correct money.

"Thanks very much" Eh say as she looks at me again we a face like a well skelped arse. She goes ta get oot oh the car and the whole queue is watching as she struggles ta get her fat arse up aff the front seat. It wouldna look so bad but she is wearing a long overcoat on one oh the hottest days we have had the whole summer. She eventually woddles oot oh the car and eh shout cheerio before she slams the door in meh face ignoring is. As she canna walk that fast due to her size eh slowly reverse the car as she heads for the back oh the queue. She's obviously haeing a bad day so there's no way eh'm aboot ta drive aff and let her leave her bad day we me. Eh shout again oot the windee and several people turn ta look.

"Cheerio, I hope you have a nice day." Eh shout a bit louder in meh polite sarcastic tone. She doesna even turn her head, the ignorant bitch. Eh shout again a bit louder and more nosey fuckers in the queue turn to see what is going on. She turns her head slightly ta see me we a big smug grin on meh face and she says through gritted teeth.

"Cheerio."

Eh laugh oot loud as eh drive aff knowing that the bitch never put a downer on meh day. Eh canna believe eh drove ah that way to pick up that miserable old cunt ta drive her aboot a hundred yards doon the street. Eh have always been brought up we the saying that manners cost nothing, a simple hello, goodbye, please and thank you go a long fucking way in meh book.

**

Right that's the Weedgie cunt in Dundee now. Eh'v text him ta go ta The Club Bar. It's the first one he'll come ta when he gets aff the train. Eh'll text him again when ta get the staff ta phone him a taxi. They use meh firm so if eh time it right the joab will come straight to me. He had better get the staff ta phone because if he uses his mobile and gets busted they will ask him how he got that number. That's me just went number one so eh'll text him now.

Good that's the joab come through. Eh drive up ootside the pub and this wee Weedgie cunt swaggers oot we a hold all over his shoulder. He is the typical wee hard man, scars, skin-head and ten bob swagger. Glasgow must be a rough place ta live because nearly every Weedgie that eh meet has big dirty fucking scars doon their face. He walks over and gets inta the back oh the taxi.

"Ahright mate, whar is it you're heading?"

"Aye awright pal, am going up the Perth Road, any recommendations" He says in his Weedgie acccent.

"How aboot The Nether Inn"

"Aye, that'll dae, am just having the one drink like and then am heading back." He says as he taks a package oot oh his hold all and leans forward putting it on the front seat.

"I'll catch you again some time pal." He says as he gets oot oh the car.

"Eh, take it easy mate" Eh say picking up the package and putting it under the seat.

Eh drive over towards Kirkton as that's whar it's getting picked up fae. As eh'm driving eh'm texting at the same time arranging the pick-up. As eh drive over the Kingsway eh see the Polis in meh mirror and the blue lights come on. Shit this is it, eh'm going doon big time. Ten ta fifteen easy, meh heart is going like the clappers. Eh pick up the package fae under meh seat and wipe it doon we a cloth before throwing it in the back. Eh'll just plead ignorant. They canna prove fuck all. The wee Weedgie cunt must have left it there, it's nothing ta dae we me. Eh wonder wha stuck is in. They must have been onta the Weedgie because it's no come fae meh side. Eh pull over and the Polis boy gets oot and walks over ta meh windee.

"What's the problem?" Eh nearly choke ta say.

"Do you have a mobile phone on you?" He says.

"What, eh how"

"Can I see it please?"

Usually eh would start ta get wide and give them loads oh shite but right now meh heart feels like it's ready ta explode.

"Eh nae bother" Eh say handing him the phone.

"Can you come and take a seat in the back off the patrol car please."

Eh get oot oh the taxi and walk over ta the patrol car and meh legs are ready ta buckle as they feel like jelly. He opens the back door and eh get in, he gets in the front next ta his partner.

"Under the traffic violation act…,we have reason to believe you were using your mobile phone while in control of a vehicle, registration number…, do you have anything to say?"

"Eh, no really no"

"We are issuing you with a fixed penalty of…"

Oh ye fucker, meh pumping heart gradually starts ta settle back doon. Eh thought eh had been busted. The Polis hand me the fixed penalty and let me oot oh their car. Eh get in the taxi and get ta fuck away fae them as quick as eh could. Any other time eh would huv got mesel lifted because eh would have argued we them and given them loads oh shite. But we that gear sitting on the back seat eh just shut meh puss and let them get on we it. And to think them daft Polis were giving me a ticket for using a mobile while driving, and eh had something on is that could have put me awa for years. It's a good joab eh wasna picking meh nose because eh'v actually seen myself looking in the mirror ta get a wee cruster oot and ending up driving on the other side oh the road. As soon as the Polis are oot oh sight eh pull over and text the cunt so that eh could get this gear awa ta fuck.

Customer No. 1698

Eh was glad ta get rid oh that gear there e'll tell ye. Eh'll dae this one last joab and head aff ta the pub. Asda for McComskie, there is a young lassie waiting we a pile oh shopping bags and eh can tell there'll no be a bar oh soap in any oh them. The lassie would look no bad if she cleaned herself up a bit but Shane was right aboot kenin by looking at somebody wah is gonna smell before they get in the car. Efter eh load up the boot she gets in the back and eh notice the musty smell straight away, the wee dirty mink.

"So whar are you going then?"

"Charleston."

"Okay"

"Listen when we get ta meh hoose, eh'll have ta pop in for the money, is that oaky?"

"Eh, but just remember and come back oot again."

Eh drive up ta the hoose and as soon as eh see the gairden eh recognise it and eh'v never even been here before. Eh mind oh Shane telling me aboot some lassie one night. She said ta him that she didna hae enough money for the fare and that he could put his hand up her skirt and feel her cunt instead if he wanted. Now Shane is no ain ta be fussy aboot getting his hole but she was apparently that bad he telt her he wouldna put his hand up her skirt if he had a fucking nuclear protective glove on. He also telt her ta pay the fucking fare or he was gonna phone the Polis. It was dark but he remembers her gairden looking like a scrap yaird we an auld B.M.W. in the driveway. Well, surprise surprise, in front oh me right now is a rusty auld B.M.W. Eh pick up her shopping oot oh the boot and follow her ta her front door. For a smelly mink she hasna half got a bra pair oh legs on her. She has got on ain oh they wee denim skirts. As she opens her front door eh'm hit we a rancid smell that fills half meh lungs.

"Come in and eh'll see if eh can find some change for ye" She says.

As eh go through the half papered, half scrapped lobby eh feel as though the soles oh meh shoes are sticking ta the car-pet.

"Do ye want a cup oh tea while yer here?" She says.

Eh look aroond the place and am shocked at the state oh it. How anybody can live like this is fucking mental. Hygiene in a woman is no ain oh meh priorities like it is we Shane, but this place is fucking stinking. Eh dinna think it takes much ta shower every day. Eh'm talking ten minutes tops and that includes emptying your sacks. Eh try ta see past ah this and look at the lassie in front oh is. She has a slim figure and a nice face, and nothing a good scrub wouldna put right.

"Sure eh'll hae a cup oh tea. Two sugars and plenty oh milk please."

Well Shane, she might no be good enough for you, but she's certainly getting it fae me. She puts the kettle on and before eh ken it, we are kissing in the middle oh the kitchen. Eh have meh hands on her arse and lift up her wee denim mini. She pulls awa fae is and gets doon on her knees ta suck is aff. Eh had a wank earlier so meh knob could be a bit cheesy. No that she'll fucking notice. She pulls oot meh knob and looks up at me smiling before putting it in her mooth. Eh feel a bit sick when eh notice the broken teeth and the yellow moldy stains on them. She gives it a wee suck but she's no very good at it. Eh pick her up and bend her over the sink. Eh lift her mini skirt right up over her waist and pull doon her knickers revealing a fuckin lovely toned arse. Eh slide meh knob in and it feels like it's no even touching the sides. Eh'm banging awa but eh stop ta take her knickers right aff so that eh could open her legs mare. Eh slide them doon ta her ankles and as she steps oot oh them, eh look doon and clock the thick yellow stains, they remind me oh curry sauce. Eh slide meh knob back in and as eh get meh rhythm back eh start ta think aboot diseases and realise eh dinna have a condom on. This is a first for me as it's never worried is before. Maybe because it's the first time eh'v shagged a burd we rotten teeth, breath like Biscuits farts, on a good day, armpits that smell like onions and a cunt that leaves moldy stains on her knickers that resemble curry sauce, then eh think, nah, eh'v had worse. There's nae point in worrying aboot it now, meh knobs ahready in. Eh feel that eh'm awa ta shoot meh load so eh grab her hair fae behind. This was ta make her groan a wee bit but ah it's done is put me aff due ta how greasy it is. Eh pull oot and start wanking, Eh shoot meh load right up her back and some drips doon her arse. Eh pull up meh jeans and get ta fuck oot oh there as quick as eh could, no even turning ta say cheerio. Eh run ta the car and drive aff feeling dirty as fuck, and no in a good way.

Chapter 11

Eh'm no looking forward ta the night, Shane has nipped oor heads the whole week ta go ta some gig night at The Doghoose because some burd he met asked him ta go. As long as it's better than last Seturday efter that run in he had we Murdo, eh ken he isna gonna let that go. Eh'v only saw Shane once this week and that was ta drap aff some cash. Every time eh'v phoned him he's been working. Eh just hope he's no been seeing that fucking Lisa efter ah the trouble she's caused.

We meet up in the East View for a few pints before heading ta The Doghoose and Jamie has been getting it tight for shagging Emma, every cunt now kens that Shane shagged her just hours before him. But as always, it doesna last long as Jamie being the smart arse that he is, the slagging soon turns aroond and now Shane is taking a bit oh stick for last week. Before we head aff eh eventually get Shane on his ain ta enquire aboot Lisa but he swears he's no heard fae her since last week, he did mention something aboot his car being damaged and thinks it was something ta dae we Murdo. Eh telt him that it wasna his style, as Murdo wouldna be that sneaky he would probably dae it in front oh him.

When we get ta The Doghoose there is a wee queue ta get in, then once we get in, we struggle ta reach the bar as the place is packed. There is a fairly young crowd aroond us but they soon move forward as the first band kicks aff. Eh stand at the bar we Kyle and Shane but Jamie, Mickey and Joey walk nearer the stage, which we ah agree is for them ta get a better look at the wee lassies dancing aboot at the front. Shane looks distracted and his eyes continually scan the whole pub.

"What's wrong mate, has she stood ye up?"

"What are you talking about?" He keeps a straight face as if he doesna ken what eh mean.

"The burd wha telt ye ta come here, has she stood ye up?"

Eh look at Kyle and we baith laugh. Shane gets a bit flustered and tries ta change the subject.

"That band sounds decent."

We ah look up at the stage ta see four young grubby hippyish looking guys. They call themselves 'The View' and their average age is aboot seventeen, hence the wee lassies hanging aboot the stage. Eh'm no even into ah that indie shite but efter hearing their first tune eh'm hooked and that's withoot any drugs yet. They play a few songs and looking at the crowd jumping aboot it makes is wish eh was a teenager again. Shane and Kyle are nattering between themselves aboot how much they sound like this band or that band, or a certain song sounds like some other fucking song. Eh was never into that kind oh music ta know what they're on aboot. Eh'm mare oh a Hip Hop man, eh like artists that tell ye how many bitches they've fucked or how many guns they hae. It's no that eh dinna like this type oh music, eh just dinna listen ta it that much. Shane and Kyle have ripped into every song that they have done and it's starting to annoy is so eh need ta say something.

"Look ye couple oh cunts, eh think they're no bad. For one thing, they're doing ah their ain stuff, which is unusual these days and so what if they sound like other bands, every other fucking group does it, and two, they are only fucking seventeen or eighteen, eh'll bet The Stones or The Beatles were shite at that age, and three, they can play better than any oh you two ever fucking will."

The two oh them look at is and then look at each other we a stupid expression before making some childish noise in a high pitched tone "wooooooo."

Jamie, Joey and Mickey come over and they all have a funny look on their pusses.

"What's the joke?"

"Have ye heard the lyrics to the song they are playing the now? It's called 'Same Jeans' it's aboot you Gaz. Eh'v had the same jeans on for four days now and eh'm aff inta the toon." Jamie makes a poor attempt at singing we a stupid look on his puss.

They ah laugh but eh soon turn it aroond.

"Eh but what aboot the ain the singer says is called 'The Don' that must be aboot you. A soft touch oh a boy wha sits on his ain while we are ah oot takin E's"

We ah laugh except Jamie as he turns ta the bar ta get another roond in before the next band comes on. When Jamie passes me a drink he asks is for a few E's and eh hand him a couple. Abody else is looking on, so eh dish oot what's left between the rest oh us. Eh obviously keep a few extra back for mesel. Before the next band comes on eh go ootside for a quick smoke we Shane and Kyle. While we are oot there eh notice that there is loads oh young people oot their nut on E's. This is strange ta me as eh'v never took E's in this kind oh environment. It's always been at a rave like the Rumba or the Glam and sometimes the occasional trip ta Weedgie Land for The Tunnel or The Arches. That was the time oh Pete Tong and the Judge spinning the decks before they became fucking celebrity deejays. They kent how ta pick ye up we the right tune when ye were waiting on yer hit kicking in. Now we just swally a few and go ta Fatties but even that's no the same now. Different people, different atmosphere, but we still go because it's the only place left that still plays half decent tunes. Just before we go back in eh see Shane's face light up as some wee dark haired lassie walks past.

"Hi do you remember me? Your taxi driver"

"Oh hi, so you made it then?"

"Yeah, I managed to persuade my friends to come."

Eh watch as Shane searches his mind for something else to say. It's only a few seconds but eh could tell he's stuck for words.

"I'll have to go and find my friends, I'll see you inside."

We ah watch her go in and when eh look at Shane he has this stupid smile on his face.

"Is that it?"

"What?"

"Is that what you brought us ah here for?"

"No, we come to see some bands"

Eh look at Kyle and we baith make a face and laugh but Shane storms awa in the huff. We go back in and eh dinna ken if it was the joint but eh feel like the crowd has become mare aggressive. There's two guys in front oh is wah are definitely on E's but are swaggering aboot like they are looking for a fight we somebody, probably anybody. That's just no what E's are ah aboot. It makes ye wonder exactly what it is that they put in them nowadays.

When Shane and I first took them they lasted the whole night and the last thing that ye wanted was ta start fighting we some cunt. Eh remember hearing once somebody describing them as the love drug and judging by the way they affected some people eh would certainly go along we that. If ye had took twa back then ye were totally smashed, if ye tak twa now you're lucky ta get a buzz. The names oh the E's changed we each different design they had on them and this was happening often, which usually meant that they gave ye a different hit. They started ta get weaker over time, which meant that ye needed mare and mare ta get a decent hit, either that or we were becoming immune ta them. It got ta the point that we were taking between six and ten in one night and still no getting the same buzz that we used ta get fae one oh them. It started ruining your night oot as we were maybe at a perty and although there were plenty oh good looking lassies there, ah ye could think aboot was getting mare E's, when we should have been haeing a banter and trying ta get our hole, instead we wasted the rest oh the night trying ta get oor hands on mare E's, and looking for that hit. When we eventually got oor hands on them we were too fucked ta actually bother aboot the lassies. It was a long frustrating night. For me it was easy ta deal we, as eh would head hame and hae a few joints, fall asleep and get up the next morning feeling great. But Shane, Shane was different, he never really smoked much hash at that time so he would go hame and think aboot loads of shite. Ah these negative thoughts going through his head, his joab, his life, ah felt worthless and it would drive him nuts. Eh offered ta get Valium for him but he refused. He says that was the first step on the way ta being a junkie. He has a smoke now when he is coming doon and he seems ahright.

Before the next band come on eh nip upstairs ta the toilet and as eh'm taking a piss eh hear a few sniffs coming from the cubicle. The door opens and two young guys eh recognise walk oot.

"Aright Gaz, how's it going?"

"No bad, yourself"

"Aye, eh'm ahright, ye wanna line?"

"Eh sure why no"

We go back into the cubicle and the young guy starts chapping is up a fair sized line on tap oh the cistern.

"Whats the crack we the music by the way"

"What do ye mean?"

"They're ah doon there oot there nut on E's and jumping aboot ta rock music."

"You've got ta keep up we the times Gaz. We've ah moved on fae techno mate. Anyway have ye never heard oh Hanney?"

"Nah mate"

"They're the next band on, probably up your street mate."

Eh tak the line in one big sniff. This coke has probably come fae the same stuff that eh drapped aff the other day. If anybody found oot eh would be banged up within the week.

"So what are they like then? Eh'v never heard oh them."

"You're joking, they're the business like."

He explains ta is that he kens the guys in the group. They are ah mates wah just play for a laugh, nothing serious, but they are actually really good. They took their name fae a mate oh theirs wah tragically killed himself.

"Wee Bobby, he was a great wee guy." He says as we head aff doon ta watch the band.

As the music kicks aff eh'm quite shocked ta find a girl on stage in front oh the band doing some strange dance, the music is great. They sound a bit like faithless, a heavy bass dance beat, a bit oh guitar and a guy at the back on the decks, scratching. This is meh type oh music. It's got a bit oh everything. The crowd has obviously been waiting on this as they are ah on their feet we their arms in the air. Loads oh the younger crowd have left, they must have only came for The View and it seems ta be mare like ah the auld ravers that are left. They must be good as even Kyle's feet are tapping away, and it takes a lot ta get him going. We ah stand nodding our heads and eh can see Shane looking aboot again, obviously on the prowl for that wee burd. Hanney's music changes we each tune, the last tune definitely had a Linking Park influence but are now sounding a bit like The Happy Mondays. It's really picking me up now and eh start ta get a wee buzz fae the E's. It's just enough ta get me going, although the singer fae Hanney looks like he's had a few. He's aff the stage and into the crowd now, while still belting oot his lyrics and tho crowd love it.

"What is he on?" Eh ask some guy wah is dancing awa next ta is.

"Wah"

"The guy on the mic, eh'd like some oh whatever he's on."

"That's Bomber, he's always like that, fucking mental"

Efter Hanney finish, the pub clears oot a bit and eh could see Shane wandering aboot looking for that burd again. As eh turn towards the bar eh see Dek Murdo and his mates standing near the door. Eh wonder what the fuck he's doing in here. Eh get the roond in as the next band comes on and introduce themselves. They look really nervous as the singer says "Hello everyone, we are Killer Angels."

Eh'm expecting mare oh the same oh what eh'v just heard but eh couldna be mare wrong. The noise is deafening, this is rock music at its heaviest. There's a few people jumping aboot ta their music but it's too much for me. Eh turn ta look for Shane when eh see ain oh Murdo's mates squaring up ta him. Just as eh go ta rush forward and stop it the cunt puts the head on Shane. He steams right back but the rest oh his mates have ah jumped in. It must have been a set up. Eh see ain oh them picking up a stool and eh lift it right oot oh his hands before he gets a chance ta use it. Shane is doon and they are ah on tap oh him putting in the boot. Eh start pulling them aff and the bouncers just stand there watching. Eh realise how when eh see Murdo standing next ta them.

"Dek, what the fuck" Eh shout across the pub ta him. He just shrugs his shoulders and gives me a smug grin. He's obvi-ously got something against Shane but we him being oot on early release he canna get in any fights or he goes back ta finish his sentence. We the help oh Joey and Mickey we pull the cunts aff him and get him oot the side door.

"Are you ahright"

"What the fuck happened there?" Shane says.

He goes ta walk back in but we ah grab him and pull him back.

"Dinna be stupid Shane."

"What was that all about, did I do something?"

"Nah the guy was just being wide. I think Murdo set it up"

"I'm going to fucking smash him when I get a hold of him."

"Come on lets head ta Fatties they dinna get in there any-way."

Chapter 12

On the way ta Fatties, Shane decides ta go up the road instead and waves doon a taxi.

"You better no go back there."

"What? On my own, I don't think so."

"They ah make attempts ta persuade him ta stay oot but when Shane makes up his mind there's no changing it. Eh dinna open meh mooth as he's ahready pulled me aside on the way doon the road and telt is ta come up efter Fatties.

While we are in the queue eh feel a good buzz coming on and eh start ta get a wee tingle doon meh spine and this sets aff the happy mood. Eh start chatting ta a group oh lassies that are behind us in the queue. Eh ken that eh'm talking a load oh shite bit the buzz eh'm getting is great and they ah seem nice enough. Jamie is helping is oot we keeping the banter going bit Joey, Mickey and Kyle are just talking shit between themselves. We ah head ta the bar as soon as we get in and Mickey gets the drinks in. As we wait by the bar we scan over the club and then Kyle gives me a tap and nods in the direction oh the bar at the far end. It's Lisa. She is looking quite smug standing we some new guy. Eh canna believe that last week she was breaking her heart, stalking and pestering Shane, now this week she's moved on an found some other mug.

"It's a good thing that Shane went up the road eh." Kyle says as he passes me a drink.

"She obviously thought Shane was gonna be here the night and start some shite we her new lad."

Eh wander aroond the club for a while and find myself in a conversation we some jumped up schemie. It's like they are a trying ta impress ya by going on aboot kicking the shite oot oh some pair cunt wah just happened ta be in the wrong place at the wrong time. These guys never seem ta get in a fight when they're on their own, it's always when it's three or four on ta one. If they do happen ta get themselves involved in a scuffle that's too much for them, that's when the bottles start getting used or in other cases, knives. They probably tell the same story aboot ten times a night ta anybody wah will listen adding things each time they tell it, pumped full oh steroids, chest sticking oot and talking as if they are hard as fuck. Eh'm in half a mind ta tell them exactly what eh think oh them but eh ken what it will lead ta and eh think, do eh really want ta get banned for these cunts. Eh'm really flying right now and the bass fae the music is flowing through meh body, Eh make meh excuses and head ta the danceflair whar eh see one oh the lassies fae the queue. She pulls meh arm so that eh'm dancing closer ta her. Eh think she looks stunning but that could be an effect from the amount oh drugs that eh'v consumed and making is think that she's stunning. Eh see Joey dancing no too far from me and eh feel like asking him if she's ahright as Joey would have had fewer drugs than me. But then what if he says she's tidy so that eh go and shag her but she turns oot ta be a total horror and every cunt taks the piss oot oh is for it. Then Joey could have had mare E's than me and actually does think she's tidy but she really is a total horror, ah fuck it wah cares, eh'm oot meh nut and she canna be any worse than what eh'v shagged before. While she's dancing she comes up and gives me a wee necky.

"Do ye want ta go ta a perty efter Fatties?"

"Eh, but can eh bring meh mate?"

"Of course"

Shane, you are getting woken up big time. Eh leave Fatties before the end so that eh could head up ta Shane's withoot anybody following us. Eh buzz up and as we walk in, Shane is on the couch rolling a joint. Now that eh see him in the light eh can see a few marks on his face.

"Have a good night then did ye?" He says making a face.

Eh offer the girls a drink and they follow me ta the kitchen. We start talking and end up in a very deep conversation but eh dinna ken what the fuck we are talking aboot. Every now and again ah eh hear is 'Ken wot eh mean' and it's starting ta annoy is a bit. Eh ken that eh speak Dundonian but these burds are owray as fuck. When eh'm smashed eh wouldna normally notice how common a lassie talks but they must be bad because it is doing meh nut in. Shane comes through we the joint but he doesna say much, he has a few puffs and passes it to me.

"I'm away to my bed, don't put the music too loud."

"Hey, no worries man"

Eh wonder what's up we him. Eh'v brought back two lovely burds wah are up for their hole and he fucks off ta he's bed. We go and sit in the living room and put some tunes on. The lassies finish their drinks and eh go ta the kitchen to refill them. Ain oh the lassies follows me through and starts necking we is.

"Do ye want ta go ta the bedroom"

"What aboot meh mate?"

"Send her through ta see Shane."

The lassie goes through ta speak ta her mate while eh fix the drinks. When eh head back through she is sitting on her own.

"Is she awa through?"

The lassie nods and smiles and eh put the drinks on the ta-ble. We start getting it on and she mentions something aboot condoms but she gets telt straight.

"Fuck that, it's like haeing a bath we yer socks on."

Eh dinna ken whar eh got that saying fae, eh just remember hearing it years ago. Eh'm on tap oh her and she's making these wee squealing noises, which eh find quite funny. We're at it for a wee while when eh start ta think aboot what eh said aboot condoms and now eh'm imagining exactly what it would be like ta actually hae a bath we yer socks on. Eh try hard ta concentrate as eh'm desperate ta shoot meh load. Eh go a bit harder and speed up a bit tae and eh could feel the sweat running doon meh face. Eh look up and see Shane standing watching is.

"Carry on, don't mind me, I just came through for a drink."

He carries on through to the kitchen and eh can hear him laughing. Eh try ta keep going but every time eh look up Shane is popping his head aroond the corner and making stupid faces, he's putting his arms up and showing his muscles. The cunt is putting me aff meh stride. The cunts been there, he kens it's hard enough trying ta come on E's withoot somebody distracting ye. He goes awa back inta the bedroom and eh try ta get back in ta it but eh keep picturing him making they faces. Eh make meh excuses and go ta the toilet. When eh get there eh canna pee but eh find mesel haeing a wank. Just as eh feel it building up eh start thinking aboot something else and it doesna happen, fuck. Eh go back ta the living room and the other burd that eh thought was we Shane has come back and the ain eh was we has got ah her clothes back on.

"What's wrong?"

"Nothing, we have ta go."

"Eh'm going awa ta skin up, do ye no want ta stay for a smoke?"

"Nah we'll just go."

They phone a taxi and by the time it comes eh decide ta go we them. Eh go hame and get Biscuit then go back ta Shane's. Eh stop aff at the shop for some munchies and then walk aroond ta his flat. He must ken it's me as he doesna even speak on the intercom he just presses the buzzer ta let is in.

"What the fuck were you thinking bringing two mingers like that up to my flat?" He says as eh walk in the door.

"What are you on aboot?"

"What am I on about? The fucking moldy orange that you sent through to my room that's what I am fucking on about."

We walk in ta his bedroom and he puts the light on.

"Look at that."

He points ta a big patch oh brown and orange stains on his pillow case. Eh burst oot laughing.

"Come on Shane ye ken me. She was groping meh bahs on the dance flair, eh just saw the tanned legs and short skirt. Ye ken when eh'm full oh it eh dinna look that far up.

Chapter 13

Shane

B ank holiday weekend and all the taxis are out in force trying to make as much money as they can. I certainly won't be working any extra hours that's for sure. More than likely it will be less, but it really depends on how fucked up I get tonight. I know as soon as I go into the pub tonight someone will say, why are you not working? It must be busy as fuck this weekend. They will be told the same as everyone else, I work enough to pay my bills and get out on the piss. I don't understand some of those drivers who sometimes work from ten in the morning until four the next morning. They must either be in a mountain of debt or are just absolute greedy bastards. What kind of life is that? Most of all its fucking dangerous, there is a good chance one of them will end of falling asleep at the wheel and knowing my luck, it will be the one that picks me up.

Customer No. 9614

My next job is to St. Mary's where I pick up two women carrying overnight bags. One has the blonde bimbo hair with the streak of dark roots quite visible down the middle and the other has dark hair but has huge tits.

"So where are you two ladies off to then?"

"The train station" Blondie says.

"No, I mean from there."

"Oh sorry, Manchester"

"Shopping" They both laugh.

"Nah it's really a weekend on the piss but we nip aroond the market for a couple oh hours before we get back on the train." Blondie says.

"We buy loads oh shite but the trick is ta make sure ye get loads oh different bags so that yer man thinks yev been busy." The one with the big tits says.

"Eh busy pulling" Blondie says as they both laugh.

"We used ta go ta Newcastle but we bumped inta too many people we kent fae Dundee so it was getting a bit risky."

"Remember that time we nearly got caught fae yer cousin ..."

They proceed to tell me some story about pulling a couple of blokes back to their hotel and kicking them out in the morning only to find that one of their man's cousins was staying at the same hotel. They went down for breakfast to find him with his family and he actually made a comment about one of the guests making some noise while getting their hole.

"He says somebody was making too much noise, it must have been you cause the guy eh was we wasna big enough ta make me scream except ta laugh it the size oh it. Talk aboot a daed ride"

What an effort just to get your hole.

***

All of my customers seem to have been in a rush today and all they have talked about is that it is a bank holiday and how good the weather is. One of them has actually mentioned that we are in for a heat wave this summer. I'm actually sweating sitting in this car and that's with the sunroof open and all the windows down. I'll be finishing shortly and it will be a quick shower, change of clothes, something to eat and up to the East View, party time.

I get to the East View and feel dehydrated due to the heat and it takes the first pint just to quench my thirst, the second flows down quite easily too. I head to the toilet and find Gaz in there getting his weekly supply of drugs from some shady looking fucker. I wait until the guy heads out before I say something to him.

"Gaz are you fucking stupid, I could have been anybody walking in here. You better watch what the fuck you're doing."

"It's usually a quick swap bit eh had ta get a bit extra this weekend, ye ken what it's like, bank holiday."

"Why didn't you go into the cubicle?"

Just as I say this, we hear a sniffing sound coming from inside the cubicle. The door opens and Kyle pops his head out.

"Ahright, you want a line?"

Gaz can't get in there quick enough. Kyle hands Gaz a credit card and he quickly goes to work chapping up a few lines. I snort half up one nostril and half up the other. My face cringes as the horrible taste goes down the back of my throat.

"While yer at it ye can pop ain oh these doon ye as well" Gaz passes the bag of E's with a big smile on his face before bending down to take his line of coke.

We all take one and then head back to the bar. After several more drinks Kyle phones a couple of taxis for us to go into the town. I head to the toilet again and when I come out I see Dek Murdo swaggering through the door. I put my head down and wait to see who he is with. Two of his mates walk in behind him and I recognise one of them immediately as the guy who nutted me last week. I run across the pub and throw a punch at him with everything I've got. It lands on the side of his jaw and he hits the deck spark out. I look up to see Murdo swinging at me and I can't get out of the way quick enough. He hits the top of my head and I step back. He puts his hand in his pocket and goes to come forward but so many people jump in between us that he can't get near me.

"EH'M GONNA SMASH YOU YE LITTLE PRICK." He shouts at me.

"COME ON THEN BIGMAN, I'M NOT AFRAID OF YOU, LET'S GO." I manage to shout back before being pushed out the door.

The hand in the pocket is obviously a threat as I know he wouldn't pull a blade in front of so many people in the pub and if he does have the bottle to do that it certainly won't be for buttering me a slice of bread that's for sure. I get outside and am pushed straight into the taxi with Gaz, Mickey and Jamie. Joey and Kyle get into the other one.

"What the fuck happened there?" Gaz turns to me looking a bit shocked.

"What? It's was just a little friendly banter that's all."

"Are you off your fucking head?"

"Did you see him going in he's pocket?" Mickey comments.

I see the driver looking in the mirror at us and I realise he is hearing all this so I make a face at Mickey and nod in the drivers direction. Nobody says a word until we get out of the taxi. We end up in a pub in the city centre, which is a total shit-hole and Kyle gets the round in while we find an empty corner. After several more drinks and discussing how stupid I am, they all change the conversation and it soon turns to shagging again in which they all take the piss out of Gaz for last week. We head off to Fatties and I suddenly feel a little strange, like I am pissed but I'm not pissed. The queue for Fatties is huge and it goes around the building and down the street, Gaz's mate is working tonight so he gets us to the front. While in Fatties I still feel a little strange, like something is just not right. We are all standing at our usual place near the top bar on the second level and I make a comment that the music seems to be better than usual. Gaz and Kyle look at each other and smile, which makes me a little paranoid and I feel that I have missed the joke or that I have said something stupid. The place is starting to fill up and every girl that walks by I feel as if they are giving me the eye. The deejay puts on an oldie which starts off slow and I now feel myself tapping my feet, my body feels all tingly like it's away to explode. Then I look at Gaz who has his stupid grin on his face.

"You spiked me, didn't you?"

"Moi, would eh dae a thing like that?" he laughs.

"You cunt" I shake my head.

The song breaks into a harder beat and then...whoosh, I get a rush that starts from my feet, comes up my body shooting through my spine until it reaches my head, now I am buzzing. I then find myself on the dance floor with my arms in the air. The beat in the song slows down and each time it bursts in I receive little rushes up my neck. I stay on the dance floor for a couple more tunes and Gaz comes over.

"Enjoying yourself are ye?" He hands me a beer.

"I can't believe you did that to me. They are really strong."

"It's MDMA."

"What does it feel like?"

"Great."

"When did you do that?"

"After your run in we Murdo, ye were starting ta piss everybody aff going on aboot it, so we thought we would help ye oot a wee bit."

It's only been an hour and the rushes have started to fade. I am immediately on the lookout for more but Gaz says he only had a little bit of it. I leave the dance floor to go up to the bar while thinking about the hit I just had. It reminds me of the hit I used to get from just one e many years ago. When I was stressed out all week in my dead end job, all I thought about was the weekend. After some good recreational drugs it would help me escape into a world where everything was great, you forgot about all your everyday petty problems and hum drum Monday to Friday existence. There was nothing better than going out at the weekend and getting fucked up. It was all harmless fun. I still got up for work on the Monday morning bright and fresh ready to face another hard week of angry bosses and miserable work colleagues. I faced them with a smile because I knew I had something on my mind to get me through the day that the other workers didn't have and would probably never experience. Mortgages, bills and household tasks meant nothing if I couldn't go out and have fun at the weekend. Some of the people that I met and got to know through the rave scene came from a well-to-do family but they still had the same reasons for going out and getting out their heads for a night or two. They still wanted an escape from whatever boring life they had at home. If some of the families of these people knew what they got up to at the weekend they would possibly disown them.

I finish my bottle and get another round in for everyone, as I pass around the drinks they all still look at me with a stupid grin. They were obviously all in on the joke, the cunts. With the feeling wearing off quickly but I pull up Gaz who slips me a couple of E's. I know however many I take I will never get that kind of hit I just had, but it's better than nothing I suppose. I end up back on the dance floor and before I know it the music stops and the lights come on. The time has passed very quickly and I feel I have only been in here for about an hour. I was given a strip of chewing gum from a girl on the dance floor some time ago and it now has no taste left but I am still chewing like mad. I stand there wiping the sweat from my head as Gaz comes over.

"So are we going up to yours then?"

"Yeah sure"

I end up in a taxi with Jamie and two young girls whom I have never seen before in my life and although I feel like talking, I can't get a word in for these girls. I don't know what they are talking about but Jamie is taking the piss by repeating what they say. I don't think Jamie realises it, but he actually talks like that too.

"Ken wot eh mean, dinna hink so, aye."

The girls take offence and let Jamie know by telling him "Shit yer puss you."

When we get to mine it is a case of, music on, joints rolled and drinks poured. Gaz appears, and as usual goes straight to the stereo to change the music. He looks up and simply says "You've got ta hae the right tunes on, man."

We all repeat "Man."

I head off to the balcony for a smoke, Jamie appears and is shocked to find me out of my nut as he never really hung around with us at the time when the good e's were going around. There are a few girls in the flat sitting around chatting and I end up in deep conversation with one of them for what seems like minutes but before I know it most people are heading home as daylight is starting to creep through. The flat starts to empty and it's only Kyle and Jamie left, then the buzzer goes, it is Gaz who had fucked off earlier to go and get Biscuit. I never even noticed that he had left. He knows I don't mind Biscuit being here but not when he jumps all over my bed with his dirty paws.

"Biscuit get to fuck." You little shit.

Later that day I manage to get some sleep but I am woken by Biscuit, pawing at me to let him under the covers.

"Fuck off."

I go through to the living room to find it is a total pig sty with bottles and glasses lying about. Jamie is slouched on the chair and Gaz is lying across the sofa. The place is stinking of grass as they pass the joint between each other.

"What have I told you cunts about smoking grass in here? Go onto the fucking balcony."

As I say this Biscuit comes running through and jumps up on the sofa.

"And your fucking dog has mud all over my bed"

They both start laughing.

"You're sniggering like a couple of poofters"

Gaz the smart arse pouts his lips and makes a smooching sound.

"Do that again and you're fucking lips will be staying that size."

"Look just because you went ta go ahead we Murdo dinna start acting the hard man we us." They both start sniggering again. Then it sinks in exactly what I did last night and I know I have got trouble ahead, big trouble. If he was a stand-up guy I wouldn't give a shit, but he is a sneaky blade man who wouldn't think twice about cutting me up.

"And you, you cunt, spiking my drink, you better not fucking do that again."

"Does that mean if eh come across some mare MDMA eh'll just keep it for myself?"

"Definitely...Maybe" I wink.

Chapter 14

I open the curtain that looks onto the balcony and I am blinded by the light from the scorching sun as it shines into the living room. Although I'm feeling like shit today, seeing the sun does actually cheer me up a little. It is unusual for Scotland to get such good weather as I am used to opening the curtains to a miserable day with the rain pissing down. Gaz has to take Biscuit for a walk so I decide to go with him to get out of the flat for a while. We have to buy more alcohol so we head to the off license. As soon as we step outside the heat from the sun hits us and it gives me good feeling that we are in for a good summer. On the way back from the shop my good feeling is soon drained from me as I notice that my car has two flat tyres. As I get closer I become aware of another scrape that goes from one end to the other.

"For fuck sake" I walk over and straight away I can see the slash about three inches long going around the tyre.

"I'm going to fucking kill him."

Gaz walks around the car checking it out.

"There's another scratch along here as well."

"That was last week. I'm going to have to start parking it somewhere else now."

"Eh canna believe that we were ah in the flat and he has come and done this. It isna like him ta dae something like this. If anything, eh thought he would come team handed and chap your door. He's a bit auld for going aboot daeing things like that. If he has a problem we ye, you're gonna hae ta get it sorted oot because this is never gonna stop."

"Exactly, he's real tough slashing someone's tyres and keying their car, when I catch up with him, we'll soon know how tough he is."

"The worse thing is it wouldna have even been him as he'll hae sent ain oh his fuckin mates ta dae it. He maybe was at the door but heard you had a hoose full so decided against it."

"I'm gonna get the cunt." I look at Gaz with my temper really starting to boil.

"Look dinna go daeing anything stupid mate, you ken he's no afraid ta stick a blade in ye. Eh'll phone a few people wah ken him and try ta sort this oot, see if he'll back aff."

I know Gaz is only saying this as a way of trying to calm me down so that I don't go looking for him.

"Do you know how much this will cost me to fix. This is a fucking re-spray job, not a fucking touch up."

When we get back in the flat Joey, Kyle and Mickey have turned up while we were out.

"You'd better pass that joint ta Shane when you've finished, as eh think he is ready ta explode." Gaz says to Kyle, who is busy skinning up.

"How, what's up?" Jamie asks.

"Nothing much, I'm going to smash Dek fuckin Murdo when I see him, that's all. The fucker has done my car again."

"Again, what do you mean again?"

"He keyed it last week down one side and sometime this morning while we were all in here he's slashed two of my tyres and keyed it down the other side."

"Fuck, eh canna believe he was up here while we were ah in the flat. Eh wonder what would have happened if ain oh us had went oot and caught him."

"What's actually bothering me is who told the cunt where I lived."

"Maybe he followed ye efter Fatties last night."

"But it was keyed last week as well."

"He must huv followed ye some other night then."

We spend the rest of the afternoon getting stoned and drinking and this soon puts the thoughts of Dek Murdo out of my head for the time being. The banter is flowing fast and it puts me in a happy mood again.

"I take it everyone's out tonight again?"

"Yeah but only if we get a chance ta spike ye again."

I laugh along with them but at the back of my mind the thoughts of fucking Murdo are still lingering. Half of my mind is all for finding him and kicking the shit out of him but I know if I go after someone like that I would have to do it properly as he is the type who will just come back again and again until I end up dead. I think I would be best waiting to see if Gaz can sort it out first before it goes down that road. We sit on the balcony drinking and talking shit until the sun starts to go down and then we head off down the Perth Road for a couple of drinks. We have to head off to Fatties early as on a bank holiday weekend the queues for nightclubs are always very long. Before I finish my last drink Gaz hands me a couple of E's in which I think nothing of swallowing them both at once.

"Did you just take baith oh them?"

"Yeah why"

"There meant to be strong, like the ains fae years back...Ah fuck it" Gaz smiles and does the same.

On reaching Fatties, the queue is much longer than we thought it was going to be as it continues around the corner and down the street. Jamie makes a quick decision on seeing the queue and decides to go to the Mardi.

"Yer ah mare than welcome ta join is" He says as he walks away.

"Fuck it, eh'm going as well" Mickey says.

Then Gaz and Joey follow them leaving me and Kyle on our own to wait in this extra-long queue. As I stand listening to Kyle talking the biggest load of shit I start thinking maybe I should have went with them but I get a horrible feeling that I am away to get my hit and have horrible thoughts of standing in the Mardi on an e, no thank you, I'll wait. I'm getting all tingly down my body but I don't want it to happen just now, I don't want my hit until I get in the club and I'm trying to fight it. It's like when you are having sex and you are about to shoot your load but the sex is so good you don't want to shoot your load at that moment. You want it to last a while longer but you can't stop it and come and the whole feeling is ruined by trying to hold back. By the time I get to the front door I am totally flying and the buzz is being ruined by having to act straight in front of the bouncers. Once we are passed the entrance and in the club, the rushes start to fade, fuck. I find myself at the bar and the tables have turned as it is now Kyle who is listening to me talking a load of shit. I'm obviously wasted and don't realise this until Kyle starts taking the piss, that's when I know it's bad.

"Shane, check her out, to your left."

I turn discretely to see two girls next to me at the bar waiting to be served. One of them is tall, blonde and has a low cut top with a large chest that I feel is staring at me. I know this is what Kyle wants me to check out, but I have seen some-thing better, much better. Her friend is the girl from my taxi. I stand and stare at her for a few seconds and realise she is the total opposite to what I usually go for. She turns her head and I lock eyes with her and can't look away. Kyle doesn't remember her from that night at the doghouse and I am too wasted to let him know.

"Hi, how are you?" She asks.

"Fine"

"Did you enjoy the bands the other night?"

"Yeah, they were really good."

"I was only there for a little while, something came up and I had to leave."

That'll be why I wandered around the place and couldn't find her. If she left then she obviously didn't see the trouble with me and Murdo's mates. I have waited ages to meet this girl again and just my luck it happens when I am fucking wasted. I want to start up a conversation with her but for the first time I am stuck for words. Kyle is a little disappointed as I usually take the lead and he would follow up with the small talk, but not this time.

"What's wrang we you?"

"Nothing"

"Why are ye no firing in then?"

I shrug my shoulder and smile.

"Oh for fuck sake, your wasted man"

The girls receive their drinks but they don't move from the bar.

"Shane they're no moving fae the bar, fucking talk to them."

I turn to look at her again and she smiles back but I am still stuck for words. I look back at Kyle again and smile. I must look really fucked because Kyle slides past me and moves in closer to the tall blonde and introduces us. He makes me think of a slithery snake the way he moves. I try to keep this thought in my head so that I can call him that from now on, the slithery snake, Kyle the wee slithery snake, slithery snake Kyle.

"Hi, I'm Kelly" She says to me.

Kyle introduces me to the blonde whose name is Sarah and then turns his back on me leaving me to stand with the girl I now know is called Kelly. Kyle looks back at me and lifts his eyebrows then leans over to my ear.

"If you're no fast you're last eh?"

Obviously he is referring to himself firing-in to the tall blonde and me getting left with the mate this time. I want to tell him I that I wasn't interested in the blonde but I cannot find the words and have to let it go. While Kyle is chatting away to the blonde, whose name I have now forgotten due to the state of my brain at this moment in time. I start to get a little paranoid as I'm standing next to this stunning girl and I can't even make conversation with her. To my relief she leans over to my ear and says

"You're really wasted aren't you?"

I look at her and don't know what to say. If she's not into drugs and I say yes, I have blown it. If I say no she'll think I am some weirdo acting like this while not on drugs so I can't win. With a half-smile I force out an answer.

"What do you mean?"

"It's okay, I just feel a little jealous. I haven't been wasted in so long."

Wow what a relief to know that she knows the score. I feel like telling her it's been a while for me too, a whole twenty four hours actually but the words won't come out. She finishes her drink and before I get a chance to offer her another one she says "Would you like to dance?"

I can't answer but she looks at me for a few seconds, grabs my arm and says "you need to dance."

The E's I have taken are obviously very heavy and are making me look a bit drunk. All I want to do is sit down and chill out. But this girl drags me up to dance and this snaps me out of my little daydream. Once I start to move it changes my frame of mind making me want to dance all night. I could do with some real dance music like last night but Fatties on a Sunday is hip hop and r and b so I guess it will have to do.

"What's your name again?" I say smiling.

She puts her hand to my face and brings her lips to my ear.

"Kelly."

As her lips brush my ear I get a sudden rush of happiness. I watch her dance around me. My feet feel like they are glued to the floor. She takes my hands and forces me to move in time with her and this gives me a feeling of being drawn to her, a closeness I have never felt before. I know the E's have something to do with it, well, probably a lot to do with it, but right now I don't give a shit. I want to pull her close and ask her if she wants to come back to mine but I don't want to sound too forward. What the fuck is happening to me? These E's have made me go soft. I would usually have a girl sized up in the first five minutes and have it worked out what type of shag she would be and what positions I would get her in, but not on these fucking drugs. I'm looking at this girl dancing around me, smiling and rubbing up against me and all I'm thinking is, I'd love to kiss her. After several tunes we head to the bar for more drinks and I find Kyle still with the blonde, slavering in her ear.

"So do you feel a bit better now?" Kelly asks.

"Yeah" I smile.

"That's the best thing you can do when you are feeling like that or you end up sitting in a corner all night." She says this like I have never experienced this before and I want to tell her that I have been there too many times to remember but the last thing I want to do is start is a conversation about drugs. The two girls talk for a few minutes and then Kelly tells me that her friend is leaving and Kyle is going with her. I feel really happy for Kyle as he never usually pulls so quick, he must have been talking some serious shit for her to leave so early with him.

"Shane, can eh get the keys ta yer flat?" Kyle gives me a wink.

"Use the spare room. I don't want any stains in my bed."

He laughs and walks away all happy with himself that he's pulled before me.

"Come on, we'll go for a walk" Kelly says taking my hand.

I watch her from behind as she leads the way. I'm oblivious to the people passing me as I stare at her lovely shaped legs. She has on a short skirt and cowboy boots and has a sexy walk that makes her hips wiggle slightly. We wander around Fatties and find a secluded corner with two vacant seats. We talk for a while but the conversation keeps going back to drugs, which in my state is not really a good thing. After another drink we go back to the dance floor and I start to feel normal again, the e's must be wearing off a little. Kelly comes up close to me and gives me a little kiss while running her hand up my back, this gives me a rush that goes shooting up to my head. She moves back and looks at me smiling.

"Are you feeling okay?" She smiles,

"I take it you've done that before."

"That's an old trick."

I eventually find the courage to ask her if she wants to come back to mine, I have never felt nervous like this around a girl in years.

"Definitely not"

She watches my expression and then comes up to my ear again.

"No but you can come back to mine if you want." She smiles.

"What about your friend, she is up at my flat with my friend."

"Exactly, I don't want them to be there when we're shag-ging."

I start to laugh and she comes closer and kisses me.

"Do want to go now?"

I shrug "Okay."

As I walk out of Fatties holding Kelly's hand she tells me her flat is not too far so we decide to walk instead of getting a taxi. She takes my hand and leads me in my hazy state of mind up Hawkhill Road towards her flat. We walk past a group of girls and I hear my name being mentioned. I turn to see a girl I know.

"Oh hi Jackie"

"Is this yer latest bimbo then?" She says as she stands with some guy's arm draped around her shoulders.

"You've got a hard neck calling anybody a bimbo" I say.

The guy takes his arm from around her and gives me the wide-o look.

"Just leave it Shane, come on." Kelly pulls me away.

"Go on, listen ta yer wee slapper."

"Wait a minute Kelly" I whisper in her ear.

"Jackie, you've got three kids to three different guys. You live with someone else who is neither of their fathers. Occasionally you have come up the road and fucked me before sneaking off home to him, and you have the cheek to call her a slapper."

Her friends start laughing and the guy who was with her has taken a step back. I walk away and stumble on up the road with Kelly's arm hooked into mine leading the way. We stop every now and again for a little snog until we get back to her flat which she shares with her friend Sarah, the same Sarah that Kyle has taken back to mine and is probably right now, doing her arse over the end of my couch. I follow her into her bedroom, take of my boots and lie on the bed. Kelly does the same after putting on some music. We start to kiss and our hands are all over each other. My hand is up her skirt and is resting on her arse. If this was any other girl, I would have had her knickers off by now but I feel something is holding me back. I have my eyes closed and I can feel her moving to slide the covers over us. She starts stroking my face and I feel myself drifting off.

"Hey sleepy head, are you getting up?" I hear a voice say.

I open my eyes to see the sunlight coming through the curtains and Kelly standing in front of me all fresh with different clothes on.

"What happened?"

"What do you mean, don't you remember? And you told me it was the best sex you have ever had."

I go to say something but stop to think for a few seconds then I see the sly grin on her face.

"I fell asleep."

"Yeah" She says with a big smile.

"Sarah is just back from your flat, she says that your other friends came up and disturbed them while they were eh'm, you know."

We both laugh at the thought of them getting caught but I know the picture in my head is entirely different from how she is imagining it.

"I don't know what kind of E's you had last night but that's the first time I have ever seen anyone fall asleep like that after taking them" She says.

"It's probably because I was out all weekend, it catches up with you" I explain.

"Or it could be the junk that they put in them nowadays."

I nod "Yeah, more than likely...well I suppose I had better take off and see what state my flat is in after those idiots."

I get up and start to put on my boots and I realise this must be the first time in years that I have went home with someone and not shagged them on the first night.

"I could give you a lift if you like. I'm on my way to Uni."

"Thanks that would be great"

We get outside and walk towards two cars at the end of the street, one is an old piece of junk and the other is a girly looking sports car. I stop at the piece of junk.

"Next one" Kelly says as she walks towards the sports car.

"Oh."

"Yeah right" She says walking back to the heap of shit.

It takes the whole time during the short journey for me to grow a pair and ask if I could see her again.

"Well I do have a lot of course work to complete over the next month but I'm sure I can fit you in somewhere."

"Oh don't go out of your way" I say sarcastically.

Before I get out the car I lean over to kiss her and she puts her lips up to mine but I kiss her on the cheek instead.

"Morning breath and that, you know."

"Yeah, you'd better go and get some mouth-wash." She says waving her hand in front of her nose implying that my breath stinks.

We both smile as I shut the car door and I walk away feeling on top of the world. But this only lasts a few seconds and then come I crashing back down to earth when I see my car again. My life seems to go from one extreme to the other. With customers who, one minute have me laughing my head off to others, who have me ready to rip their head off. I will get the tyres fixed and get myself back on the road but that paint job is going to take some work.

Chapter 15

Customer No. 9814

I receive a job to The Hawthorn Bar on the Hilltown for Ramsay and with the rain pouring down I need to make a run from the car to the entrance of pub. When I open the door the waft of smoke and stale beer hits me full on. There are about ten people in the bar, all older men and each one of them looking shadier than the next. The place is silent and several of them look around at me and then look back at the bar. I shout the name, no answer, I look around to get some-one's attention but they all stare into their drinks or at the T.V. watching intently at the horseracing. I shout again, no answer, the barmaid looks over and nods in the direction of a man sitting directly in front of me. I shout one last time and the man who is about six feet away from me slouched on a stool at the bar turns his head slightly and grunts. The man is in his late fifty's and is clearly a bit pissed. I walk back out in the pissing rain and quickly jump back into the car. I wait for what feels like a long time and he doesn't appear. I'm thinking that I should just go as I can tell that he is going to cause me more bother than he is worth. I am about to drive off when the guy stumbles from the bar and opens the front passenger door. He basically falls into the seat and kicks the speaker on the way in and cracks the plastic cover.

"For fucks sake, watch what you're doing" I snap.

He doesn't say a word, no apology, nothing.

"Right mate, where are you going?"

He slowly turns his head and looks at me through his slanted eyes and gritted teeth

"Fuckin hume"

I feel the hair's standing up on the back of my neck but I keep telling myself to be calm and don't bite as he's just being wide.

"I need to know where you are going mate."

He turns his head again, but this time he leans over only inches from my face and I can see his smirk as he says again "Fuckin hame"

In the split second that these words come out of his mouth I lean forward and nut him, which catches his top lip. I get out the car and bolt around to the passenger door. Opening it with one hand, I reach in with the other and grab him by the throat to pull him onto the wet pavement.

"Do ye ken wah eh am?" He says as he struggles to get up.

I have heard this saying so many times when I was growing up but it was usually by some young teenager who thought he was some sort of hard man, but they were always found out. I never usually hear it from a fifty something old man. He gets to his feet and tries to throw a punch but I move back slightly and throw one of my own into his already bloody face. He hits the deck with a thud and I look around to see people across the street wondering what is going on. I suddenly realise how stupid this must look. It is just after one on a Tuesday afternoon, in the pissing rain and I have just nutted and punched some fifty odd year old drunk. I see the door of the pub opening so I quickly get back in to the car and drive off leaving the cunt lying on the pavement with his face covered in blood.

Customer No. 6815

I know who my next customer is and exactly where she's going. She is a snobby bitch with a big fancy house, well I say snobby but I really mean a fucking wannabe snob. She obviously come into a bit of money and bought the big fancy house, now she thinks she is fucking high and mighty. I can't stand people like that, there is big difference between bettering yourself and thinking you're better than everyone else. Money does not make you a better person, your actions do. She tries to talk polite but I can tell that it is forced, like she is trying to lose her Dundee twang and it just sounds all wrong. It is not hard to talk polite but still keep your Dundee accent. It sounds a hundred times better than this stupid bitch's snobbish patter. Before I turn the corner I dig out a heavy rock CD and put it on. An annoying little trick that I learned, the last time I had her in my car she moaned at me that my music was too loud. I turned it down but she seemed to get herself worked up because I was laughing at her. So what did the bitch do, she phoned my office to complain, who in turn called me and were then told to 'fuck off.' The stupid cow did not realise that I was actually laughing at her stupid snobbish accent that was continually changing with every word she said. There were obviously certain words that she could not pronounce in her fake, polite, newly acquired accent. When I pick up people like that now, I put the music to a level where it is not low but not loud enough for them to complain. Some heavy rock with loud guitars or even hard techno with some strong bass or a high pitched beat is good for this. If you are not into that type of music I know it can be quite annoying.

I drive around to the side door of the shopping centre and I notice her face straight away due to the amount of make-up that is caked on it. She is dressed as if she is about to go to a fucking wedding. Don't get me wrong, I would rather have someone with clean clothes in my car than some of the smelly minks I usually pick up. She has plenty of shopping bags with all the top high street labels on them. God forbid she is ever seen with a discount clothing bag in her hand. I get out and shout her name and as soon as she sees me I can tell she's pissed off that I have been sent for her. I open the boot and usually I would take the bags from people and put them in myself, but not today, as she is not most people. She looks at me to help but I take a step back and look away so that she has no option but to do it herself, oh if looks could kill. She gets in the back and just as I am wondering if she will have anything to moan about today she says "Could you put that window up please."

The front passenger window is open about six inches, it's quite warm today and this bitch asks me to close the window.

"Sure" I say as I push the button to put the passenger's window up and at the same time my window comes down.

I can see her looking at me in the mirror with pure hatred and I am fucking loving it. I arrive outside her house and park at the start of her driveway. I drove here quite slow so that the music would start to get really annoying.

"That's four pounds sixty please" I say with a smarmy grin.

She hands me the fiver and waits on her forty pence change, which I knew she would. I go to the boot and take out her bags, dumping them on the ground at her feet. If it was any other customer I would have taken them to their door, but fuck her.

"Cheerio" I say as I walk back towards my car door.

She doesn't answer but looks at me in total disgust. She picks up her bags and I watch as she struggles with them up her driveway.

Customer No. 448

As I pull up to Asda I see several people waiting in the taxi rank and out of all the people there, I can tell which customer will be mine. Although there is a nice looking blonde girl who could possibly be going a good distance, I know that it is going to be the smelly one that's only going around the corner. I shout the name and this very rough looking woman, dressed in clothes that are either too big or have been stretched in a tug-o-war competition. Her face has the distinguished features that you can tell she has had a hard life, but that's not to say she didn't choose it. Her trolley is overloaded and as I struggle to fit it all in my boot, I notice it is packed with junk food and alcohol. Unsurprisingly, her destination is less than a mile away. I pull up outside her house and can see this tiny little man watching her from the living room window. I think he's been waiting to help her with the shopping. I couldn't be more wrong. As I start taking the shopping up the front path this pathetic little man opens the front door. He has a dirty white vest on that shows off his ugly man boobs and loads of pointless homemade tattoo's all down his arms. He stands in the doorway with a tin of cheap lager in his hand and an expression on his face that looks like he's trying to squeeze a shit out of his arse. Judging by the stench from him I think he's actually done one in his pants.

"Alright" I say.

He answers with a grunt.

"Whar have ye been?" He shouts to his missus.

She ignores him and looks at me. I can see fear in her eyes as she walks past him into the house with some of the shopping bags.

"Eh asked ye. Whar have ye been? And how's meh dinner no ready?" He shouts back into the house.

She goes to walk past him to get back out of the house and he says to her

"Just tak them fae there, the driver can bring them ta the door."

I have never wanted to smash somebody so much in such a long time. There is a vast amount of bags, which means I have to make several trips back to the car. All the time this little runt of a man stands at his top step staring at me. Each time I return to the door I have visions of hitting this cunt. Just one word, one little comment, please, you know you want to, just give me the slightest excuse and I will fucking dance on your head you miserable little bastard.

I drop the last of the bags at the door as his missus walks back out to pick them up. He shouts more abuse at her telling her she had better have got this or she had better have got that. He walks back into the house and stares at me from the living room window while shouting at his missus to hurry up and get his dinner on. I stay there for a few minutes looking at him and at what I would have done if he had given me enough reason. I think he is the type of person that if I hit him, I wouldn't stop. I drive off thinking to myself, what the fuck have I just witnessed there?

Customer No. 1048

The Cutty Sark pub used to have one of the most feared reputations in Dundee. My on board computer that sends me the jobs has a note that says, do not send car 15, 27, 45, 81, 124, 129. These numbers are taxis that are refusing to pick customers up from here. The few years that I have been working on the taxis I have had several calls here every week. Out of all those times I have never had or even seen one bit of trouble in the place. Don't get me wrong I know it's full of guys, and women might I add, that don't take any shit from anyone. This pub has had a violent past including shootings, stabbings and many serious fights. The people I pick up from here always go out of their way to make conversation with me no matter how short the journey is. I never get any attitude from them and they always leave me a good tip with a 'cheers' or 'thanks' as they get out.

I open the door of the pub and a few hard faces look around but most of them nod in my direction and turn back to their pint. I am about to shout the name when I recognise my customer sitting at the end of the bar looking quite pissed. He is the movie man, who sells pirate DVD's and CD's.

"Did you phone for a taxi?"

"What? Oh, eh, cheers" He picks up his hold-all and follows me out.

"So what have you got today then?" I ask as he gets in the car.

He opens his hold-all and the first DVD I see is a copy of the latest blockbuster at the cinema. Seeing this reminds me of an advert I came across the other day warning people against buying pirate DVD's due to their poor picture and sound quality, but every time I have bought a film from this guy, you could not fault it. He always says he wouldn't sell them if they were not good quality as nobody would buy them again from him. The same advert went onto say that the money you spend on them is going into the hands of drug dealers and smugglers. But people are obviously going to buy a product at a fraction of the price rather than the high street stores no matter where the money goes. The government spends thousands of our money from tax on adverts telling us that we are lining the pockets of criminals. What about them? They put so much tax on everything we buy, for what? So that politicians can line their pockets or spend our money on giving free drugs to junkies. To go to the cinema to watch the same film would cost a fiver or more. If you go with your partner, that's more than a tenner plus food and drinks. This guy sells the same film for three pound and you can watch it in the comfort of your own home. You don't have to put up with people munching crisps and sweets in your ear all the way through it and at least if you need to go to the toilet you can press pause and don't have to squeeze through half a row of people.

I drop the guy off in his usual destination in the city centre and as usual, instead of paying the fare I take a couple of discs from him. My intensions are for one to watch with the guys when we are all getting stoned and one for curling up with Kelly for either before or after I have had my hole.

Customer No. 1268

I drive along Dundonald Street slowly as I look at the numbers on the vandalised tenement block doors. There is a group of young people hanging around up ahead and just my luck they are right outside the number I am looking for. One of the young guys in the group walks over and leans his elbow on my car. I roll down the window and politely tell him to move off the car.

"Shut yer puss. Eh'll lean on it if eh fucking want" He says kicking his heel on the passenger door.

I get out of the car to confront him, and clock the others as I walk around the car. There are three guys and two girls and all of them are in their late teens to early twenties.

"Who the fuck do you think you are?" I say as I inspect the damage.

His hands drop to his sides and he puffs out his chest giving me the hard man look.

"Wah are you talking ta ya fucking arsehole?" He says squaring up to me and pushing his arms out wider and his chest a few more inches.

"What, do think you're some sort of a hard man?"

"Eh ken eh'm a hard man" He says as he comes close and is now in my face. I can smell the alcohol off him and this is obviously the reason behind his hard man act

"Get out of my face." I shove him back towards his friends.

"Do ye ken wah eh am?"

Oh fuck, here we go again.

"I couldn't give a fuck who you are?"

He takes a swing at me with his arm that is far behind him. I move out of the way and due to the momentum of the swing, he falls towards me. I step past him and push the back of his shoulder making him fall to the ground. I see one of his friends go to step towards me when my customer comes out.

"Is this my taxi?" He says.

"For Anderson" I ask. He nods and we both get in the car but before I drive off one of the group kick the back of my car as they all shout abuse. I speed off before anything else happens.

"Bit of trouble there was it?" My customer says.

"Just somebody that's had too much to drink"

I play it down and make small talk but as soon as my customer is out of the car I am back up to the same street looking for the little wide-o bastard. I see the group not far from where they were standing. I keep my distance and park up, waiting patiently for the right opportunity. After twenty minutes of watching him swagger about shouting abuse at anyone walking past he decides to break away from the group. I watch him walk up a small alleyway in between two other tenement blocks. I get out of the car and run as fast as I can towards the alley. I cross the road and slow down to a jog, keeping my head down as I pass his group of friends who don't even notice me. I enter the pitch black alley and have slowed down to a fast walk as I hear him zip up. I see the swagger a few feet in front of me and without saying a word I launch forward with a barrage of punches to his head. As he falls to his knees in front of me I grab his hair at the back of his head and throw several more punches to his face. I swing my leg back and bring my knee forward to his face. I let go off his hair and watch his shadow fall back into his own piss. I walk back out of the alley, passing his friends once again without detection and cross the road towards my car.

I can only imagine him tomorrow when he has sobered up telling his exaggerated story of how he managed to sustain a black eye and possible broken nose. I would like to say that I taught the little cunt a lesson but I can tell he will be back out doing the same thing next week with more drink on him and a bigger chip on his shoulder. He will no doubt be back in the same place giving abuse to anyone who happens to be in his way, a possible Murdo in the making.

Chapter 16

Over the next few weeks I met up with Kelly several times. She was nearing the end of her course at university and was always busy finishing course work or studying for exams. I would sometimes receive a phone call late at night from her saying that she had been studying for hours and wanted to talk as she was stressed out and needed a break. We would talk on the phone for a long time and eventually she would ask if I wanted her to come up for a while, of course I did, but I would obviously play it cool by answering 'If you want' as if it was no big deal. With the amount of shit I listened to from people all day it was actually good to meet someone who never really complained about anything. It was strange meeting a girl who didn't bitch about everybody and everything; she must be a rare breed.

On the odd occasion I would be in my bed and she would come up unexpectedly. She would strip down to her underwear and jump in next to me. We would lie for a bit and after a little touchy feely I would be eager to shag her but I would somehow hold back. I always let her make the first move and most of the time she did. These were two things I had not done in years, one was to wait for a girl to make the first move and the other was to actually talk and get to know someone. Well the second was only in part, as although we talked for hours I somehow never really got to know that much about her. I never asked her personal questions but if a subject came up she would sometimes work her way around it or just change the subject altogether.

She was very strange as she wouldn't come out to meet any of my friends, although Kyle and Gaz have seen her, they can hardly remember what she looked like. If I was in the East View and she was picking me up to go somewhere with her, she wouldn't come into the pub to get me. She would wait outside in the car and give me a one ringer on my mobile to let me know she was there. Nothing was ever planned and it was always a last minute phone call to ask if I wanted to meet up. It didn't bother me that much but it did bother the life out of Gaz. If we were out on the piss and I received a phone call from Kelly I would be off like a shot to go and meet her. I never saw her regularly so by the time she phoned I was anxious to see her.

One day, I was sitting in the East View having a few drinks not long after I met her, and she randomly phoned me to ask if I would like to go to a U2 concert that night as her friend had pulled out. Of course I said yeah. I was never a big fan of U2 but as soon as I announced this Kyle and Mickey were calling me a lucky bastard, but not Gaz. He started his big spiel about how he wouldn't go to a U2 concert if you paid him.

"Bono, trying ta save the fucking world because he canna cut it we the new bands nowadays. Oh eh, he still sells millions oh albums but that's only because oh ah his loyal fans fae years back. But if ye asked any oh them aboot his politics most would say that they couldna give a fuck. The only time ye hear oh the cunt is when he's aboot ta release a record. While other bands are oot on the toon pulling burds and getting pissed ta get themselves in the papers. He goes and gives some speech aboot saving the fucking world, and as for that slimy fucker Geldof, does he really think the average person gives a fuck aboot people going hungry in a country thousands oh miles awa...no, but what they do give a fuck aboot is if they hae enough change left for that last pint oh lager before they head hame, or if they will hae enough ta pay their electric bill it the end oh the week before it gets cut aff, or if they hae enough ta feed their ain bairns because they huv just put the cooncil tax up again. Even mare important is if their team will win the league or on the other hand get relegated. The average person doesna live like him we ah his millions in the bank and royalty cheques every year ta depend on. Wha the fuck gives him the rights ta ask people ta go on a march. What is he on? Does he no ken most folk hae jobs ta go ta. Is he gonna pay their wages or employ them if they get sacked for taking the day aff ta go on his fucking march. Cunts like Bono and Geldof should concentrate on rock n roll music and living like a real rock star, fucking champagne socialists. Look at the Stones or even mare up ta date, Oasis, you never see them on T.V. pleading ta put money inta this charity or that charity. That's because they sell oot their gigs without ah that shite. The fans respect them for what they are, no going aroond pretending ta be something they're no and being up their ain arse. Real bands are busy shagging and getting oot their nut, like us. If only we could play or sing we would make better rock stars than they cunts."

"Thanks for putting a downer on going, I'll go and phone her back and cancel. I'll explain to her that due to Bono's politics I'm refusing to use the sixty pound ticket that I'm getting for fuck all." Revealing the cost of the ticket was enough confirmation to Gaz that his rant was justified.

I assumed Kelly would change once she finished university but she became even stranger. If we met up in a pub or restaurant in town for dinner she would always be looking around and couldn't relax, like she didn't want to be there. She hardly ever went out at night in Dundee and when we did go out it was as though she didn't want to be seen with me. I would occasionally ask her what was wrong and she would subtly change the subject. I was starting to get a little paranoid that it was something to do with me. When we were together we were always having a great laugh as, like me, she appeared to have a cheeky sense of humour and I didn't want to push the subject and ruin it. It did cross my mind that she had another boyfriend as she would sometimes disappear for a few days but then she would call me from Spain as her father runs a nightclub out there. We would talk for hours and she would tell me she was missing me.

Dundee was now in the middle of a heat wave and with us not having a good summer in years I was starting to believe what people had said about my flat before I bought it. There were several different styles in the one block on offer and two of the more expensive ones had balconies. Apparently I was stupid for paying a lot of extra money for a balcony that I would only use a few days a year. It's always pissing down here and I would not make much on it if I was to sell it. This advice was from people who had rented their homes all their lives. I started off with a flat that cost fifteen grand and am now living in one that is worth a hundred and fifty grand, and they are giving me advice.

Due to this unusual heat, I would wake up early and go to work but on bright sunny days people choose to walk more, the knock on effect for me was that I would have to wait much longer between jobs. If I received a phone call from Kelly it did not take much persuasion for me to finish work and meet up with her. We would go for a drive in her heap of shit and for someone who didn't like a lot of attention she would have the windows down and the music up, but this only happened once we were outside Dundee. She became so relaxed and appeared so much happier.

I knew I liked Kelly from the first night I met her, which was maybe the reason that it took me weeks to eventually shag her. It was a

Saturday night and I was in Fatties, out of my face wasted on E's as usual. I had already discussed with Gaz through my altered state of mind that we were going back to mine for a party when the club finished. I was sitting down in the chill out area next to a girl I knew who appeared to be in the same frame of mind as myself. We were in the middle of a deep meaningful conversation about something that I have no clue about whatsoever when I felt this tingling sensation in my balls. It reminded me of when I was a kid on a carnival ride like the Waltzers and it spun around really fast. I remember getting the same feeling and not wanting it to stop. Although this tingling sensation only lasted for a few seconds and then it would stop for a few seconds, it did this several times and then it would stop for about a minute and then it started all over again. The conversation with this girl started to sound even better as the tingling continued. This appeared to go on for quite some time until I reached over to the table in front of me for my drink and the tingling moved to my leg. I then realised that it was my phone vibrating in my pocket. I was hoping that the phone call was really important as whoever it was, would continue to call me, thus keeping the tingling sensation going through my balls. I went to the toilet and I took out my phone to see that it had been Kelly that had been calling me. I answered but it was very hard to make out what she was saying. I did decipher that she had been phoning for the last half an hour. She had not had a good night and wanted to see me. I knew she was going to a party with her friends that night but she said she would either see me in Fatties or more than likely meet me after it. That's why I didn't answer the phone as I thought it was one of my friends asking if I was having a party. I didn't even bother to look around for Gaz or anybody else to explain that the party was off. I flagged down the first taxi I saw and headed straight to Kelly's flat. As soon as I got to the door she opened it and put her arms around me.

"What's wrong?"

"I saw someone I didn't want to see tonight" She said, knowing full well that I was going to ask who.

"Well...are you going to tell me?"

"It was my ex-boyfriend. He turned up at the party."

"And what happened?" I asked, not really knowing if I wanted to hear the answer. I was expecting her to say that she went off with him or something, but she I guess she wouldn't have called me up to her flat if she did.

"Look, he's caused so much trouble for me. It was a bit of a shock seeing him tonight"

"What happened? Did he say anything to you?"

"No I left before he saw me. Well I hope he didn't see me."

I could tell that she was scared so I put my arms tighter around her. I had the thought of some young prick giving her shit and taking advantage of her and it made me feel angry.

"Do you want to talk about this?"

"Not really."

"Good because I was having a good night until now and I was coming up here for it to continue."

"Oh you were, were you?" She broke into a smile.

I had seen Kelly a few times and although being with her had got quite heavy on occasions it never really went to the stage of shagging. With everything going really good with her I was a bit worried about shagging her as it wouldn't have been the first time that I had really liked a girl, and once I had shot my load up them the feelings disappeared as quick as I ran out the door. I was beginning to get a little paranoid by thinking that if I didn't try to shag her soon she would start thinking that I was some sort of a nonce.

She climbed into bed with her clothes on and pulled up the covers. I went to do the same.

"No, no, yours has to come off" She said with her eyes peering out over the top.

"Oh they do, do they" I smiled.

I kicked off my boots and pulled up my t- shirt, but when it came to my jeans I started opening the buttons very slowly and she started making silly noises. I was down to my boxers and she opened the covers to let me jump in beside her. Our arms were wrapped around each other. Then she got out of bed and gave me a show by taking her own clothes off but she only went down to her knickers and bra and tried to get in the bed.

"No, no, carry on."

"Let me in." She said grabbing a pillow and hitting me over the head. I threw back the covers and she climbed into bed with me. After a quick hug and a little touchy feely we were nearly ripping the rest of our clothes off. I hadn't had sex in weeks and I was hoping that the few wanks that I had had in that time would have done the trick as I didn't want her thinking I was some sort of two-minute-wonder. I then realised that I had taken several E's that night and the chances of me coming quick were slim and none. The sex was good, intense, no fancy positions and it didn't go on for hours. It felt different from the sex I'd had recently and I couldn't tell if this was because I really like this girl or that I just had too many drugs that night. We lay together in each other's arms for a while and I thought to myself that anyone who says that the high from drugs is better than sex is obviously not doing it properly or I'm not taking the right drugs. Back in the East View the next day Gaz grilled me for trap-dooring it out of Fatties.

"So whar did you fuck off ta last night?"

"Kelly's, she had a bit of bother."

"Thanks for letting us ken like. We hung aboot for ages waiting on ye"

"Fuck, sorry man. Where did you end up anyway?"

"We went back to Jamie's mates hoose. What a laugh. As soon as eh walked in, the people were asking me for E's. Do eh look like a drug dealer or something?" We both raised our eyebrows and smiled.

"Eh had a couple on is and eh wasna awa ta just hand them over so eh decided ta raffle ain oh them. Made mesel twenty quid aff one E. Eh had a competition for the other ain."

"What kind of competition?"

"Well eh had ah we look in the kitchen and saw a box oh Weetabix, so eh telt them ah, that if anybody can eat a whole dry Weetabix they could hae the last E for free."

"You're sick. Did any of them go for it?"

"Every single one oh them. You wouldna believe what some people would dae for a free E. They were ah boking but still trying ta force this Weetabix doon their throat. There was only one person that finished it so eh gave him the E. He was walking aboot the perty like he was the fucking world champion or something."

Chapter 17

Gaz

Tin the park is Scotland's largest music festival whar people pay way over the odds for a ticket ta gather in a field oot in the middle oh nowhere ta watch their favorite bands play. This is not a rock concert as there are bands from every different type oh music performing. For me it means a weekend oh drinking, smoking and taking as many drugs as possible. We hae a mini bus that taks us there and brings us back both days. There are thousands wah camp ah weekend and eh have tried it in the past but, eh like meh hame comforts. Especially when eh'v been on it ah day and night. The last thing eh need is ta go looking for a tent in the pitch dark, in a field we thousands oh other tents. It's only a short journey on the bus and eh'm home in the comfort oh meh own bed curled up we Biscuit. Eh waken up ta meh Kate's cooked breakfast as she makes sure eh have a good meal in me before eh go and do it ah over again.

Eh hear her shouting on is ta get up, she's mental meh gran. Eh telt her the bus was leaving at eleven so waken is at ten but eh ken it's only nine thirty. This is her way oh making me have enough time ta get a shower and eat meh breakfast, bless her, she means well. She kens ah the shite eh get up ta, well no the specifics but she kens eh'm always up ta no good. She lets me smoke grass aroond the hoose. She occasionally moans aboot the smell but secretly eh think she pinches some oh it for her and Danny. That doesna bother her but if eh brought back a lassy ta stay for the night she would go aff her fucking nut. Eh always take care oh her and Danny as they're ah eh'v got, well except for Biscuit, Meh mother died when eh was really young, eh never new meh dad. Eh'v asked Danny aboot him over the years when eh was growing up but he didna really ken much aboot him. They have always made sure eh never wanted for anything though, eh wasna spoiled or that and while Kate taught me right fae wrang and Danny covered most oh the grey areas, the past few years eh'v got inta a lifestyle that eh ken if eh got caught they would be so disappointed, no ta mention eh would be locked up for a very lang time.

Eh get oot the shower and can smell the bacon cooking, Eh rush doon the stairs ta a plate oh sausage, eggs, bacon, tomatoes and twa slices oh toast. Kate pours both oh us a cup oh coffee and sits next ta is. Biscuit comes in the front door and rushes inta the kitchen, although he is wagging his tail and looks happy ta see me, it's actually only because he smells the food. He doesna bark or pant, he hovers aroond ye hoping ta get something, the wee grubber. The smell oh the bacon and sausages cooking has probably been driving him nuts. Danny informs me that he has been ta the shops and got is meh carry oot for the bus. Plenty oh cans oh lager and two half bottles oh vodka. One bottle for each day, slipped doon the jeans, if eh get caught trying ta sneak them in they'll only take them off is. For the low price oh ah fiver, it's worth the risk.

Jamie turns up at the door and we are too early so the tins oh lager get started on, Danny joins us and eh'm tempted ta ask if he wants ta come we us but eh dinna even say it as a joke cause the auld cunt would take is up on the offer. We head ta the East View and wait on the mini bus and there are a number oh faces eh'v never seen before but they are ah mates oh mates and by the end oh the day, once the drugs kick in and the gibbering starts, eh'll probably ken them ah quite well. While we are waiting for the bus Shane phones and says he's running a bit late. Some cunt has damaged his car again, he starts ranting an raving doon the phone aboot Murdo but eh hang up on him as eh feel like he's putting a downer on is. We are ah on the bus and ready ta go when this rust bucket oh a car pulls up. Shane gets oot and his burd leans oot ta give him a kiss and eh ken eh seen her that night at the doghoose but eh'm sure eh recognise her face fae somewhere. Shane gets on the bus and is still going on aboot his car being damaged. He's being a bit loud and mentions Murdo's name again. Eh tell him ta shut his puss as he doesna ken wah could be on the bus listening. Eh hand him a can oh lager and a few E's.

"There, sit on yer arse and get them doon ye. You'll no be giving a fuck aboot yer car in half an hour."

It's only a forty five minute journey ta Kinross fae Dundee but once we are there it taks aboot another half an hour for oor coach ta actually reach the field whar the festival is held due ta the amount oh traffic. As we approach the site aff the main road we can see the field oh coloured tents and in the distance is the the big wheel. As eh look aroond the bus eh notice people a bit excited, either that or they are ah bursting for a piss. Shane appears ta have cheered up and is blabbing awa in somebody's ear in between puffs on a joint that eh passed him. The E's eh gave him are obviously taking effect. There is a massive queue ta get through the gates inta the park so a group oh us from the bus find a space on the grass and sit in the sun until it goes doon a wee bit. We hae several cans left so they are knocked back while we bake in the melting sun. Shane mentions something aboot E's so eh hand him another couple. We go through the main gates and head straight for the main stage whar we find the rest oh the people wah were on oor bus. There is a good line-up here the day but there are loads oh other acts that eh want ta see on some oh the other stages. The only problem is what state eh'll be in later ta actually go and see the other acts. There is a strong possibility eh winna be moving too far fae this spot. Weller is on stage two in aboot four hours, His stuff isna meh cup oh tea but the rest oh them have said that he always plays a few Jam numbers, which will do for me. He is the Modfather efter ah. Four hours is not the problem as eh could take it easy until then. The problem is that stage two is in a tent, which means that we will hae ta go there really early if we want ta get in. If we go in like an hour early, we will hae ta stand and suffer whatever shite act is on before him.

The Arctic's are playing the main stage just now and they have really got the crowd going. Shane is looking smashed and eh'm wondering just how much he's took ta get in that state. Eh hope he's no took ah they E's in one go, eh warned him that they were really strong. Eh'd better keep meh eye on him for a while. He's sitting on the grass in our big group from the bus, and he's gibbering a load oh shite ta some lassie wah appears ta be trying ta speak but canna get a word in. She was on oor bus we her lad but eh think he has fucked off and left her in Shane's capable hands. Eh canna believe the state Shane is in. Eh partly feel responsible as eh gave him the E's in the first place. Eh want to go and seeThe Streets on the NME stage but eh canna tak Shane we is while he's in that state. Eh overhear Joey mention watching The Streets, that'll do for me, eh'm off we him. Eh pull him aside and tell him that eh'm going we him but to keep it quiet likes as eh dinna want Shane ta come. It'll be like babysitting if we bring him. We sneak awa and go ta the beer tent on the way. Eh still hae loads oh E's on me but eh dinna want ta take anymare just now. Eh'm jealous as fuck oh the hit Shane has hud as eh'v no hud one like that for years but eh'm just wondering how many it took ta get in that state. We get ta the N.M.E. stage an there is a fairly large crowd ah standing aboot in the sun waiting on them ta come on. We find a space deep in amongst the crowd but no too near the front. Our drinks are placed at our feet as we struggle ta skin up withoot making it look too obvious. The band comes on and the crowd in front oh us go wild. We picked a spot far enough back so as we are no shoved aboot. There are lassies on top oh peoples shoulders we just their bras on. Eh wouldna mind if they took them aff and flashed their tit's a bit but eh guess that's just meh dirty mind at work again. The Streets are only half way through their set when eh feel eh'm going ta explode as meh bladder is aboot ta burst. Eh take meh tap aff and tie it aroond meh waist, leaving the knot hanging specifically at the front. Joey holds meh drink as eh pick up an empty cup. The cups that you get your drinks in are made oh paper but they're big enough ta hold a pint. Eh stand we one hand holding the cup and we the other eh casually open a few buttons and pish in the cup. Nobody bats an eyelid as eh fill the cup and place it back on the groond. Eh button my jeans back up and eftir Joey hands back meh drink he goes ta pick up the cup oh pish and eh ken exactly what he is awa ta dae.

"Nah Joey, ye canna dae that."

He pours some oh it oot so that it is only half full. This is so that he can fold the tap oh the cup together withoot it spilling over. He looks at me and gives me a sly grin.

"You're a dirty bastard."

He taks a swing and launches the cup upwards towards the stage. This sprays the crowd we meh piss until it lands on some poor cunt wah ends up soaked as the cup opens up when it hits them. Getting hit we a cup oh cosy beer goes hand in hand we being in the mosh pit, but a cup oh piss is just no on. Eh stand and watch The Streets storm through the last oh their set we Joey next ta is, he has his fucking pigeon chest oot looking ah proud oh himself that he has just ruined some poor cunts whole day. On the way back ta whar the others are sitting, Joey stops some lassie we a programme and asks if he could hae a quick look at it. As he chats awa ta her eh flick through the pages until eh see that The Modfather is on Stage Two in an hour. That'll dae for me. Eh ken rap and hip hop is mare meh thing but eh used ta be right inta The Jam when eh was growing up. Eh hand back the programme and tell the lassie thanks as eh grab Joey and drag him awa before he ends up sneaking awa we her.

"Fuck sake Gaz eh was in there."

"Were ye fuck, she was only aboot fifteen anyway ye fucking beast."

We go ta the bar for mare drinks before heading ta the main stage ta find Shane when eh spot him staggering past us.

"Oi, whar are ye going?" Eh shout ta him.

"Alright mate" Shane says looking at us we eyes that he can hardly keep open. Jamie is no far behind and makes a face at us when Shane isna looking. It's a looks that ye can tell he is pissed right off we Shane. Shane tries ta put his arms aroond meh shoulder and eh end up dropping one oh the drinks.

"Shane, get a grip"

"Sorry mate, I'll get you another one."

"Get yourself ain. It was fir you anyway."

He goes ta the bar and while he's getting served Jamie tells us that he has been babysitting since we left them. He took him for a walk ta try and straighten him oot a bit.

"We're going ta see Weller, ye coming we us?" Joey asks

"Yeah sure, what aboot Shane?"

"Just keep an eye on him, eh ken this is probably wishful thinking, but at least if he's we us he isna gonna get inta any bather."

How things change. It used ta be Shane that had ta look efter me. We look aroond and Shane turns from the bar we two drinks and is struggling no ta spill them. He hands one ta Jamie and we walk towards Stage Two.

There is a queue ta get in when we turn up and there is a band ahready on, but we ah ken that most people are no here ta see them, they are just getting in early ta make sure they see Weller. We eventually get in and eh swallow two E's at once, eh'v ahready taken a few but eh'v no felt anything. Eh should get a good hit by the time Weller comes on though. We ah stick together in the tent and work oor way ta get closer ta the front. The crowds getting tighter so we stop ta finish oor drinks before we end up wearing them. The band that was on finishes their set and surprise surprise, hardly anybody moves. They are all here for Weller.

"Whar's Shane" Joey says looking aboot.

"Ah whar the fuck has he went ta?"

We ah look aroond but the tent is too dark and crowded ta find anybody.

"He kens whar we ah stand at the main stage and if it comes ta it, he kens whar the bus picks us up." Eh say thinking to myself that eh'm no awa ta spend the rest oh the day looking for him.

We drink what is left in oor cups and squeeze oor way through the crowd until we canna go any further. We are only aboot four or five rows fae the front which isna too bad. The lights on the stage go on and before Weller actually appears the crowd erupts. Weller walks on ta a thunderous noise. The sways in the crowd kick right aff. This is what eh was hoping for as it means eh can work meh way closer ta the front. Eh look back ta see Joey and Jamie no too far aff ta meh left but they are still pushing forward. Eh ken Jamie will get ta the front as he would shove past his ain Granny the evil wee cunt. As the crowd sways eh notice Shane ta meh right and he's closer to the front than me. He's we some lassie wah looks ta be in the same state as him. Eh work meh way closer ta him and eh'm just aboot ta slap him ta get his attention when eh notice he has his hands on her hips and is rubbing up against her arse. So much for him being loved up we his new burd. Eh'm aboot twa foot awa fae him and can see that the lassie wah he has his hands on actually has her hands on the guy in front oh her. Eh'm aboot ta reach over and drag him awa but eh stop as eh think ta myself that eh'll just watch and see what happens here. His hands work their way aroond ta the front oh her jeans and end up inside them. Her man in front is turning his head ta kiss her then when he turns his head back to face the stage she's turning aroond and kissing Shane, what a dirty bitch. Shane's arm is reaching further. Hmm, eh wonder what he's doing, her face says it ah really. She is now reaching back we her hand and is groping Shane's bahs, oh oh, she's opening his buttons now. Eh dinna ken what's happening on stage or what tune Weller is playing as eh am too busy perving at this spacer. She has her hand in his fly and is obviously wanking him aff. Oh fuck, her man has just turned aroond and noticed what's going on.

"What the fuck are you doing?" He says in his Weedgie ac-cent as he throws a cracking punch from a fist full oh sovereigns catching Shane's forehead and bursting it open.

The blood is trickling doon his face and the Weedgie goes ta throw another one but Shane grabs his wrist. He throws the other fist and

Shane grabs this one as well. Shane now has baith the guys' wrists and eh'm waiting for the head ta get stuck on him and lay the Weedgie cunt oot but it doesna happen. Shane is still full oh it and is trying ta talk ta the guy telling him ta calm doon. Eh would step in if Shane was getting a hiding but it's one on one and it looks as though he's handling it ah by himself. The E's have made him ah mellow so he's no fighting back. Shane lets him go and the guy shouts at him ta get ta fuck. He turns towards the stage and places his burd in front oh him this time. It looks as though it's ah over and eh go ta grab a hold oh Shane but he's obviously still got the horn and is hanging aboot trying ta get the lassies attention when the guys no looking. He taps the guy on the shoulder and eh move in behind him but eh still dinna let on that eh'm there.

"Here mate what was all that about?" Shane says looking quite confused.

"Are you still fucking here?" The guy shouts and his fists start flying towards Shane.

Eh grab the guy by the throat and squeeze hard, he suddenly stops. He looks at is and eh nut him in the bridge oh his nose. He puts his hands up covering his face and crouches doon. Eh could have hit him again but eh grab Shane and drag him awa fae there as quick as eh could. Shane keeps stopping and turning roond and eh canna tell if this is cause he wants ta go back and hit the guy or ta go get the guys burd. Eh find a place further back whar the crowd is no so tight and eh smile ta myself when eh see the state oh Shane's head. He has a bump sticking oot oh his forehead we a cut in the middle and blood trickling doon his face. Eh look at the state he is still in and eh'm wondering how the fuck it hasna hit me yet. Eh'v took mare E's than Shane now including twa at once before eh came in this tent and eh'm still feeling straight. Noel Gallagher has just walked on stage as a special guest and this has lifted the crowd again. They perform twa songs, finishing we 'That's entertainment' which for me it certainly was.

We head ta the bar for a drink whar we catch up we Joey and Jamie wah are shocked ta find Shane we a bump that has now swelled ta the size oh a half a golf bah. His recollection oh how it happened is somewhat different ta how eh remember seeing it.

"The guy just hit me for nothing." He says.

"What, and ye didna hit him back?" Jamie says ah serious.

"Eh, no"

"What does he look like? We'll go get the cunt." Jamie says keeping his serious face ta Shane but gives me and Joey the sneaky grin.

"I can't remember." Shane says looking quite confused but is missing the point that trying ta find somebody in the middle oh a field we forty thousand other people is the joke. Eh'm tempted ta tell them exactly what happened but eh'll save it for a rainy day. We go back and find the others ah sitting aroond on the grass catching the last oh the sun. We dinna get weather like this up in Scotland too often so every second is soaked up we ah the sun worshipers. Eh lie back on the grass haeing a smoke and finish meh drink. Razorlight have just come on stage and most oh the crowd are standing up now, but me, eh think eh'm going ta stay right here a bit longer. Eh close meh eyes for a while and eh guess eh must have dosed aff, either that or Razorlight have only done three songs and are onto their finale. Eh'm shaken by somebody tripping over is and eh stand up ta catch the last song 'America' The band sing the chorus and the music stops so that the crowd have ta sing it back ta them. Hearing thousands oh people sing a chorus in tune back ta the stage sends the shivers doon meh spine and it's nothing ta do we drugs. The closing band on the main stage the day is the Strokes but as much as they are probably a top act but ta me every ain oh their tunes sound the same, they are just no meh cup oh tea. Eh have ta finish the day at the N.M.E. stage as New Order are closing the show and eh dinna care if eh have ta go on meh ain that's whar eh'm heading. Eh announce this ta see if any cunt wants ta join is but it's only Jamie wah taks is on. Eh look over at Shane wah has a drink in each hand and it looks as though the E's are finally starting to wear aff.

Eh head ti the bar on the way ta the N.M.E. stage and while eh'm being served Jamie gets chatting ta a couple oh lassies wah eh can make oot are Weedgies judging by their strong accent. Eh hand him twa drinks and as we head aff he offers them ta come we us, which ta meh annoyance they oblige. The band have no started yet so eh work my way doon the side wah until eh find a good space ta sit doon. Eh put meh drinks ta one side oh is and get myself ah comfy on the groond. Eh start skinning up while Jamie is next ta is in serious chit chat we the Weedgies. Eh spark up and feel content we meh back against the wah and meh drink ta one side as eh tak long slow puffs on meh joint. Eh ken there's an unwritten rule aboot the twa puffs and pass it, fuck it's usually me that enforces it, but no this time, and it's no cause eh'm being greedy or that eh'm running low on grass, it's cause eh grudge passing ta a couple oh hangers on, especially a couple oh Weedgie mingers. As eh sit and listen ta their conversation eh cringe at some o Jamie's comments ta them. Ain oh these Weedgies is quite slim but has a face like she's been chasing parked cars, the other has a nice face but is fuckin enormous, the layers oh fat are hinging over the sides oh her jeans and her stretch marks look as though some cunt has drew them on we a highlighter marker. Eh catch Jamie passing them a couple oh E's and eh'm thinking, what the fuck are you doing? Eh eventually pass the joint efter Jamie gives is a funny look and just as eh guessed he takes a quick puff and passes it straight ta them. They are camping oot here and have asked Jamie if we want, we can sleep in their tent the night, hmm eh wonder why?

"Are ye up for it Gaz?"

"What?"

"Staying in their tent"

"We dinna hae camping bands."

"That's ahright, they'll sort it."

Eh really dinna fancy sleeping in some smelly tent we a couple oh Weedgies when eh can jump on the bus and be curled up in a comfy bed in less than an hour but eh wouldna leave Jamie in the lurch as eh ken he wouldna dae it ta me.

"Gaz, they said they have loads oh drink in their tent and baith are up for their hole" Jamie says still trying ta convince is.

"Eh'll even take the fat ain." He says as he puts his bottom lip oot we a sad expression on his face.

These lassies are only aboot seventeen which doesna sound bad for Jamie as he's only nineteen but at twenty five, this doesna look good for me. Eh nod and tell him that eh canna really leave him on his ain so eh'll hae ta stay. He gives me a big cheesy grin then says "Eh kent that you would be up for it if eh mentioned you would get yer hole, ye dirty cunt."

"If we get caught sneaking in the campsite we'll hae ta run like fuck ta catch oor bus hame." Eh tell him.

"Dinna worry aboot it. Eh'll pay for a taxi, if need be"

Chapter 18

We get ti the campsite gates and the security is checking for the wristbands as people pass through. The twa weedgies go through first and the fat ain snaps her wristband and the skinny ain comes back oot we it. She puts it aroond Jamie's wrist and taks the chewny oot oh her mooth and puts it on the ends oh the wristband huding it together. She taks Jamie's hand and they walk through, nae bather. She then comes back and does the same we me, Weedgies, they ken every trick in the book. We walk aroond the campsite for a while as the lassies canna find their tent. Eh pass a few people that eh ken and they offer me ti stay and hae a beer. As much as eh would like ti stop and hae a banter we them meh hand is tugged fae the skinny ugly lassie as we struggle ti keep up we Jamie and the fat burd. We eventually find their tent and as soon as eh sit doon they pass me plastic cup.

"What the fuck is this?" Eh say as eh tak a sip.

"Fuck. This is cider. Do ye no hae any beer?"

"Naw, that's aw we've got."

Eh'm now thinking that eh should go an find they cunts eh seen on the way here and hae a beer we them, ken what, eh'll stay and hae a smoke first, then eh'll go looking for them. Eh sit in the corner oh the tent rolling a joint when meh phone goes.

"Hello."

"Gaz, where the fuck are you?"

"Ahright Kyle, eh'm in the campsite we Jamie."

"That's good. The bus has only been waiting here for half an hour on you two."

"Sorry mate eh forgot ah aboot it. We are gonna stay here the night. We'll see ye the morn."

"Yeah, see you."

"That wis Kyle. He sounds a bit pissed aff that we didna tell him."

"Fuck him. If he had the offer he would be here tae." Jamie says trying ta justify the bus waiting on us.

Eh light up and hae a few puffs before passing it ta Jamie. He is lying curled up ta the fat lassie. Eh down the cider and ask for mare. Eh'm hoping they've none left so eh could use the excuse ta escape. The skinny lassie pulls oot a three litre bottle and comes over and pours some inta the plastic cup. She pours herself another ain and moves in closer ta is.

"Hey Gaz have you got any E's left?" Jamie asks.

"Yeah a few but they're for the morn."

"Gonna give is a couple and eh'll phone Kyle in the morning ta bring some mare."

Eh pull oot meh stash and realise eh hae aboot ten left but eh dinna let on ta Jamie as eh ken the cunt will nip meh head until they're ah finished and he'll probably only dish them oot ta these mingers. Eh hand him twa and he puts baith oh them in his mooth at once and swallys them we a moothful oh cider.

"Fuck it." Eh dae the same.

As soon as eh swally it eh canna help but think that was a waste as eh huvna hud a proper hit ah day. Eh think eh must be gitting immune ta them or something. Eh think eftir this week-end eh should hae a break fae these, especially eftir seeing the hit Shane hud fae them the day. We sit aroond for a while as we doon cup eftir cup oh this pishy cider. Jamie and the fat lassie are now in the same sleeping bag and are whispering in each other's ears so eh guess they are giving it a bit oh foreplay. As eh'm talking ta the skinny lassie she reaches over and starts kissing me, but eh think this is just so eh will shut meh puss as they twa E's must be making is gibber shite ta her. Everywhare she touches me eh feel ah tingly and eh start getting turned on. Eh keep thinking that this is ah wrang as this lassie is too young. Before eh ken it she has meh jeans open adn she's wanking is aff. Eh open her jeans and put meh hand in her knickers. Eh try ta slide meh fingers further doon but am findind it hard as she has the hairiest fanny eh huv ever came across.

"Eh think you need yer bikini line done hen." Eh whisper in her oar.

She cniggers so eh guess she thinks eh'm joking. Eh eventually manage ta slide meh fingers doon and slide ain in her, then another ain. This gets her going a bit. She pushes up meh tap so eh tak meh hand oot oh her knickers and tak meh tap aff and she does the same. Eh put meh hands on her sides and she is that skinny eh feel her bones. She must be ain oh they anorexic lassies, either that or eh'm just used ta the big fat burds.

Eh dinna say anything and we carry on taking the rest oh oor gear aff. We her knickers aff and her legs open, eh climb on tap oh her and am banging awa. Just meh luck, a screamer.

Eh'm in a tent, in the middle oh a field at T in the park and am shagging a screamer, but no just any screamer, a wee gadgie Glesgay screamer. Eh look ta the right oh is and through the dark eh can see Jamie's shadow. He's oot o the sleeping bag and kneeling over the fat lassie.

"Suck it then." He says in a low voice.

Eh snigger as eh heard it loud and clear. The skinny lassie is still groaning and screaming every time eh thrust inta her. Eh can hear a loud cheer in the distance we each scream that she makes and eh'm now giggling awa ta myself.

"Ye huv ta keep sucking till it goes hard." Jamie says in his low voice again. He obviously canna get a hard on and is getting stressed oot.

"How do ye no just hum meh bahs instead?" He says a bit louder.

"What, what do you mean?" The fat lassie asks.

Eh hae a wee muffled laugh as eh try to hud it in.

"Eh mean just put yer mooth aroond meh bahs and huuuuu-um" Jamie says dragging it oot.

Eh start ta loose meh rhythm as eh struggle ta concentrate we this going on next ta is. Eh lift myself aff the skinny lassie and tell her ta turn over.

"Yer no putting that up my arse" She rages.

Eh laugh at this "Dinna be daft of course eh'm no gonna put it up yer arse."

She turns over and eh lift her boney hips so her arse is sticking up in the air. Eh'm back in and banging awa feeling like eh'm the fuckin man. Eh can see Jamie's grinning in the dark and he's making faces at me. Eh start making porn star noises and we both burst oot laughing.

"Keep humming, dinna stop" Jamie says.

But the lassie does stop and says "Ah don't want tae dae this anymore. Ah want you tae shag me like he's shagging her."

"Just shut it and keep humming, myabe if you werena so fat and ugly eh would hae a hard on, and eh would be shagging you like that."

The smile is drained fae meh face as eh canna believe that Jamie has said that ta her. Eh feel sorry for the lassie as eh think Jamie was a bit oot oh order saying that. But the lassie has a mooth on her and fires right back at him.

"If you were any sort oh man your dick would be in me making me scream like her anyway" She says we a bit oh attitude in her voice now.

"Oh ho, she's got ye there Jamie" At this point eh stop and sit back

"What's wrong?" The skinny ain turns ta is and says.

"Nothing, eh just need a drink."

Eh sit back and pour myself a cup oh this pishy cider as meh hard on settles doon ta a semi. The fat lassie isna slow as she blurts oot "Are we swapping over then."

Eh ignore what she says and ask Jamie ta hud the phone near is so eh can use the light ta skin up. The lassies are at one end oh the tent drinking and whispering and we are at the other drinking and passing the joint between oorselves.

"Eh hud nae intension oh shagging her" Jamie whispers in meh ear.

"Eh only said that ta persuade ye ta stay."

"What do you mean? If you said eh was on the fat ain eh would huv stayed anyway."

We both laugh like a couple oh bairns.

"Well you can shag her now then cause she's no gonna let me near her."

"Was that the plan then, was it?" Eh say but dinna get a reply.

Eh hae one last puff and then pass it ta the lassies wah are pouring themselves mare cider.

"How do we go aboot this Jamie?"

"Eh'll show ye" He says moving towards the lassies side oh the tent.

"Right fatty, you're now we Gaz and you. You're now we me" Jamie says as he taks his tap aff and moves towards the skinny lassie.

Eh finish meh cup oh cider and move towards the fat lassie wah is lying doon. Although she's quite fat she does hae a nice face so eh start kissing her. Eh'm still naked and hae meh hands up her tap and she has her hands on meh arse. She works her way aroond and it's no long before oh'm hard again. Eh help her tak aff her tap ta reveal her big saggy tits but eh dinna ken what ta dae next as eh slide meh hand doon her waist onta the layers oh fat folding over her jeans. Eh'm aboot ta try and open her tap button that is buried in her stomach but she moves meh hand and does it herself. She taks aff her jeans ta reveal her big granny pants an when eh help her tak these aff they feel like a pair oh they lycra running shorts.

Eh guess that's ta help hud in some oh the fat ta make her appear thinner. She must be really turned on as eh put meh fingers doon she feels really wet, either that or she's pissed herself. Eh slide a finger up one eftir another until eh hae three up nae problem withoot her even making a noise, fuck sake, am eh in trouble or what? The saying when eh was growing up comes ta mind 'It's like throwing a mars bar up a closey." Eh pull them oot and climb on tap oh her and as eh dae this eh hae a wee sneaky smell oh meh fingers, ahh, the lovely smell oh a sweaty stinky fanny. She grabs meh willy and rams it in but she still doesna make a sound. Eh've heard the saying fir years aboot no even touching the sides and eh hud visions oh this but it doesna appear ta be the case. She still doesna move or even make a noise, and as eh thrust harder and harder she lays there like a sack oh tatties. Eh lift up one oh her legs so that eh can reach her arse cheek. This is no so that eh can grope her fat wrinkly arse but eh do hae an ulterior motive. Meh middle finger finds it's way through the layers oh fat and eh play aboot by rubbing the tip oh meh finger ah aroond her wee browner. She starts ta groan a bit and this encourages me ta keep going. Eh rub her fanny again which is dripping wet and eh squeeze meh finger in ta moisten it and then go back ta her arse. Eh circle aroond it then just ram it up. This results in a much louder groan fae her, still nae movement bit at least it lets is ken she's still alive. Eh'm thrusting meh hips hard and wiggling meh finger up her arse and just as eh start ta get the feeling eh'm aboot ta shoot meh load meh mind wanders and eh start thinking aboot some weird shit because oh they fucking E's. Eh start ta think that eh'v been kissing that lassie eftir she wis hummin Jamie's bahs and eh'm now feeling a bit sick. Eh forget whar eh am for a bit as the sweat runs doon meh face. Eh somehow get inta a wee rhythm again when eh hear Jamie moaning at the skinny lassie because she winna give him a blow job. It starts ta get a bit aggressive and then in the dark eh see Jamie shove the lassie across the other side oh the tent near me. The lassie shouts at him and eh see Jamie's arm go back as if he is awa ta hit her. Eh stop what eh'm doing and reach over and give Jamie a hard slap in the puss.

"Dinna you fuckin dare." Eh say, ready ta give him another ain.

"What the fuck are you doing?" He says.

"Dinna you ever lift yer hands ta a woman."

Eh'm aboot ta get aff and tell the fat lassie ta forget it bit eh think this wee cunt is no spoilign it for me. Eh struggle ta get going again and think ta myself eh'll give her it fae behind but then eh think oh the size oh her arse and think better oh that idea. Eh get going again and feel myself building up and am aboot ta shoot meh load but eh dinna come up her. Eh pull oot at the last minute and wank until eh shoot meh load ah over her.

"Oh thanks and how am I supposed to clean myself."

"What do ye mean? Yer a weedgie. You lot dinna wash any-way."

Eh hear Jamie laughing at this and eh reach over putting the finger eh hud up the fat lassies arse under Jamie's nose and rub it hard above his lip. This is kent as a tangy porker. We used ta dae this type oh thing when we were at skale. Eh guess some people just never grow up.

"What are ye doing? Ooh what the fuck is that?" He says sitting up ta wipe his face.

Eh sit back in the corner and canna stop laughing as Jamie storms aboot the tent trying ta get the smell oh shit fae his nose. Eh pick up the first thing at hand that happens ta be the fat lassies tap and eh give meh finger a good rub ta clean it. Eh put on meh clothes and start ta pour myself a cup oh cider. Jamie opens the zip on the tent and taks aff his condom and throws it oot in the distance. As usual eh never even bathered we ain, and none oh these twa Weedgies asked is ta put ain on.

"Eh'm gonna get you back for that Gaz." Jamie says.

"That's for starting on the wee lassie ye fucking bully" Eh say pushing him lightly. He doesna say anything back. We hae a few cups o cider and Jamie opens another bottle, the lassies hae a wee moan and seem to be getting a bit nippy so eh think it's time for us ta find a another tent ta crash in.

"Eh think we should make a move Jamie, eh really dinna want ta waken up here in the morning. Its ahready stinking oh stale smoke, drink, sweat, spunk, an now shit fae your face."

"Dead funny, ye prick."

Eh pull up the zip on the tent an throw oot ain oh the full bottles oh cider withoot the lassies kenin. Eh fucking hate cider but that's ah they hae so eh guess beggars canna be choosers. Without even saying cheerio, we get ta fuck oot oh there we nae intension oh returning. We stretch oor legs as we look aboot in the dark wondering which way ta go. There are several lit areas whar we can hear groups oh people talking and we decide just ta try and find somebody we ken, which shouldna be too hard. Eh pick up the bottle oh cider as we go.

"Eh thought ye didna like cider?"

"Oh that's no for us, that's for bargaining we."

Eftir walking aroond in the dark for a few minutes we hear some distinguished Dundee accents. We dinna ken them but eftir ah trade oh some grass and a bottle oh cider for a few tins oh lager we are welcomed inta their company. Twa tins oh lager, a good smoke and eh'm comatose in a clean tent feeling safe in the company oh some real Dundee schemies.

Chapter 19

Shane

I waken up as Kelly walks in and opens the curtains.

"Come on sleepy head, get up."

She passes me a cup of coffee and by the looks of it she's been up for ages as she looks fresh and ready to go.

"I have as surprise for you later."

"Oh you do, do you?" I say smiling at her.

"You were in some state last night" She says.

"Was I?" I reply while trying to actually remember yester-day.

"At least the bump on your head has gone down" She says nodding to my forehead.

I put my hand up to my head and feel a slight bump sticking out. I get a flash back of some guy punching me, but cannot remember why. I vaguely remember trying to push my way to the front for Weller coming on so I guess he wasn't happy about it. I wonder why I didn't hit him back.

"Come on, get in the shower and we'll go somewhere for breakfast."

I finish my coffee then quickly jump in the shower and the whole time I am still trying to remember most of what happened yesterday. It's been a long time since I got myself in such a state where I can't remember the day before. I get changed and we head downstairs to Kelly's car. She points in the direction of my car, which has been fixed.

"Was that you?"

"Who else would go and sort your car?"

"You didn't have to do that."

She smiles and says "I just wanted to help you out."

"Thanks."

Kelly asked me yesterday when she dropped me of at the bus if I knew who was doing it but I didn't tell her. The last thing I want to do is let her know I have someone like Dek Murdo on my case. She takes me into the town and we go to a café for some breakfast. I don't feel hungry in the slightest but she is making such an effort I don't want to tell her. I play safe and order a bacon roll and Kelly orders the same. I mention we will have to be quick as I have to catch the bus shortly.

"Don't worry about it." She says with a big smile, which makes me think she wants me to miss the bus so I won't go.

"I can't believe the state of your head." She says, changing the subject.

"Don't worry about it."

"What if you see the guy again today, I hope you won't start fighting with him."

"Kelly there is forty thousand people a day at the park, not to mention that I can't remember what the guy looks like, so the chances of that happening are quite slim. Anyway the bus leaves in twenty minutes so we had better make a move soon."

"That's alright I'll give you a lift."

"What do you mean?"

She looks at me and smiles and pulls out a Sunday ticket from her pocket and puts it in front of me.

"What, are you coming too?"

"A friend of mine offered me it last night, so I thought I would surprise you."

"Brilliant" I say leaning over and kissing her.

"But this means you will have to meet all of my friends, I hope you realise that."

"Oh I think I can handle it."

We take our time finishing our breakfast and I text Kyle to say that I am getting a lift from Kelly and that I will meet them later. Although I have explained to Kelly that there is no chance of seeing the guy that hit me she has warned me that if the situation occurs she will walk away and I would never see her again as she absolutely hates violence.

"I understand that but what if someone is about to attack me, or you for that matter, I will have to fight to protect you, would you still walk away."

"That's different, and you know fine well what I mean."

"I know, I was just testing you" I say smiling at her but thinking the total opposite as in my mind if I saw the cunt again I would fucking smash him.

Gaz

"Jamie that's Kyle just phoned me. They're on their way but Shane's not on the bus. Apparently he's phoned ta say he's getting a lift fae his burd and he'll meet us when he gets here. Huv you met her yet?"

"No, how"

"Eh'm just wondering how he never brings her oot ta meet us, it's like he doesna want us ta see her. Are we no good enough ta meet his new burd or something."

"That's no what's bathering you, it's the fact that when he is we her you hae naewhar ta go eftir a club for a perty."

"Nah that's nothing ta dae we it, well maybe a wee bit but if he's happy being we her then good luck ta him. Eh would just like ta meet her once and see what she's like, that's ah."

"Eh right, like her fae the taxi office, ye were on his case constantly for seeing her."

"Eh, but she was a fucking idiot."

"That's no the point, every time Shane gets ah serious aboot some burd you lot always tak the piss oot oh him and he ends up dumping them."

"That's because he always ends up getting serious aboot lassies that are fuckin idiots, dae ye ken what? Eh bet its some burd eh'v shagged before and he doesna want us geeing him stick for it."

Jamie changes the subject and eh think ta myself that in future eh'm no gonna say anything ta Shane aboot the burds he meets and we'll soon see what fuckin trouble he gets inta.

Shane

It's not long after the park opens that we arrive and meet everyone from the bus. They are sitting on the grass in their usual place in front of the main stage. I introduce Kelly to everyone and Gaz makes a comment that he thinks he knows her from somewhere.

"So you're the ain that's keeping oor mate occupied." Kelly smiles politely back at him.

"She's a right wee pumper is she?" Gaz comments

There are two ways that you can take it when someone says your girl is wee pumper. I have already pre warned Kelly of what they mean as this has been an ongoing thing between me and Gaz for years. In one way it could be said by meaning that she is a wee slapper and she will pump anything, hence 'wee pumper'. In another way it could mean she is a lovely looking girl and that you would like to pump her. Kelly laughs as Gaz says this knowing full well that he is winding me up that he would like to pump her, well I fucking hope that's how the cunt is meaning it.

"And you, you're looking a bit rough mate" He says inspecting the bump on my head.

The banter is flowing fast of the stories from the past twenty four hours. Someone mentions that they saw Gaz and Jamie with a couple of horrors yesterday but although they try to deny it. Jamie puts Gaz right in it by pulling out a pair of knickers from his pocket and holds them up to everyone's amusement. These knickers are the biggest I have ever seen so I can just imagine the size of the girl that was wearing them. Jamie proceeds to explain in great exaggerated detail about what Gaz got up to with this girl. Gaz stands and takes it as he knows he will bide his time and wait for the right moment and get him back again.

Gaz

Shane's burd is a lot smaller than eh remember fae that night at the Doghoose. Eh end up speaking ta them again and eh find oot that she is a really nice lassie but eh suddenly realise whar eh remember her fae. If it's the same person wah eh think it is, Shane's in a lot oh trouble. She's obviously no telt Shane aboot her past if it is the same lassie or he wudna be standing there huding her hand and parading her aboot like that. Nae wonder she doesna come oot often ta meet people. He walks awa ta talk ta the others still huding Kelly's hand but if eh manage ta get him on his ain he'll no be doing that for very much longer. Eh watch them walk aff ta the bar kissing and cuddling up ta each other and eh realise that Shane must really like her as he would never be that forward we a lassie in front oh his mates. The last time eh saw him dae anything like that we were still at skale, but eftir a good slagging fae us, for some reason he never done it again. Eh get Shanes attention and tell him eh need a word we him but his burd drags him awa. They're awa ta see that Dundee band 'The View' on another stage. Eh canna believe that cunt. He stood in the Doghoose and ripped into every sang that they done and now he's awa we his burd ta go and see them. Eh'll bide meh time and try and get him on his ain later before the wrang person sees him we her.

Shane

"So do like this new band then?" Kelly says as she puts her arm into mine as we walk towards one of the smaller tents where the new up and coming bands get to play.

"Yeah, they're great, I didn't think much of them when I saw them at the doghouse that night but I was pretty wasted. Mickey handed me a copy of their demo C.D. from Mickey, I play it all the time when I am working. They've got some catchy tunes."

As we enter the packed tent the band are on stage just about to start, and for a new band who haven't even released a song, they have quite a number of fans. As soon as they kick off the tent erupts with their army of wild fans. I stand with Kelly further back as the drinks start to get thrown about. This young band have the crowd going more than some of the headliners and are up on this small stage ripping into all that shit with their powerful tunes and lyrics. We end up squashed at the back of the tent halfway through their set due to the amount of people trying to squeeze in to see them play.

"They should be on a bigger stage" Kelly says.

"I know, definitely a future headliner."

As they announce their last song, some of the fans end up on stage and are dancing away. Somehow I can't see that being allowed to happen if they get a slot on the main stage

We walk back to find everyone still sitting around at our usual area near the main stage. Kelly has to go to the toilet and I am about to go with her when Gaz tags along as he is going to the bar. We reach the toilets first and the queue is very long.

"I could be a while so why don't you two go to the bar and I will meet you back here?" Kelly says as she gives me a kiss on the cheek before walking off to join the queue.

I order a couple of drinks and we stand around watching the main stage from a distance. Gaz is being a bit funny and I ask him what's up, thinking he's away to take the piss about yesterday.

"Shane, eh, Kelly's dad wouldna happen ta own a nightclub would he?"

"Yeah in Spain, do you know him?"

"No but if your burd is wah eh think she is, then you're in a lot oh fuckin trouble."

"What are you talking about?" I smile nervously.

"Shane, eh think Murdo could be on yer case cause oh Kelly."

"What do you mean?"

"Eh think Kelly could be Murdo's ex burd"

"Fuck off" You're on the wind up.

He doesn't say anything but his smile drops and he looks at me serious.

"This is a piss take right."

"Come on Shane, you ken eh wouldna wind you up aboot something like this."

"Yeah right, he's old enough to be her father, and anyway Murdo's been in the jail for the last four years and Kelly's only twenty-one, which would make her about seventeen if he did happen to go out with her."

"Actually eh think she was only sixteen when he went oot we her."

"Gaz, what are you talking about?"

"Shane, do you remember the nightclub a good few years ago called Velvet. It shut doon and it is now a day centre for junkies or something."

"Yeah, it was a shit hole."

"Kelly's old man used ta own that."

"And what"

"Look Shane, Murdo used ta be her dad's mate and was the head bouncer on the door there."

"Yeah I remember him, he wasn't actually allowed to work the door because of his criminal record so they gave him a different title but everybody knew he was in charge. If any trouble kicked off he stepped forward and sorted it out."

"Yeah well, eh used ta end up there sometimes when eh was oot we a few dodgy characters. Eh think you were busy doing up yer flats at the time. Well eh remember Kelly, she hud long blonde hair and always wore ah the tight short clothes. Eh dinna ken the full story but the four years Murdo has just done, was for stabbing her cousin."

"Are you sure it's the same person Gaz?"

"Eh hope eh'm wrang mate, but if it is her, just watch what you say. Eh ken her and her family hud a hard time. Murdo was ain oh they jealous people and didna like her talking ta other guys. That's what started the fight we her cousin, the pair cunt was actually beating Murdo until he pulled the blade and chibbed him a few times. Kelly and her auld man hud ta go up in court against him, it was ah on video but the sick cunt pleaded 'not guilty' just so they would huv ta testify. Apparently the footage on the video looked as though Murdo was punching him until he pulled his hand back and there he was standing we this big blade in his hand. Her old man hud ta eventually sell up an move due ta the amount oh trouble he hud eftir that."

"That's why she doesn't go anywhere" I say to myself.

"This is what eh'v tried ta explain ta ye every time you've mouthed aff at him. This is the type oh person yer dealing we. He's been in jail twice for stabbing and it was only luck that he didna kill them."

"Well you know what they say, third time lucky." I joke but Gaz doesn't laugh.

"If that is her ex, what am I going to do?"

"Eh dinna ken mate. Eh could try and hae a word but Murdo is a nut job he's no gonna listen ta anybody."

I see Kelly coming back from the toilet and I make a face at Gaz who quickly turns around and gives her a big smile.

"Those toilets are disgusting" Kelly makes a face

Gaz leads the way back to the other and we make small talk along the way but my head is in serious deep thought at my situation. Back at the main stage it is starting to get really crowded as the final act is due to come on. Gaz mentions he's away to head to the N.M.E. stage as Primal Scream are closing it and he makes a sharp exit through the heavy crowd. I stand with Kelly as we wait for Faithless to come on and close the show on the main stage. I actually feel like asking her about all this now but I have had a good day and really don't want to spoil it. Faithless kick off while the sky is still bright but after a few songs the sun goes down. This makes the stage look great as it is all lit up in the dark. The lights and lasers move around in time with their music as the crowd cheer with each uplifting tune. They finish their set to a massive cheer from the crowd. As we walk back through the field we are treated to a firework display and as each rocket is shot up into the sky you can see the disappointment on the crowds faces that it is all over for another year.

Chapter 20

The long walk out of the park to Kelly's car gives me time to think about what Gaz told me. I have to find out if it's true but how I am going to bring this up.

"Are you okay?" Kelly grips my hand tighter.

"Yeah of course, why"

"You have hardly said a word all the way out."

"Sorry, I'm just thinking about something Gaz said, that's all."

Kelly smiles at me and I smile back but I'm actually looking at her thinking how could she have been with a prick like him. I am actually picturing the two of them together and it is making me feel sick. I will wait until tomorrow when both of our heads are clear. The queues of traffic are locked and we sit in the car park for nearly an hour before it starts to move. We eventually get onto the main road and Kelly asks me again what's wrong.

"I have never seen you so quiet."

"Sorry, I have something on my mind, that's all."

"It must be important."

"Eh, nah, well...Fuck it, Kelly I need to ask you something?"

"Sounds a bit serious, I suppose it depends on what it is?"

"Did your dad used to own a club in Dundee?"

"Yeah, why"

"Eh'm, it's just something Gaz told me."

"Why, what did he tell you?"

"He says your ex is Dek Murdo."

I don't get a reply and there is silence in the car for what seems like a long time.

"Well, is he?"

Kelly pulls the car over to the side of the road and brushes her hands up her forehead and through her hair letting out a long sigh at the same time.

"Yes, yes he is."

This is obviously something that she didn't want me to know so I try to reassure her.

"Look Kelly, I'm not bothered about your past." I say as I put my arm around her.

She leans over and puts her head into me and both her arms around me. This lasts for several minutes then we break off.

"So what else did Gaz tell you?"

She listens to me as I tell her exactly what Gaz had said. When I finish she doesn't say anything.

"Well is it true?"

"Yes." She says in a very soft voice.

"But there is a lot more to it than that."

"Look you don't have to explain it to me. I'm just disappointed you didn't tell me sooner before I found out from a mate."

"Look I need to explain so you know what really happened. Yes I did have long blonde hair and dressed in the tight clothes but I was sixteen and I didn't know any better. I got a lot of attention and most of it was from Dek. He was a friend of my dad's and he was always nice to me. I knew his reputation but when you are young and naïve you can be attracted to that. My dad went nuts but that encouraged me even more. Until Dek started to get jealous and it got to the point that I couldn't even talk to anyone, even girls. He would march over to me asking what I was saying to them. If I had a skirt on he would be constantly on my case and shout at people that he thought were looking at me."

"Why didn't you just leave him?" I ask getting myself worked up thinking about this beast with her.

"Believe me I tried, but he came up and smashed up my Dads house and threatened me that if he saw me with anyone he would kill them."

"Did he ever hit you?"

"No but he put a knife to my throat once."

"WHAT?" I shout.

"It was after he stabbed my cousin and he was out on bail. Do you believe it, my cousin was in hospital on a life support machine and he gets out on bail. Anyway he kept coming up to the house to try and speak to me. You know, bringing flowers saying he was sorry and sending stupid gifts. I just ignored him but he started following me around. I would go into a pub to meet up with friends, all females by the way, and then he would appear and accuse me of meeting other guys and make a big scene."

"But you weren't seeing him anyway."

"I know, but that didn't register with him. I told him to leave me alone and he would try to drag me out of the pub. The other bouncers wouldn't go near him as they were all shit scared. One night I was out and there was a large group of us. My friends' boyfriend was talking to me and Dek appeared and started ranting and raving that I was seeing him. It got so bad that I had to persuade Dek to leave with me before he hit my friends' boyfriend. I didn't think for one minute he would do anything to me. Yeah he would hit guys and smash things but I never thought for a minute that he would harm me. I got outside the pub and phoned my dad to pick me up but there was no answer so I started walking towards the taxi rank. He dragged me into an alleyway by the hair and I was shouting and screaming to let me go then he pulled out a knife and put it to my throat telling me to shut up. He said if he couldn't have me then no one could and that if he ever saw me with anyone this is what they would get and so would I."

I look to see the tears in Kelly's eyes and I pull her close to me to comfort her but comforting someone is the last thing I feel like doing right now.

"That's why you wouldn't go anywhere with me?"

"That's right" She says looking straight at me.

"Kelly I'm not scared of him. I can look after myself." I say trying to sound hard.

"But it's not just him, it's his mates, if he snaps his fingers they go running. That is why we had to move away. After he put a knife to my throat I went to the police as there were conditions with him getting bail that he was not allowed to approach me or any of my family. I had plenty of witnesses to say he was harassing me so he was put back in until the trial. That's when it started getting really bad for my dad. If it wasn't the house being broken into and our cars being smashed up it was the club. My dad couldn't get bouncers to work the door as Dek knew them all and they refused to work for him."

"Your dad must have known some other firm to work it."

"He did, he brought in a Glasgow firm but this caused more trouble as the fighting got worse. It played right into Dek's hands as he was locked up with all these gangsters and he obviously had a word with whomever run the Glasgow firm and they pulled out. The club was losing customers every week and eventually my dad had enough and sold it. The trial was creeping up so he decided to move abroad."

"Why didn't you go?"

"I did, but I missed my friends and I wanted to go to Uni. After Dek got sentenced my Dad opened another club abroad. We both thought it would be safe enough for me to go back. I thought I would be finished Uni by the time he got out."

"And then what? Hurry on back to Spain before he finds you."

"Something like that."

"I can't picture you two together, well I can but it doesn't seem right."

"Believe me if I could change it I would, but remember I wasn't the same person back then, I was just a very naive young girl. I didn't even look the same."

"So what happens now?"

"I don't know, my intensions were to move back to Spain and work for my dad, but I've met you and I don't know what to do. I really like you Shane but I can't live here. You could always come with me."

"Yeah right, just pack up and walk into the sunset."

There is a long silence and Kelly starts the car and drives off. From the side of her face I can see the tears in her eyes. This makes me feel really sad seeing her unhappy, but at this moment I cannot think of anything to say to her. We arrive at my flat and I go to get out of her car.

"Do you want me to come up?"

"What do you mean? Of course I want you to come up?"

I get into the flat and head to the kitchen and put the kettle on.

"Do you want one?"

Kelly nods. "Please."

I put sugar and tea bags in the cups and as we wait on the kettle boiling she puts her arms around me tightly.

"Kelly, can I ask you something?"

"Of course, what is it?"

"Are you still intending on leaving? I mean, you finished Uni a while ago and you are still here."

"I had to wait on my exam results and one thing led to an-other so I decided I was going to hang on until my graduation."

"When were you going to tell me all this"

"I don't know. I was always happy when I was with you that I didn't want anything to spoil it. I always told you I was going to work for my dad anyway."

"Yeah, I know but I..."

"What?"

"Oh, nothing"

"You thought I would change my mind and stay here to be with you."

"Something like that!"

"So when I asked you to leave, is that not the same as you expecting me to stay" Kelly smiles.

"Why don't you stay? He's been out for months now and he's not bothered you."

I now feel glad I have never mentioned the hassle I have been having with him or that when she fixed my car the other day that it was actually Murdo that done the damage.

"He has not seen me with you yet, actually since he's been out he has not even seen me yet."

I would love to tell her the truth that I think he's already seen us together.

"I'm not afraid of him."

"That's the problem Shane. Neither was my cousin and look what happened to him."

"Look Kelly I can get someone to sort him out if you want and he will never come near us." As soon as I say this I realise how stupid it sounds. I don't know anybody that would take him on. Every other hard case is an acquaintance of his and they certainly wouldn't tell him to back off for me.

"Shane don't you think my dad tried all that? He even offered him money to stay away from us."

There is a silence between us for a few minutes as my mind is going around in circles thinking of something to say that would make her change her mind.

"Look I really care about you, that is why I have to leave as I don't want anything to happen to you."

"Listen Kelly" I say holding her tighter.

"He is a coward. He won't do anything to me."

"Look you know it is not just him though, I don't want to get a phone call one night saying something's happened to you and I have to live with it."

"So that's it." I say, releasing my arms from around her gently.

"You are just going to leave and if I want us to continue I have to move to Spain."

"It's not like that Shane, look, maybe I should just go."

Kelly goes to walk away from me but I grab her arm and pull her tight towards me.

"Look Kelly, this is a lot for me to take in, in one night. I would love to say I will sell my flat and come with you but it's not as easy as that."

"I don't expect you to do that for me, but the fact is I can't stay here. Why don't you come for a few weeks and see what you think?"

"I can't just up and leave. I have my family, my friends and my job. I also have this place which I have worked really hard for. What if it didn't work out? What if I didn't like it over there?"

"Shane you don't know until you try, you can rent your flat out for a few months. It will pay your mortgage and give you some extra income."

"You have got this all figured out don't you?"

Kelly hugs me again

"I don't expect you to do anything Shane, I am only asking you to think about it."

She takes my hand and leads me to the bedroom

"Come on, it's been a long day, let's go to bed."

Chapter 21

I can't believe Kelly just left like that without saying anything. Three days after asking me to move to Spain and live with her. She packs her bags and leaves. I get a text saying she's away to her dad's as she needs some time to think and that she would be in touch. I went around to her flat and her friend let me in. All her stuff was gone. To top it all, the next day my car gets paint stripper poured over it. It wouldn't take a rocket scientist to figure out who did it. I was ready to go after Mudro but Gaz calmed me down. It's not just the cost of the re-spray but it is the days off work that is more of a problem. By not working it's made me sit around thinking more about all this shit with Kelly and Murdo.

I have been to the gym with Joey two days in a row as I thought a good work out would get it all out of me, no chance. Joey pushed me harder than ever but I don't think I worked out. I just worked myself up. I did phone the office and left a message for anyone who needs a driver for a couple of days but nobody got back to me. I hate working for other people and handing over half the money but at least it would have kept me occupied. I now find myself out on the piss. I'm the first one in the pub so I get myself a drink and stand at the bar. I would go and sit down but I would get a bit paranoid if anybody walked in and saw me sitting in the corner of the pub on my own. Gaz and Jamie walk in together and the rest of them follow. I can tell by the look on their faces as they walk past me that something is going on. I shout the round up then follow them to our usual corner and find them all sniggering between themselves.

"Right what's going on? What am I missing?" I say before I start to get pissed off.

"A few screws fae what eh hear" Jamie says.

"That's good coming fae you, you're just as bad" Gaz comments

"What do you mean? What's going on?" I ask, getting a little anxious as they all snigger to themselves.

"What did that guy hit ye for at T in the park?" Jamie asks.

"So this is why you lot are sniggering like a bunch of poofs, I have already told you I can't remember. But if you guys want to make up some shit and whisper it between yourselves like a bunch of wee lassies then that's up to you."

"So ye canna remember trying to shag the guys burd?" Jamie says.

"What guy's burd? What are you talking about?"

"The guy wah hit ye."

"Yeah right, who said I done that like?"

They all look at Gaz.

"Gaz" I say looking at him then turning back to Jamie.

"And you believed him?"

Gaz puts his hand on his heart and pleads.

"Ye did mate, eh swear. Eh stood and watched ye."

"You're full of shit."

I get up and head to the bar and when I come back with the drinks Gaz has now moved the discussion to Jamie who is now taking some stick due to his gentle words and ways of foreplay, also at T in the park.

We stay in the East View for several drinks before heading off to the city centre and into a disgusting hole of a pub. Gaz goes into the toilet and insists I follow him. He goes into the cubical and pulls out a small wrap of coke and asks for my credit card, something he has never had before. Actually, I don't even think he's had a bank account in his life. He goes to work and starts chapping up a couple of lines with my card.

"Could you make mine a bit bigger?" I say, being sarcastic.

I have only ever taken coke with Gaz and the lines he's given me in the past are about a quarter of the size of the ones he is putting out now. He obviously knows they are big as all he does is turns and smiles at me.

"What's with the coke anyway? That's not really your thing Gaz."

"Eh ken but eftir taking ah they E's last weekend and hardly getting a hit, eh thought eh hud better tak a break fae them."

"What? And start on the coke, smart move." I raise my eyebrows at him.

Gaz rolls up a note and snorts half a line up one nostril and changes to the next for the other half. He passes me the note and nods towards the cistern where there is another large line waiting on me.

"By the way Shane, ye wouldna happen ta hae left a message at the office saying ye needed a car ta drive would ye?"

"Yeah, it's just for a few days while mine is in getting a re-spray."

"Wully, the auld guy eh work for. He kens that eh ken you, well he telt is ta pass on a message. Somebody has started a rumour aroond the office saying that you rip every cunt aff and that ye drive their cars like a maniac."

"What? No need to guess who that would be, Lisa."

"Well, maybe no, as he's also heard that there is a lot oh talk aboot ye banging Lisa and that she was sending ye extra work. The directors are gonna be looking inta it."

"Fucking hell, you wait until I have had a line before telling me this."

He knows once this coke kicks in none of this will bother me as all the bad thoughts will be pushed to the back of my mind. But tomorrow, tomorrow will be a different story as it will all come crashing back into my mind and I will feel ten times worse. But fuck it, I will just have to make sure I have a good night to justify it. We start a little pub crawl around the city centre and realise why we drink up the West End. It's not really to do with the actual pubs but the people that drink in them, Scheemies. These are the guys who are barred from all the clubs, sometimes just for wearing the wrong clothes, the stripy Lacoste or Henry Lloyd jumpers, The Burberry caps and the Timberlands with the laces open and the tongues hanging out. They now have a socially acceptable name, Chavs. It is those type of people that have given E's a bad name, saying that, most of them have moved onto coke now anyway.

We eventually reach Fatties a bit worse for wear, and after several drinks and line after line of Gaz's coke, I am flying out my head. Everything that has happened to me in the last week is pushed to the back of my mind. The time in the club goes so fast and before I know it I am in the back of a taxi with Gaz and Jamie heading to my flat for a party.

"Eh invited Emma and her mates up ta yer flat by the way." Jamie says.

"Oh did you, well why didn't you just hand out flyers and invite the whole of fucking Fatties up while you're at it. Did you not think of asking me first as I might not want them up to my flat." I say, winking at Gaz.

"Is that so that you can try and get in Emma's knickers again just remember an let Shane shag her first, like last time" Me and Gaz both laugh.

"Ah shut yer pusses" Jamie shouts from the front seat.

We take a detour on the way to my flat and stop at the twenty four hour garage.

"What are we stopping here for?" I ask.

"Emma's bringing up a bottle oh vodka, and she asked me ta get juice and also Gaz is needing skins."

"Ooh she's got ye right under her thumb ahready, sending ye for juice."

Jamie tells us to fuck off as he storms out the taxi and joins the queue outside the garage. There are a lot of people around as all the clubs finish at the same time. A group of girls go past the car and a couple of them have very short skirts on but Gaz and I don't think anything of it as they look really young. The taxi driver's eyes light up.

"Look at them. I wouldn't mind getting one of them in the back of the car" He says in a strong Irish accent as he leers out the window.

"She's a bit young thought mate, even for meh liking" Gaz says sounding a bit straight now.

The driver looks over his shoulder slightly with his face looking a little distorted and says "The younger the better though eh."

"What are ye? Some sort oh a paedophile." Gaz's tone changes

The driver laughs and then says "Don't tell me you guys weren't thinking the same thing when you saw them."

Gaz and I look at each other and lift our eyebrows

"Well eh, no we didna actually, as girls wah look aboot fourteen dinna actually dae it for us" Gaz says sounding angry.It must be the coke as I have never seen him get worked up so quickly.

"Don't give me that, if you had the chance you would be off with them" The driver comments

I am in shock as I don't think this guy realises what he is doing. Gaz looks at me and I can see the anger in his face. I shrug my shoulders and lift my hands up to let him know that I don't know what to say to him. Gaz has an answer. He launches forward as fast as I have seen anybody move and punches the guy in the side of the face. Gaz gets out the car and storms around to the driver's door. He pulls the handle but the driver has locked it from the inside, smart move. I get out and pull Gaz away thinking the Irish cunt will drive off and that will be it, all over, but no, the Irish cunt gets out the car and starts mouthing off. He appears to be a lot bigger now that he's out of the car.

"That's right, get that trouble making bastard out of here" He shouts at me.

"Why don't you get back in your car get and fuck off before both of us smash you, you fucking idiot" I shout back while still holding Gaz from getting near him.

Everyone is now staring over from the garage queue to see what is going on and the driver is still mouthing off.

"What because you have a drink on you, you think your some sort of a hard man." He says.

I am trying my best to stop Gaz from going over and he suddenly stops struggling to get away. I look around to find Jamie walking over. He puts the bottles of juice that he's just bought on the ground near the taxi and is walking up to the driver with his arms out wide and his hands up telling the driver to calm down but he starts ranting and raving at Jamie and is now in his face.

"What are you…?" Before he finishes his sentence Jamie nuts him straight in the nose and the driver crumbles to the ground. He walks back and picks up the juice. The driver is out cold and I look at Gaz as we stand in shock.

"Eh tak it we're walking up ta yours now" Jamie says.

Chapter 22

The walk up ta Shane's flat didna actually look that far but eh feel fucked now that we're here. At least one good thing is that it has given me time ta get that Irish cunt oot oh meh head. Eh canna wait ta get in, sit doon, hae a smoke and listen ta some tunes. The rest oh them can go and dae whatever they fucking like. Eh just want ta sit back and get stoned. Shane's phone has been ringing ah the way up the road we people asking whar he is. First it was Kyle and then that daft burd Emma and now Joey. They are ah standing together at the bottom oh Shane's flat, yet they tak it in turns ta phone and ask whar he is.

"It's aboot time." Mickey says as we turn the corner ta Shane's block.

We ah pile inta the flat and it looks as though Shane has got over his burd as he sneaks awa inta the kitchen we that Stacey's hands on his arse. Eh head straight for the stereo and put on some good hip hop tunes that eh brought we is. Eh dinna fancy listening ta ah that indie shite. Naebody likes meh taste in music, but fuck them. Eh find a space on the sofa and start skinning up and eh look over ta see Kyle sitting ah comfy in the corner skinning up as well, he obviously had the same idea.

"Gaz. Beer?" Joey shouts as he pops his head through fae the kitchen.

"Too fuckin right eh will." Eh ken there are only a few bottles oh beer left so eh might as well get ain before there's only Vody thats left. Eh head oot ta the balcony we meh beer as eh spark up the joint, Don Juan in the kitchen there doesna like the grass stinking oot his flat. Eh can just see him fae the balcony through the kitchen windee, whispering sweet nothings in that Stacey burd's ear but good luck ta him. At least it's taking his mind aff Kelly for a while.

"Hey Gaz, how is it going?" Emma says as she steps oot on ta the balcony.

"Ahright"

What the fuck is this daft wee burd wanting? As if eh didna ken. Well she can wait cos it's just been lit and Joeys wanting it eftir me. She starts talking ta is and eh dinna ken what the fuck to say back as she is thick as shit and she's E'd oot her nut. Eh feel eh'm nodding and agreeing we everything she is saying but eh dinna ken what the fuck she's on aboot. Eh shout Joey through and pass him the joint thinking this will be meh sharp exit, but no. She involves Joey inta the conversation and ah he does is makes faces behind her back and the actions as though he's humping her. Every time eh look at her legs Joey catches me and starts taking the piss, the cunt. He has a few puffs and passes it ta Emma, then sneaks back inta the living room leaving me we her again. Eh keep looking doon at her legs and they're making me thinking aboot shagging her. She has on a wee short skirt we the tanned legs an according ta Shane she's a decent shag. But that's the problem, eh tak the piss oot oh them cos they both shagged her in the same night. How is it gonna look if eh go and shag her as well. Eh smile ta myself as eh think aboot this. She must be wanting shagged as she's coming on ta is big time, nudging me and laughing as eh mak meh smart arse comments aboot whatever the fuck it is she's trying ta tell me. Does this daft burd no ken that ah eh'm interested in is smoking and shagging. She has her arm aroond is and eh'm starting ta get a bit paranoid as this appears ta be too easy. Eh wouldna put it past Shane and Jamie the wee shite ta tell her ta come on ta is, just ta see if eh would go for it. Then blow is aff in front oh thum. That's their sense oh humour, the cunts. Actually it's probably more like something eh would dae. She is now cuddling up ta me and eh'm now thinking fuck it, eh'll tak it as far as she'll go. We start necking and eh huv meh hands on her arse. She has the loveliest tight wee bum eh have ever felt. Eh pull her closer ta me and eh could feel myself getting a semi. She pulls awa and looks aroond like somebody is watching us.

"It's ahright the curtains closed, naebody can see us" Eh say, hoping this will be enough ta persuade her ta keep going.

She's ahready shagged twa oh meh mates in this flat and she's worried aboot somebody seeing us necking. Eh go back inta the flat and head for the kitchen while Emma wanders inta the living room whar the banter is flowing and people are starting ta get louder by the minute. Eh find Shane still in the kitchen talking ta that Stacey burd and they go ah silent when eh walk in. Shane gives is a funny look behind her back as if she's doing his head in. Eh smile at him as a pour myself a Vody but its mare cause eh realise he's no set Emma up ta tak the piss. But eh'm no counting oot Jamie though, he could've done it on his ain. But the mare eh think aboot this the mare eh think the wee cunts no really got the brains ta think oh a wind up like that. Eh pick up the glass and shift oot oh there before Shane uses me as an excuse ta get awa fae Stacey. As eh go inta the living room the only place ta sit is right across fae Emma. Eh look over ta her and she tilts her head in the direction oh the door. She announces she has ta pee and heads aff ta the door giving is a look as if ta follow her. As she heads through the door Shane appears we Stacey and they walk past everybody and oot the door inta the bedroom withoot anybody batting an eyelid. Eh probably could've done the same thing we Emma but that's just like saying ta every cunt in the room that we are awa for a shag. No that anybody here would bather but eh just cannae dae that, eh guess eh'm just mare oh a sneaky cunt. No lang eftir Shane and Stacey go through, eh follow them but eh stand ootside the toilet and Emma appears.

"What are you waiting on?" She says trying ta be a smart arse.

"Eh'm just waiting ta use the toilet." Eh say, covering myself in case it's still a wind up. She grabs me we both hands and starts necking we is. She tries ta pull me towards Shane's room but eh tell her that somebody's in so she pulls me inta the spare room. We end up lying on the bed, still just necking like, and she puts a hand doon and rubs meh wee semi. Fuck, this lassie's no shy man. Eh dinna ken what it is, if it's because eh ken her a bit we going back ta pertys or something but eh feel different we her than eh'v felt we other burds. It's like, eh kind a like her a wee bit mare and eh dinna want ta just shag her. Eh'm kind oh happy just lying here we her and cuddling in. Eh ken she's got a bit oh a reputation and that but that doesna bather me. Eh canna say anything bad eftir some oh the things eh'v got up ta. It's ahright for a guy ta go aboot shagging wahever he wants, and if he's got a burd and shags something behind her back he thinks he is the man. If a bird does anything like that she would be called ah the slags and slappers under the sun. Emma has stopped rubbing me and is cuddling in closer now. This is weird cause eh'm lying here we a really sexy burd and eh'm dying ta shag her but eh canna move as eh dinna want ta spoil this. Eh slide meh hand doon under her wee skirt and eh stroke her leg right up ta her thong. Eh feel a few sprouters sticking ootside oh her thong and eh always hud a mental picture oh her haeing a nice wee trimmed or even shaved fanny, but it's no ta be. She starts ta get inta it a wee bit and moves onta her back. Eh get on tap oh her and start kissing her as eh work meh way doon ta her skirt. Eh lift it up ta reveal her wee thong barely covering her fanny. Eh kiss on tap oh her thong and eh get a wee wiff. It's no that bad, it's just a normal fanny smell but when eh pull her thong ta the side the stench hits is full on. It's like a cundie. Any other time it wouldna bather is. Meh tongue would be in aboot her but somehow the night eh just canna dae it. Eh dinna want ta be rude and tell her that her fanny's stinking, so eh kiss aroond it and work meh way back up ta her face again. Eh feel disappointed that a girl as sexy as that, wouldna clean her fanny a bit mare. Eh start kissing her again and we fumble aboot fir a wee while. Before eh ken it meh boxers are at meh ankles and she's on tap oh is moaning and groaning. Eh feel that eh'm awa ta shoot meh load and eh dinna want her ta think eh'm a two minute wonder but eh canna help it. It could be cause eh've no took any E's the night.

"Eh'm awa ta cum" Eh say.

"No...hold on" She says.

Too late..."ahhhh"

She lays doon aside is and cuddles in but now eh'v shot meh load eh canna really get inta it now. Meh mind is thinking aboot the stench that has now filled the room fae her fanny being fully exposed. Eh'll hae ta remember and ask Shane aboot this. We lay for a wee while then she starts ta snore a bit so eh slide myself oot fae under her and put meh jeans back on. Eh hope she didna think eh would dae a Jamie and cosy up we her ah night. Eh hae a wee look at her thong afore eh sneak oot the room, as eh had visions oh stains like curry sauce or even cottage cheese like that burd fae a while back, but eh'm relieved ta find they are ah clear. As eh come oot the bedroom, eh hear somebody at it in the toilet. They are obviously pissed and dinna realise eh can hear them. Eh thought that eh would hear Shane and Stacey at it but there wasna a peep fae his room. Eh walk through ta the living room just in meh jeans and eh get a wolf whistle fae Joey, the big poof. Eh sit across the room fae him but eh could hear him speaking aboot is ta one oh they daft burds. He's talking aboot meh build and meh six pack the fuckin weirdo. Em sure he's been taking it up the arse working in that gym we ah they body builders. Studied for a degree and thinks he kens it ah. Ah he ever talk's aboot is weights and training, what ta eat and what no ta eat. Eh eat whatever eh fuckin want and eh'm fitter than that poof that's never oot oh the fuckin gym. Eh skin up and head ta the balcony for a smoke when Mickey appears saying that eh beat him to it, for the spare bedroom.

"Ye should have asked Shane for his, it didna sound like there was anything going on in there anyway."

Eh go back inta the living room and tell them that eh'm heading and Kyle starts laughing at is.

"What are you laughing at?"

"You, you do that every time, you get your hole from some bird and then sneak off to leave Shane to get rid of them."

"Listen if eh meet a burd that is worth hanging aroond for, eh'll stay, but until that day comes...anyway eh'm coming back."

"What, with Biscuit?"

"Ye ken me too well."

Eh'm aboot ta head oot the door when eh walk past the mirror in the lobby and notice meh hair ah sticking up, it must have been fae shagging. Eh grab Shane's baseball cap as eh go oot, only ta be grabbed by Jamie.

"Whar the fuck do you think yer sneaking aff ta?"

"Eh'm just nipping oot ta get Biscuit."

"Hud on eh'll come we ye. Eh need some munchies fae the shop."

We get a taxi and the driver taks us over ta Kates, he stops ootside her hoose and eh tell Jamie ta wait in the taxi as eh'll no be lang. Danny is obviously up as Biscuit is oot in the gairden. He sees me and right awa his tail is going like a wee helicopter ready ta tak aff, at least somebody is always happy ta see is. Eh go in the hoose ta pick up his lead.

"What ye up ta?" Danny asks sitting back we his cup oh coffee.

"Nothing much, just pumped some wee slapper and sneaked awa ta pick up Biscuit. Eh'v got Jamie we is in the taxi. Eh'll be back later on."

"See ye son" Danny says. Eh'm obviously no his son but he's always said that since eh was a bairn.

We dinna go straight ta Shane's. We stop at the shops doon the street so Jamie could get some munchies, plus it gees Biscuit a wee walk up the road. Eh stand ootside and can smell the fresh rolls as the door is opened we the paper boy's going in and oot. They stroke Biscuit as they walk past and his tail starts going again, he loves ah the attention. Jamie comes oot we a bag oh rolls, bacon, juice, various bars oh chocolate and mare skins. As we walk up the road ta Shane's flat, Biscuit is a good bit in front oh us. There is a patch oh spare groond at the back oh the block whar he usually sniffs aboot so eh ken that's whar he's heading. Me and Jamie walk aroond the block slowly and eh could see him sniffing aroond a tree and lifting his leg. We stand talking shit for a few minutes but my mind is actually thinking aboot sitting back in Shane's flat and getting served ain oh they bacon rolls, mmm. Meh thoughts are suddenly interrupted when eh hear somebody behind is saying "Oi Shane you cunt."

"What, eh'm no Sh..."

Eh feel a sudden pain in meh lower back, like eh'v been punched hard, very fuckin hard. Eh go ta turn and see wah it is but the next thing eh ken, eh'm on the deck struggling ta breath. This feeling is strange, it's as if somebody is pinning me doon and eh dinna hae the strength ta get them aff. Eh look up but eh could barely open meh eyes and eh could see Jamie struggling we somebody. Fuck, he's doon as well, meh eyes feel really heavy like eh'm drifting aff ta sleep. It's like eh'v took too many downers or something. One good thing is the pain in meh back has gone awa. Meh body just feels ah numb. Jamie is shouting at is ta wake up but fuck him, naebody is interrupting this sleep. The wee cunt is slapping is now. If eh huv ta get up eh'm gonna boot his bahs. Eh'll bet that wee cunt has spiked is we Vally's. Well if he has, they are fuckin good ains. He can slap me ah he wants, cos eh'm just gonna cosy up here an enjoy them. Night night Jamie.

Chapter 23

Everybody seems to have left at the same time. First Gaz and Jamie sneak off without saying a word to anybody then the rest of them phone taxis and leave me here on my own. I'm not complaining though as I usually can't get rid of them. I thought Gaz would have come back up with Biscuit, that's not like him. Well maybe I wil get to my bed now...fuck there's the buzzer, I guess it was wishful thinking.

"Yeah"

"Shane, help we've been stabbed" Jamie says in a faint voice.

"Yeah right, just hurry up and come in."

"Nah seriously, phone an ambulance, Gaz is in a bad way."

I grab a t-shirt and put it on as I run down the stairs but all the time I am thinking that if they are taking the piss I will fucking slap them. I open the front door to the flats and find Jamie semi-conscious and in a pool of blood.

"Where's Gaz? What's happened?" I shout while lifting his head up.

He doesn't answer but as I move him I go in his pocket and take out his mobile. I put him in the recovery position and dial 999 on his mobile. I follow the trail of blood around the block until I find Gaz. He is lying there not moving, Biscuit is next to him licking his face and making whimpering noises. There is blood on him but it does not appear to be his. I get through to emergency and ask for an ambulance. I tell them the situation and they give me some advice before I am cut off, it is always when you most need it the battery goes.

"Fuck."

"Gaz...waken up...Gaz" I shout as I slap him hard in the face.

I take his arm and feel his wrist for a pulse but I have never done this before so I don't really know where to find it, nothing. I look up and see one of my neighbours' at their window.

"Help, my brother has been stabbed, he's at the front door, I have phoned the ambulance."

I lift Gaz to put him on his side and as I do this thick blood comes out from underneath him. This is not the red blood you see when you cut your finger, it is a thick dark red almost burgundy. As I move him the amount of blood coming out is frightening. My neighbour, an older woman in her dressing gown comes rushing over with a pile of towels. She nudges me out of the way and puts her fingers on his neck.

"He's doesn't have a pulse." She says as she puts a towel on the wound and slides him on his back. She gives him mouth to mouth as I stand back thinking I am in some sort of nightmare. She gets on top of him and starts pushing his chest.

"Your friend around the corner, he has a pulse so go and keep pressure on his wounds, talk to him and try to keep him awake."

The ambulance finally arrives and as they take over I manage to get a hold of Biscuit and put him in the flat. I rush back down the stairs to find the police have arrived. Jamie and Gaz are in the ambulance and the police are trying to get me to stay behind to talk to them. Their attitude is disgusting and they are told where to go, which sees me being handcuffed and put into the back of the police car. My neighbour talks some sense into them and I am let out to travel in the ambulance. I enter to see them giving Gaz the shock treatment, which to my relief gets his pulse going. Jamie is unconscious but breathing. I take Gaz's phone from his pocket and the ambulance guy tells me I can't use it here, I ignore him and use it anyway. I call my mother and tell her what's happened. She rushes off to tell Gaz's gran. I also phone Kyle and tell him to get his arse up to my flat as quick as he can as I left without locking the door or even picking up my keys. If the police walk in I am fucked with all those drugs lying around.

"I'll take care of it" He says.

"Biscuit, he is at mine too."

"I'll take care of it. I'll be up as quick as I can."

"Okay, cheers."

As I sit in the waiting room a nurse brings me a blanket and a pair of these horrible plastic slip-ons with elastic around the ankles to wear. I only had on a pair of boxers and a t-shirt, which are covered in blood. I struggle to put them on as my hands are shaking so much. The nurse said she would try to find me something else to wear but I tell her it's alright I will get someone to bring me up some clothes. I still have Gaz's mobile so I walk outside and phone Kyle again who is just arriving at my flat. He asks what happened but I don't know and at this moment it is the least of my worries as I wait on the news that both of them are going to be okay. My mother arrives with Kate and Danny and their faces drop when they see me covered in blood.

The questions from my mother and Kate all come at once. 'Are you okay?' 'Where are they?' 'What happened?' 'How bad is it?'

"WAH DONE IT?" Danny says in his deep voice towering over them.

I try to answer them but it is Danny's question that rings through my head. Who did it? My first thought is Murdo but then he has nothing against Gaz or Jamie. Although it is his style to creep about outside someone's house in the early hours waiting for them. My thoughts turn to the taxi driver, the Irish cunt from last night, nah it couldn't have been, could it?

We sit for a long time staring at the walls until a doctor appears. We all stand when he comes over to us as we listen for the good news that both will be fine, but it doesn't come.

"Jamie is stable, he had five puncture wounds but they missed any vital organs, although he has lost a considerable amount of blood."

"What about Gareth?" Kate says with a croaky voice and tears rolling down her face. Kate is the only person that I have ever heard Gaz being referred to as Gareth.

"Gareth was stabbed once but it punctured a lung. His heart had stopped by the time the paramedics arrived. Although they managed to resuscitate him we don't know how long his brain was starved of oxygen. We have to operate and only then will we know his condition. If he manages to breath on his own there could be a chance, but that does not rule out the possibility of brain damage."

The doctor says what he has to say and fucks off. Kyle, Mickey and Joey turn up and not before time, they hand me a bag of clean clothes.

"I have taken Biscuit to mine. I had a hard time from the police trying to get into your flat, but your neighbour persuaded them that I was your mate." Kyle hands me the keys to the flat.

"What's happening?" Joey asks.

We sit down away from everyone as I tell them what hap-pened and also what the doctor has just said.

"I can't believe we were all there not an hour before it happened" Kyle says.

"Any idea wah done it?" Joey says.

I pause for a few seconds before answering as the thought has been flashing through my mind constantly.

"I don't know, my first thought was Murdo, and then the Irish taxi driver, but I really don't know."

"Mare than likely it was Murdo" Mickey says.

I shrug my shoulders as I think of all the possibilities. It could have been something Gaz was involved in, but I can't mention any of that in front of them. We sit for what seems like hours then we are told that we can go and see Jamie. The police are still hanging around but I know Jamie won't tell them anything before he has talked to me. Jerry, Jamie's dad, has turned up after being called away from his job. He and my Mother go in first. They are not in long before they come out with my mother sobbing in Jerry's arms. Kyle and I go in to see Jamie wired up to machines and ventilators but his eyes are open slightly. I get the small talk out of the way then I ask the questions that have been going through my head constantly since I arrived here.

"What happened? Did you see who done it?" I say trying to sound as calm as possible but it still comes out in a fast mumble. Jamie opens his mouth but I can hardly hear him. I put my face closer to his ear and he says "They thought Gaz was you."

I step back and look at him very confused.

"What do you mean? They thought Gaz was you."

Jamie opens his mouth so I move in closer again.

"He come fae behind and said yer name ta Gaz before stabbing him" He says in a weak voice. "He hud on yer baseball cap, they thought he was you."

I sit down in the seat next to the bed in total shock that all this has happened when it was intended for me. The only vision I have now is Dek Murdo. I have a picture of his ugly distorted face in my head. I can't believe he has went this far because I was seeing Kelly. She was right all along. Jamie is back snoozing away before we leave the room and the machines are beeping away showing a strong pulse. I walk back to the waiting room and sit down. My mother tells me to go home.

"Eh'll phone ye if there is any news on Gaz."

"No mum, I'm staying here until I know he's going to be okay."

I go for a walk with Kyle, Joey and Mickey around the hospital to get some fresh air but the real reason is to have a joint. We pass it between ourselves as we talk about what happened. Joey mentions again who it could have been and I give Kyle a stare and shake my head for him to keep quiet about what Jamie said. As soon as I get the news that Gaz is okay I am going straight for Murdo to get this sorted out. I'm not waiting around looking over my shoulder on him to get me. The joint relaxes me a little and when we get back to the waiting room I feel my eyes getting really heavy and I want to go to my bed. I nod off for a while when Joey nudges me awake.

"Shane, the doctors just took Kate and Danny awa"

I jerk up feeling very groggy but that soon disappears when I hear a scream from around the corner, which can only mean one thing. It is the news that we have all been dreading. Gaz is dead. Kate walks back into the waiting room with Big Danny's huge arms around her, consoling each other.

"They couldna save him" I hear Kate say through her tears.

We all stand up, frozen, staring and speechless. A moment later the doctor comes back and asks if they would like to go and see him. Kate shakes her head but I ask them if I could go. Kate walks over to me and wipes the tears from my eyes, I hadn't even realised I was crying.

"Dinna you go doing anything stupid now Shane."

I don't answer but Danny puts his arm around me and walks me off to see Gaz. The nurse leads us to a room that is filled with equipment and the walls are full of charts and diagrams. I see Gaz lying on a table. He has a white sheet over him that has been dyed red with blood. It goes up to his chest leaving his tattoo on his shoulder exposed. It is one he had done recently of Biscuit. I walk over to the table and Big Danny walks around the other side. We both stare at him for a while half expecting him to open his eyes and start laughing or jumping up and calling me a big poof for crying, but I know that's not going to happen. I stare at him and can't help but think that it should be me lying there instead.

"Hey Gaz, you don't have to worry about Biscuit I'm going to look after him. I know I used to moan when you brought him up to the flat but secretly we both knew I liked having him there. I'm really sorry Gaz, it should be me lying there."

I look up to see Danny in flood of tears.

"Shane do you ken eh had to bury meh daughter when she was aboot the age Gaz was now. When she was dying, Gaz's Dad wanted ta tak him awa but meh daughter telt him he would be better aff in oor care. Eh promised her eh would tak care oh him. She trusted me that he would hae a better life than we that waster oh a father he had. Life sure has a sick sense oh humour does it."

I have known Gaz nearly all my life and this is the first time I have ever heard anyone mention his father. I think that was one of the things we had in common. We both had absent fathers. Of course I had Jamie's dad but he wasn't a father he was just some bullying bastard. I feel like a big kid sitting here with Danny as he was probably more of a father figure than the wanker I had to look up to. This brings back memories of when I used to run across to his house after Jamie's dad slapped me around. He would let me stay at his for a bit until it all calmed down. He was tempted to march across the road and slap him around but Kate always stopped him as it was none of his business. As things turned out, Danny didn't have to worry about it, as a few years down the line I did it myself and it was nothing to do with him hitting me. I caught him lifting his hands to my mother. He still tries to order Jamie about but with the evil streak that Jamie has I can't see that lasting much longer. To me, Danny has always been one of those proper old school tough guys, a man's man, but right now, he looks as though he is ready to crumble and fade away.

"Danny I know Kate said not to do anything about this and I always listen to both of you, but I'm going to get whoever did this."

I am sort of expecting him to go along with Kate and give me the talk of, not to be so stupid, whatever I do is never going to bring him back or that I could be the next one lying there but I know Danny better than that.

"Eh thought ye would. If ye need meh help just let is ken, eh'll be there" He says.

Through the tears and anger I smile to myself when I hear this as it's exactly what Gaz would say.

Kyle drives me to my flat and the first thing I notice is the incident box the police have now set up not far from my block. I guess it is now a murder enquiry. Kyle, Joey and Mickey offer to come up but I send them on their way as I feel I want to be on my own for a bit.

"Just phone if ye need anything mate" Mickey says.

I nod and turn towards my flat. The whole place is cornered off with tape but I am allowed through without any harassment. I walk around to the door to see the pools of blood and one of them that leads all the way up to my front steps from Jamie dragging himself to use my intercom. I go straight to the shower and wash off the rest of the blood that is on me. I make myself a cup of tea and roll a joint. I lie back on the couch and stare at the TV but watching nothing in particular. I eventually drop off to sleep with all the crazy thoughts of last night and the many different ways that I would change it. I can't decide if I would like to be there just before it happened to stop it but also to see who it was that done it, or have the whole night changed so that none of it happened but then the same thing could have happened on another night. My much needed sleep is broken several hours later when the buzzer sounds and wakens me.

"Hello this is D.C. Richmond, I'm looking for…"

I don't let him finish, I press the button to let him in. I rush over to the coffee table and hide the hash and empty the ashtray. I open the door and tell them to come in and have a seat. They have their notebooks at the ready but I feel like telling them not to bother. They introduce themselves and proceed to ask me details about the previous night. They appear to be a lot more civilized compared with the other arrogant cunts this morning, and I let them know this. Although they do apologise for their colleagues behaviour and give me an explanation with big words that mean absolutely fuck all to me. I can tell they are trying to be nice but they know, that I know, that they can't fucking stand me and I have very little if any respect for them or any of their colleagues. They leave disappointed with their notepads full of useless information and I shut the door after them. I watch them from the window as they walk into their incident box. I am soon back lying on the sofa, only I am wide awake this time. I sit and think about Gaz for a while and it suddenly sinks in that I am never going to see him again. He has been my best friend since I moved here as a kid and now he's been killed because of me, because of some girl I was into. If I hadn't been seeing her, none of this would have happened. If this had been Kyle, Mickey or even Joey that had been killed I would be sitting here with Gaz planning on how to get the cunt back. I have always known he was a blade man but I always thought that it was just for show to build up his reputation to make people fear him. I have never feared him, but reality is setting in fast that I could be in a hospital bed next to Jamie or even next to Gaz in the morgue. At least now I know just what he is capable of and how cunning and violent he can be and that he is not going to stop until he has hurt or even killed me. Well I'm certainly not going to wait around on him coming for me. I'm going to get the cunt first. I know I'm usually a stand up and square go type of person but to beat him I will have to think like him and lower myself to his level. I don't have Gaz to help me out and the only other person I can really trust is Kyle. He's not much of a fighter to back me up but he has a lot of bottle. Mickey has too much of a big mouth and I wouldn't trust Joey as far as I could throw him.

Chapter 24

I am just not in the mood for working today but if I don't, I only have two options. One is to go to the pub and the other is to sit in the flat and get stoned. Both of these options will result in me getting wasted and doing something stupid. I have to keep a clear head if I am serious about getting back at Murdo because if something goes wrong then I am well and truly fucked. I went for a run this morning before going to the gym to try and tire myself out but all it did was get me fired up even more. Joey was working and kept hanging around trying to talk to me. He was asking loads of stupid questions and telling me the gossip that he heard going around the gym. One thing's for sure, that whatever I plan; Joey will never get to know about it. He just can't keep his mouth shut.

Customer - # No. 1274

I receive a job to the Old Bank Bar where two old men are waiting outside. They come over to the car and actually struggle to get in due to them being too drunk. I don't have a problem with that as I know I have probably been in the same state before. What I do have a problem with is the damage they do to my car when try to get in or out, the most annoying part is that they look you as if it's my entire fault. These two have kicked the seats, the doors and the one in the front has also managed to kick the panel under the dashboard.

"We're heading up the Lochee Road Jim."

Jim my names not Jim, why do these old gits insist on calling all taxi drivers Jim? The guy in the front is pissing me off already and I haven't even moved yet. He's trying to reach for the seat belt but he can't turn his body around for his fat gut to grab it. I'll bet if it was a pint of lager he would turn quick enough though. He pisses me off that much that when I stop at traffic lights I reach over and grab the thing myself, nearly choking the cunt in the process. Next thing he starts to un-wrap a boiled sweet and pops it in his mouth.

"Excuse me but there is no eating in the taxi" I point to the sign on the dash in front of him.

'NO FOOD OR DRINK TO BE CONSUMED IN THE VEHI-CLE'.

"Ach it's only a wee sweetie." He says.

These signs are mostly put up so that kids don't get a chance to leave sweets, crisps or chewing gum stuck to the floor or on the seats, but the reason they are put up in my car are for my pet hate, people like this old cunt who has his mouth open letting everyone hear it clatter between his false teeth. Then it gets worse, he starts sucking on it while talking to his friend in the back. All I hear is the sweet clunking around his mouth as he slurps and talks at the same time. They are having a conversation and both of them are talking at the same time about two totally different subjects. I can't get to their destination quick enough but what makes it worse is that I don't know where they are going.

"Tak a left here, then at the tap oh the road tak a right"

"Where is it you are actually going?" I ask.

"Left here"

"Yeah but where are you going?"

"LEFT" He shouts at me.

I am starting to get really pissed off with this old cunt, why can he not just say his fucking address"

"Alang here and it's the fourth lamppost on the right" he says in between crunches on his sweet, or hopefully it's just the annoying cunts teeth fucking crumbling away. Instead of watching the road I am now trying to count fucking lampposts. A journey which at the start was to go up the lochee road has now ended in St. Mary's without me actually being told. He pays me and turns to face the door.

"Eh canna fine the honl" He says.

"What?"

"Eh canna fine the honl."

"I don't know what you're saying."

Is this cunt taking the piss.

"The honl, whar's the honl?" He shouts at me as he swipes his hand up and down the inside of the door.

It eventually registers, he can't find the handle. A honl, a fucking honl. How can someone go from a handle to a fucking honl.

Another job comes through the computer; it is for John-stone at The Highway Man. This used to be one of the roughest pubs on the Hilltown. It closed down several years ago and reopened as a day centre. It was intended as a community centre type of place but that only lasted a few weeks before the junkies took it over. I pull up outside and there is a small group of people gathered near the front door. They are all junkies and I recognise one of them from years ago. She was at school at the same time as me and I remember her having a really pretty face and a great body. Now she looks like she is riddled with every disease known to man.

"Is that taxi for Johnstone?" A tall, skeleton looking guy shouts over.

"Yeah"

He puts his index finger up to signal to me that he will be there in a minute as he gets the last few puffs on his already beefed roll up. I look over at the girl I knew and feel quite shocked at the way she has turned out. It makes me wonder how she managed to get herself in such a mess.

"Eh'm going to Greenbank Place mate." The skeleton guy says as he gets in the back of the car.

During the journey the guy talks the biggest load of shit and every time he opens his mouth a disgusting smell comes past his rotten teeth and fills the car. I drive into his street and he goes quiet and starts to fidget a bit in the back. I know what's coming.

"Eh'll just hae ta nip up for the money." He says as he opens the car door and goes to take off. I grab his smelly shell suit top by the arm.

"You're going nowhere" I say.

He pulls his arm away and runs. I am out of the car and only feet away as he runs behind a block of flats. I grab his top from behind and he turns to punch me. It lands on the side of my face. This just makes me angrier and I throw one of my own. He stumbles back and I launch forward throwing punch after punch. He is on the deck with blood pouring from his nose. I grab him by the hair and as my grip tightens I can feel the greasy strands slide through my fingers. I step forward bringing my knee up to his face.

"You junkie bastard" I shout as I lay into him on the deck with a barrage of punches and kicks. I step back but before I walk away I run at him with one last kick to the head leaving him motionless on the ground. I get back into the car and speed off back to my flat. After I wash the greasy smell from my hands I change my blood stained clothes, I go for a walk with Biscuit who has now become my permanent lodger. I calm myself down and put all the violent thoughts to the back of my mind. After a cup of coffee I am back to work as if nothing happened.

Customer - # No.894

I decide to work late to try and tire myself out and I find myself being sent to the bingo in Douglas. Before I arrive I am picturing my customer to be an old woman standing with a headscarf who has just gambled half her weekly pension but I couldn't be more wrong.

"Taxi for Bennett" I shout out of the window to large queue of people.

"That's us." I hear someone shout.

Two women stagger forward who look a little bit worse for wear. They are in their late thirty's and are dressed like teenagers, or hookers.

"Right driver, we're going ta the Bowbridge on the Hulltoon" One of them says as she climbs in the back.

"Oh look, it's a young driver." The other one says as she puts her arm through the gap in the front seats and starts pawing at me.

"Excuse me, but could you not do that while I'm driving please."

"Oh he's getting offended cause eh touched him."

"Maybe he's gay?"

"Are ye gay? Do ye no like wimen touching ye?"

"No it's because if I was drunk and touched you, you would be the first person to go running to the police and get me done."

"Eh you drivers are ah the same. Taking young lassies up ah they back roads late at night."

"I don't think so "

"It's no that when you lot are making rude comments to us and using yer mirrors to look up oor skirts when we're drunk."

Fuck, these women must have been in Gaz's taxi before. I smile to myself as I think what Gaz would be saying to these women. My smile soon fades as I feel one of the women's hands touching my neck.

"Could you stop that please?"

She then slides her hand around and starts rubbing my leg.

"Could you move your hand please or I'll stop the car and put you out."

"What's yer problem? Ye should feel privileged that women as good looking as us are touching ye."

Their attitude starts to become quite aggressive and I know that most guys would probably think I am being stupid as they would love to get that kind of attention but I know if it was the other way around any man would be banged up for it. Maybe on another day I would just laugh this off but not today.

"Ye big poofter" One of them says with her face looking quite angry at me.

"Look here missus, if you had got in this car and I turned around and touched your leg. I would be charged. Lose my licence and no doubt put on the sex offenders list for the rest of my life. Now you have got in my taxi and touched me and I'm supposed to just laugh and think nothing of it."

"Ah shut yer puss. Yer just a big poofter"

"Do you know what? Just get to fuck out" I stop the car in the middle of a busy road.

"Fine, we fucking will get oot"

They slam the doors shut and I drive off leaving them walking along the side of the road. I am about to switch off the computer and head home before I lose the plot, but I am sent another job and I reluctantly take it.

Customer - # No. 415

I sit outside a tenement block in Fairbairn Street as I wait on my customer. Two guys walk out of the block and one of them is well over six foot wearing a long over coat. The other is quite small and is wearing a bomber jacket. I had one the same when I was a kid but back then they were known as N.F. jackets. This was due to skin headed thugs in the National Front that wore them. Somehow I don't think you could go around calling them that now. Back in those days none of us actually knew what any of that stood for. We were just young and they were in fashion.

These two guys do have the skinheads and some of the worst growler looking faces I have ever encountered. They swagger towards the car like they are about to smash me, so naturally I am on the defensive. This is the reason I don't like working late at night, you never know what you are going to pick up. I get myself ready as I don't know what kind of shit they are about to give me. If they start, I am certainly not going to sit back and take it no matter how hard they think they are. Both of them get in the back and straight away I'm thinking that they are about to grab me from behind. I look in the mirror to see the tall one with the long coat putting his seat belt on. This I find to be strange as nobody does that unless they are about five years old.

"So where are you guys off to then?"

The reply I receive is not what shocks me but the way it is said.

"The bus station please." The small guy with the N.F. jacket says in a most camp voice.

Twenty seconds ago my heart was pounding as I prepared myself to take on these two scary looking psychopaths and now, I am smiling as I drive off with the now, two ugly poofters. As I drive off down the road I can't help thinking why they said they were going to the bus station as I know they are going to Liberty's, the gay nightclub across the road. I drop them off at the bus station and sure enough they cross over the road and walk into Liberty's. I look up to see the rainbow flag outside. This reminds me of a trip we had down to Manchester for an Oasis gig. When it finished we headed into town to catch a few bars before closing. I found myself chatting to a couple of girls and a guy whom I thought was one of their boyfriends. Gaz and Jamie were just over from me, standing at the bar and Kyle, Mickey and Joey had disappeared to another bar along the road. The girls invited me back to a party so I go back over to Gaz and Jamie to tell them. They found this really amusing.

"What's the joke? I don't get it."

"Have the girls asked you back to a party or has the guy asked you back to do your ass?" Gaz said with a big grin.

"What are you talking about?"

"Have a look. I think the girls have started without you."

I turned to see the girls kissing and the guy who was with them was nodding at me to come over. Then it hit me that we were in a fucking gay bar. The guy had been chatting me up, I felt violated.

Gaz clocked the guy nodding at me and put on a camp voice

"Come on now Shane, run along, your new boyfriend is waiting on you."

The both of them were pissing themselves as I stood mortified.

"How did you know it was a gay bar?"

"Jamie told me before we came in. The whole street is full of gay bars so it would be interesting to find out how the rest of them are getting on."

Back at the hotel I asked Jamie how he knew it was a gay bar and he tells us about the rainbow flags all the way along the street.

"Yeah but how do you know they were gay flags?"

"I eh, saw it on the Simpsons"

On the way home the next day I was waiting on the wind up about being chatted up by the gay guy but it never came. It was all vented towards Jamie for being in the know about the rainbow flag and using the feeble excuse that he saw it on an episode of the Simpsons.

Customer - # No. 715

With these happy thoughts in my head I decide to drive home but on the way I am flagged down by two guys. They are in their mid-thirties and as I pull up they stagger towards me. One of the guys gets in the back and one gets in the front.

"We're going to Monifieth mate." The one in the front says.

The one in the back starts to give me shit before I even drive off.

"Look I'm not taking you guys anywhere."

"He's pissed mate, just ignore him" The guy in the front says.

"Aaron, shut it or he's not going to take us."

"Yeah he fucking will because we are paying customers so he has to take us" The guy in the back mumbles to himself.

"Fuck this, get to fuck out of the car, I'm taking you no-where."

"Ah look mate, he's drunk, I'll apologise for him."

I know I should just throw them out now but I stupidly decide to drive them. This is the wrong time and I am the wrong person for them to get wide with right now. I only drive about half a mile up the road and the mouth in the back starts again.

"Hey I have never been in a taxi like this before. It's a bit sporty looking to be a taxi. You taxi drivers, always pleading poverty, but not by the looks of this."

I ignore him but I feel myself getting agitated. I know at this point I should stop the car and ask them to leave but once again I let it go.

"That's a great tune" The guy in the front says as he reaches over and turns the volume up really loud.

"Do you fucking mind?" I say turning it back down.

Both of them start laughing and the guy in the back nudges his mate in the front and signals for him to do it again. Due to him being drunk he obviously thinks he is invisible to me in my mirrors. I know of a small piece of wasteland up ahead and I start to speed up as my heart beats a little faster anticipating what lies ahead. The guy in front leans over and puts the volume up full blast. This time I leave it up. As they nod their heads to each other and laugh they don't realise I have left the main road and am now seconds away from any witnesses. The guy in the front is now pushing buttons on the stereo to change the tracks. I drive around the back of a derelict industrial unit and screech the car to a halt.

"Right you couple of cunts" I get out and run around to the other side of the car. I open the rear door and drag the first drunken guy out by his shirt. I punch him to the ground as the front passenger door is opened. The guy in the front gets out and attempts to throw a punch. I land mine first. He doesn't go down but his body falls back onto the car. He lunges forward at me and grabs my shirt with both hands. I put my head back and launch forward nutting him in the mouth. He falls to his knees and puts his hands up to his face. I turn to see the other guy on his feet and watch as he stumbles towards me with both fists flailing. Not one of them land on me as I put my hands up to block them. I throw two straight punches to his head and he falls back on to his arse. I give him a kick to the head and he falls back. I turn back to the other guy who has his face in his hands which are covered in blood. I reach over him closing the passenger doors. Everything goes quiet as I realise the music from the stereo has been blasting out the whole time. I get in the car and speed off with the wheels skidding on the gravel. I switch off the computer and drive home still raging. As I walk into the flat, I am met by a friendly face with his tail whizzing around all my rage suddenly disappears.

Chapter 25

I've been trying to get a hold of Kyle all day but he won't answer his phone. He knows what it's about so maybe that's why he is not answering. I will try Mickey.

"Hello."

"Is that you Mickey?"

"Yeah"

"Where are you?"

"Eh'm sitting in meh room we Kyle haeing a smoke."

"What, Kyle's with you?"

"Yeah"

"I have been trying to get a hold of him all day."

"Yeah his battery's dead."

"I'll be up in ten minutes."

His battery's dead, my arse, the cunts avoiding me. I know he agreed to help out but when I explained exactly what that involved I could see the fear in his eyes. I already told him if he doesn't want to do it, to tell me straight away.

I pull up outside Mickey's house and his Mum lets me in. I head up to Mickeys room to see them both pretty stoned.

"How is it going Shane? Here ye look like ye need this." Mickey passes me the ashtray with the burning joint in it.

"No thanks. I have too much on my mind and I don't want something to hinder it"

Kyle stares at me as he knows why I'm here.

"Do ye no want ta sit doon?" Mickey gestures towards the edge of the bed.

"No I'm fine here."

Tho two of them sit and stare at me as I stand in the middle of the room.

"Mickey, I need to ask you something."

I look at Kyle thinking he might have already told him but I know Kyle is not like that.

"Sounds serious"

"Don't be afraid to say no, I'm away to do something really stupid and I need your help. If you say no I will understand."

"Depends on what it is I suppose."

Kyle puts his head down and Mickey realises I am not fucking about. His eyes widen and he looks back at me.

"I can't tell you what it is. If you don't want involved it's better off you don't know what it is."

I gave the exact same speech to Kyle and I don't think he realised what he was agreeing to help me with. If you say something like that people are obviously more interested in what it is than what they are agreeing to do.

"Yeah sure, whatever it is, eh'm in." He says moving to the edge of the bed wanting to know more. I sit down to relax a little as I proceed to tell Mickey exactly what I need him to do.

"...so all you have to do is drive my car around for a while with the computer on like you're working."

"Eh dinna understand."

"Right the computer in the car is fitted with a device called a G.P.S. It is like a tracking system. It means when it is switched on, whatever area the car is in, it will send a signal to the main computer via satellite to the taxi office. This lets them know exactly where the car is. If a job comes up in that area it automatically sends it to the computer in the car."

"So what dae ye want me ta drive yer car aroond for?"

I look at Kyle and he smiles and shakes his head.

"You're not too bright Mickey, are you? While you are driving my car around, I will be elsewhere."

"Ah, now eh get it. That's yer alibi."

"That's right."

"This wouldna happen ta be anything ta dae we Murdo would it?"

I don't answer but give Mickey a serious look again.

"Wait a minute, what if someone gets in the taxi?"

I look at Kyle again and realise why I picked him to do this, because if this goes wrong I would be in even more trouble if Mickey was with me.

"Don't worry about that I will give you instructions when the time comes."

I might even get Joey involved by phoning up as a customer and letting Mickey drive him around for a while.

"Are you sure you know what you are doing Shane?" Kyle asks.

"Guys, that fucker killed our best friend and both of you know now that Gaz was mistaken for me. If I don't do some-thing, I'm going to be next."

"When is this gonna be happening?"

"Tomorrow night."

"The day before Gaz's funeral" Kyle mumbles to himself.

Both of them go quiet and I feel that I have said what I came to say. I stand up to leave as Mickey starts skinning up again. I make a sharp exit before I end up staying for that much needed smoke.

***

We meet up at my flat and I throw Mickey the keys to my car. I hand him a list of instructions, all written out of where to go and at what time. I decided not to involve Joey as he is too much of a big mouth and I just don't trust the cunt.

"The instructions are all there."

As Mickey heads out the door I go to the bedroom and start to change my clothes.

"What are you waiting on Kyle? Get changed. We're on a limited time here."

Kyle pulls out his old tattered clothes from a hold all that I asked him to bring along and he starts to get changed. Kyle makes a comment that I am supposed to be in my old scruffy clothes but look like I am dressed to hit a fucking nightclub. I pull out a black bin liner from under my bed and from this I take out a wooden baseball bat and a metal pole that has been shaped at both ends. One end has been shaped for gripping and the other is shaped with sharp edges that stick out for a purpose that I can only describe as to inflict as much damage as possible to the recipient.

"Which one do you want?" I say as I hold one in each hand.

He shrugs.

"You would be better with this." I hand him the metal pole with the evil looking shaped edges.

He takes it from me and holds the gripped handle with both hands.

"Kyle you're taking on fucking Darth Vader."

I take it from him and place one hand on the shaped edge and one half way up.

"You'll get more leverage to hit somebody if you hold it like this."

"Whar did ye get these?"

"Jamie's wardrobe"

He smiles nervously "Whar did he get them?"

"I gave him the baseball bat. It was a holiday present from years ago. He made the pole himself when he was involved in all that gang fighting shit. Me and Gaz had a word with him and told him to get rid of it. It was about the same time Gaz got him to start hanging around with us. I didn't mind at the time as it stopped him from getting the bloody jail."

"A bit ironic is it not?"

"What?"

"You telling him ta get rid oh it to keep him oot of jail and now you hae it and are aboot to risk the same thing."

"You're forgetting something."

"What?"

"I'm not about to use it, you are."

"Come on, we'd better go."

Kyle drives towards the Hilltown and on my instructions of lefts and rights he is now lost as he has never been down any of these streets before in his life.

"I can only guess why Murdo lives in a secluded area full of narrow streets and high walls." Kyle comments.

"Yeah well just think of his lifestyle and the amount of people waiting to smash him."

We stop in a one way street with high walls all around us. I turn around and point to a tall gate no far from where we have parked up.

"Do you see that tall gate back there?"

He looks in the mirror and nods.

"Behind that gate there is a path and some steps. The path leads to the lower house but there are no windows looking onto the path so no-one in the lower house can see us. The steps lead to the flat above, that's where Murdo lives.

"How do you know all this?"

"I'm a taxi driver, I know everything."

I reach in the back of the car and hand Kyle the pole.

"Look Kyle, I'm not asking you to do anything here, I'm going in there after Murdo, I want you to keep your distance behind me. If it gets out of hand I want you to run back here to the car and take off. You drive to end of this street take a left and you will know where you are from there. Phone Danny and tell him what's happened, he will know what to do."

"What do I have this pole for then?"

"Protection, there could be five of his mates up there."

"What if they all jump on you? Would I not be better phoning the police?"

"And how do you explain what we were doing here? They're not going to be much fucking help when I'm nailed to the fucking floor are they?"

I check my watch, and then from Kyle's mobile I call the taxi office and order a car in name of smith, from the Swallow Hotel heading to Broughty Ferry. We Leave the car running and casually walk up to the gates with the weapons by our sides. I know most people doing something like this would plan it late at night or the early hours of the morning. It's seven at night in the middle of summer and the sun is still cracking the pavements, this could possibly be the best time to catch him unaware. I have already been here and checked his door, there is a Yale and a Mortise lock but there is more chance of it only being the Yale on at this time. We walk up the first flight of steps and I tell Kyle to wait while I crouch down and crawl up the next flight. There is a small window situated next to the door and I peer through for a few seconds. I see him lounging on his couch watching T.V. with his top off. A sudden rush of fear comes over me and for a split second I am ready to take off and forget the whole thing. Then I think about Gaz and Jamie and what he done to them. I picture him with Kelly and the fear is soon put aside as I look at this big, fat, ugly, bullying beast of a man and I know I have to end this now. I look through the keyhole of the Mortise lock and there is no key, I know nine out of ten people who lock it from the inside would leave the key in it. I go back down to Kyle.

"Right Kyle, I have just seen him, I think he is on his own."

"So what are you going to do then?"

"Stay out of sight but keep close enough to watch my back."

"Shane it's not too late to turn away. Are you sure you want to do this?"

"Kyle seeing him lying up there has encouraged me even more."

I smile at Kyle and then turn to bolt back up the second flight of steps two at a time. Once at the top there is a distance of nearly twelve feet to the front door. I look behind at Kyle who is standing with the pole in both hands the way I showed him. I turn back towards the door in a pure rage with gritted teeth I bolt forward, and using my momentum and with as much power as I can, I place a kick as near to the lock as possible. It bursts open and Murdo jumps to his feet. Before he gets a chance to do anything I strike him on the side of the head with the baseball bat. It splits his head open and the blood splatters across the room onto the walls. He falls to the floor and I drop the bat and dive on top of him throwing punch after punch to his face, which is now also covered in blood. I grab him by the throat and nut him several times.

"LOOK AT ME...LOOK AT ME" I shout, tightening my grip around his throat.

"WHY DID YOU DO IT?...WHY DID YOU KILL GAZ, EH?...ALL THIS OVER A FUCKING GIRL."

"WHAT ARE YE ON ABOOT?...EH NEVER KILLED GAZ." Murdo splutters back through broken teeth and a mouthful of blood.

"YOU KILLED HIM THINKING HE WAS ME."

"EH NEVER KILLED GAZ, EH SWEAR."

I stand up and pick up the bat again and start smashing it into any part of Murdo's body that's exposed as he curls up trying to protect himself. He stops moving and I stand and stare at his limp body curled up on the floor. I turn to see Kyle standing in the doorway with the pole by his side shaking with fear. I see his eyes widen and as I turn back I catch Murdo taking a swing at my leg. He has a blade in his hand and it cuts through my jeans and slices my calf. Before I get a chance to raise the bat he is on his feet with the blade in his hand. I swing the bat hitting his wrist but he doesn't drop the blade. He comes forward and I have no option but to drop the bat and grab his wrist to stop the blade from going near me. There is a struggle as I try to get the blade out of his hand and we both end up on the floor. He is on top of me and I way underestimated his strength as I struggle to push him off while keeping the blade away from me. I eventually prize it from his fingers and it slides across the floor. He gets to the bat before I get a chance to get up and as he swings it clips the top of my head sending me back to the floor. I look up as he holds the bat above my head with his face like a horror movie and one eye shut.

"Eh could assure ye, eh had nothing ta dae we Gaz's murder. Ye should have looked mare in the direction oh yer last we slapper, the ain wah asked me ta do ye in for her. And as for ye seeing Kelly, well, ye had it coming."

He goes to bring the bat down over my head and I am about to try and move out of the way when the bat stops in mid-air and Murdo falls to the floor with the pole sticking out of his back. Kyle stands rigid in the middle of the room. I stand up and pull the pole out of his back and he makes a low whimpering noise which to Kyle's relief he knows he hasn't killed him. I pick up the bat and grab Kyle's arm.

"Come on, we have got to get out of here."

I hobble to the door and turn to see Kyle repeatedly kicking Murdo in the groin.

"Kyle that's enough, let's go."

We get to the car and after wrapping the bat and pole back in to the bin liner Kyle gets into the passenger seat.

"I take it you want me to drive."

He doesn't answer but puts his trembling hands out in front of me. I drive off slowly back to my flat. Once inside I turn on the shower and strip off. When I pull my jeans down the cut is bleeding freely. I tear up a towel into lengths and use one of them to cover the cut. I tie it tightly to stop the bleeding until I have a shower. After washing off Mudro's blood I come out and put a fresh length of the towel over the cut.

"I think that needs stitched mate."

"Yeah I know but I will have to leave it for a few days. I can't exactly show up at the hospital can I?"

Kyle puts all the blood stained clothes in the bag with the weapons.

"I could really do with a smoke."

"I'll skin up now if you want" Kyle's says.

"No let's just get to yours and get this over with. Phone Mickey and tell him to meet us at yours."

We get down to the car accompanied with the bag of clothes and a cloth soaked in disinfectant and start to wipe all the places that I have touched with Murdo's blood. When we get to Kyle's, Mickey is already waiting, he is full of questions but neither of us answers him. Kyle walks into his house with Mickey following. I hang back and swap the bag over to my car. I enter Kyle's house and watch as he tries to skin up with his hands still shaking.

"Give it here, I'll do it, you go put the kettle on."

Kyle gets up and goes through to the kitchen and Mickey keeps at me asking what happened.

"Look Mickey, the less you know the better, just leave it okay"

I spark up the joint and have a few puffs before passing it to Mickey. Kyle comes through with the tea and the joint is passed again until it comes back to me. I have another smoke but I feel I can't relax with the evidence still in my car. I quickly drink my tea, make my excuses and leave. On the way home I drive by the docks and park up. I make sure no-one is around and take out the bag. I tie it tightly before throwing it as far as I can into the water.

Chapter 26

I really don't want to go to this today. I hate funerals and try to avoid going to them at all costs, but this is different. This is my best mate whom I have known since I was a kid. Kate phoned me the other day and asked which song I would like played for him. There's not going to be any prayers or hymns or any of that shit as Gaz hated religion. I know everyone else will pick all the sad songs but that's not how he would want remembered. He was so full of life all the time so I told her I wanted Slade's 'Cum on feel the noise.' This actually made her laugh down the phone and she understood straight away why I chose it. Well he always said he never understood why they had a minutes silence for people that had died. If it was him he would want as much noise as possible for a whole minute. He once said he would want everybody clapping and cheering to celebrate his life rather than mourn it. She also asked if I wanted to say a few words at the funeral. But I didn't think I would be up to it.

If I sit too long thinking about it, the guilt starts to get to me as I still feel it's my entire fault that he's gone. I look at Biscuit and sometimes wonder if he knows why Gaz's not here. I know it should have been me instead of him but I know that Gaz wouldn't want me to feel guilty. 'It's meh fate' he would say. 'What's meant for ye winna go past ye.' I smile as I think about him saying this. That's my buzzer. It must be Kyle to pick me up.

"Hello."

"Hi Shane"

Shit its Kelly. What the fuck will I do?

"Oh eh, hi come in." I push the button to open the door.

I walk out onto the landing and watch her coming up the stairs. She's all in black so I guess she is here for the funeral.

"I thought you were in Spain." She gives me a smile but it is not a happy smile, it is one of those forced sympathetic ones.

"I thought you might need some company. Do you mind if I come with you?"

"Don't be daft. Of course not" I put my arms around her.

"It's good to see you Shane."

We go back into the flat and Biscuit rushes over wagging his tail and lifts up his paws on to her.

"I'm sorry about Gaz."

"How did you find out?"

"A friend called me."

I could probably ask her a hundred questions right now but I am so happy to see her that I don't want to scare her away so I play it cool.

"Is that the only reason you're back?"

"I was intending to come back to see you. It's just a bit sooner than I had planned. I know we have a lot of things to talk about and you probably have a million questions for me but I think its best we wait until after the funeral."

"Okay sure, but just so that you know. I am really happy to see you."

"I know."

"I was supposed to be getting picked up from Kyle as I'm taking Biscuit with me. Do you want to take us in your car instead?"

"Yeah okay, wait, why are you taking Biscuit?"

"I think Gaz would appreciate it."

"Will he be allowed in?"

"I don't care, he's coming."

I phone Kyle and tell him not to pick me up but to meet me outside as I will need his help to sneak Biscuit in.

We arrive at the crematorium and there is a large queue outside. Kyle sees us and comes over with Mickey and Joey. Jamie is here too but is up at the front with my mother. He is still on some serious pain killers to help him move about. I pick Biscuit up and we all huddle together to hide him as we all walk towards the door. There are a few funny looks from people but I hear the whispers behind me commenting that it's Gaz's dog. We find a space at the side to stand as all the seats are taken. Kate told me there would be a seat kept at the front for me with them but I told her I was sneaking in Biscuit so I would be best to stand at the side. She laughed and cried at the same time. We find a space in amongst the packed room and I put Biscuit down on the ground. A strange looking guy stands up on the platform next to the microphone and explains to everyone that this is not a service but a gathering to celebrate the life of

Gaz as he wasn't religious. Too fucking right he wasn't religious. If anyone brought up religion Gaz would be the first person to join in on the conversation and get himself all worked up. 'How can they justify saying they are men oh god when their ain priests use their position ta tamper we ah they wee alter boys. Every other week there is a story aboot abuse or some sort oh preacher embezzling money fae some pair cunt. And what aboot the preacher in America wha set up cameras in his neighbours' hoose and was watching them and their bairns get the toilet and stuff. Then you have ah the other religious cunts abroad blowing things up and killing hundreds oh innocent people and they have got the hard neck ta say it's for god. What a load oh shite. And dinna get me started on them fucking Rangers and Celtic cunts wah sing ah them religious sangs at the game. They dinna even ken what they're on aboot. Gaz would go on for hours about all that. Kate would tell him stories about his great granny, who was brought up by the nuns and how wicked they were to her. These were people who were supposed to be doing the work of god but all they really did was use it as an excuse to bully and beat up kids that were in their care. These stories were obviously passed down through the years and Gaz would fill our heads with them.

The strange looking guy introduces Danny who says loads of funny things that give me a massive lump in my throat. He mentions his daughter dying really young which left him and Kate to bring up Gaz. No mention of his dad though, which makes me wonder if he is here. Danny introduces a song that he says reminds both him and Kate of Gaz. Perfect Day. The song kicks in for about thirty seconds and people are bursting into tears. I feel close to tears myself and I am glad I chose not to go up and say anything as I don't think the words would come out. The song finishes and then the strange looking guy introduces me, Jamie, Kyle, Mickey and Joey.

"These people have been friends of Gaz for many years and have written something for me to read out to you."

I actually wrote it myself and read it to the guys before submitting it to Kate.

"If Guz was here today to see us with tears in our eyes feeling sad that he's gone he would say 'look at you, greeting like a big poof'."

The crowd laughs at this as it sounds so funny hearing this scary looking guy say our speech.

"If anyone knew Gaz, they would know Biscuit and know how much he meant to him. It was his 'bairn' as he would put it and if anyone should remember anything about Gaz they should picture him with Biscuit. We want you to remember him as we have always known him, loud, funny and the most genuine person any friend could have. The song that we have picked sums up the way in which we want to remember him."

There is a short silence of a few seconds and Kelly looks at me with tears in her eyes until Slade's 'Come on feel the noise' kicks in. Her face breaks into a smile and she puts her arms around me. I look around and can see a smile on so many people's faces. Before the song finishes I head towards the exit door with Kelly's hand gripping mines tightly. There is another strange looking guy guarding the door but I nod in the direction of Biscuit and he quietly opens it and lets us out.

"Is everything okay?" Kelly asks as we walk towards her car.

"Yeah, I just don't like funerals and I know the other song that is about to be played, it is sad and depressing and that's not how I want to remember Gaz."

Kelly comes closer and puts her arms around me.

"Who wrote the speech?"

"Me."

"I'm sure Gaz would have loved it."

I feel a lump in my throat again and the tears trickle down my cheek.

"Hey it's okay." Kelly hugs me tighter.

"No. No it's not."

"What do you mean?"

"Gaz...Gaz was killed for me."

"I don't understand."

"Someone thought that Gaz was me. That why he was stabbed."

"What. Why?"

"I don't know, look can we take off? I really don't want to see everyone when they come out of there."

"Yeah of course"

I open the door to my flat and Biscuit goes rushing past me sniffing around the place. It makes me feel sad when I see him wagging his tail. He is obviously looking for Gaz and wondering what's going on. He jumps up on the sofa and makes himself at home. Kelly sits next to him, patting his head. I make us both a cup of coffee and we go out onto the balcony to catch the sun as it breaks through the clouds. We sit for a while as I try to explain what's happened the last few weeks that she's been away. I tell her about going after Dek but I leave out the part where it might not have been him after all.

"Oh my god, I can't believe all this. When I heard Gaz had been killed I never imagined it was to do with any of this. I thought it was a random fight, like he was in the wrong place at the wrong time or something. I hope you know this is never going to stop until one of you is killed."

"I know. I should have ended it last night when I had the chance."

"I'm glad you didn't."

"Why?"

"Because that would make you just as bad as him and I know you are better than that Shane."

I guess she doesn't know me at all. There is a long uncomfortable silence. One of those where no-matter what you want to say, you know it will be the wrong thing.

"I left here so that nothing would happen and nobody would get hurt, but he goes after you anyway. You're best friend is killed. Your brother is nearly killed and it's my fault."

I take hold of Kelly's hands and look her into her eyes, which are now filling up with tears. I know straight away before I open my mouth that I am about to tell her a load of shit but...ah well, here goes.

"Kelly this has nothing to do with you, if it wasn't Gaz it would have been someone else."

"What do you mean?"

"Dek was a maniac. He is the type of person who looks for excuses to cause trouble. I had a few run-ins with him before I even met you. He is a nut job. It's not your fault. This could have happened even if we never met."

She has her arms around me and is crying into my shoulder.

"Shane, I have something to tell you."

"What?"

"I'm pregnant."

Wow, I did not see that coming. I move from her and again I feel one of those uncomfortable silences.

"Say something."

"How, when did you?"

"I found out the first day that you were at T in the park."

"Why didn't you tell me the next day?"

"I was going to tell you when we got home but then all that came out about Dek, I was too upset and couldn't think straight so I took off to get my head sorted out."

"You could have told me before now."

"And what would you have done? I had to figure out for myself what I wanted. I was planning to come back in a few weeks to tell you but because of all this I thought I'd better do it now."

"I don't know what to say."

"Well I need to know if you want to be with me."

"Of course, I have thought about you nonstop since you left."

"I was hoping you would feel like that, as there is something else."

"I'm listening."

"I want you to come and live with me in Spain. I don't want to bring my child up here."

"What? You're joking."

She doesn't answer but her expression says it all. There is another long silence, but there are so many thoughts going through my head right now the silence is welcomed so that I can let everything sink in.

"Do you know what you're asking me to do?"

"You could give it a try, if you don't like it you could always come back."

"But I have my friends and..."

"...I know, you told me all this before and I know it's asking a lot of you but I don't want my baby growing up here. You can rent your flat out for a while. It will be here if you decide to come back. Shane I don't want anything to happen to you, I don't want my baby growing up without a father."

"I know, it could turn out like me" I smile.

"We would have our own place to live. My dad could give you a job. This is a great opportunity for you to get away from..."

"Okay." I cut her off before she finishes. "Okay. I'll do it" I smile again.

"You will."

"Yeah I'll give it a go"

"I thought it would have taken more persuasion than that."

"Yeah, you certainly picked the right time to ask me."

I have never really thought about leaving Dundee before, I mean everybody dreams about moving abroad and living in the sun but how many people actually just get up and do it. I know when you are young and you have your two week holiday with your mates. You save up for months and the minute you arrive you are on the piss. The first week is crazy, you go out and drink for Scotland and you meet all these knew people. There are maids cleaning up after you and barmen who laugh at your drunken abuse because your spending money in his pub and not forgetting you are getting your hole from all these young girls who are out for the same reason that you are. The idea comes into your head that you want to stay there and get a job, all in the space of a week. Then your money runs out, the barman doesn't laugh at you jokes anymore and he stops taking any of your shit. Your room is a tip because the maid hasn't been seen for a week and you can't stop scratching your balls because of some slapper you slept with the first night you arrived, the same one that you've been buying drinks for since you got there. The job situation doesn't look good either as it's either touting to get punters into the pubs and clubs or selling drugs to pay for some shit hole of a one bedroom flat that is actually sleeping four. Yeah the moving abroad thing is very short lived. But somehow I think this is a bit different. During one of our many heavy smoking sessions, where Gaz liked to have his little rant now and again. Someone had mentioned about moving abroad and I remember him being really stoned and saying 'Eh wouldna leave Dundee in a million years. Eh think Dundee is a fucking great place ta live. Eh always hear people moaning aboot how shite it is an how it's full oh junkies and ah that shite, but ye can go anywhar and you'll get that. The only thing bringing Dundee doon is they Labour cunts running the cooncil. If people open their eyes ta what they're ah aboot we could get them voted oot and maybe the toon would hae a fighting chance. They Labour cunts must be loaded we ah they back handers they must get fae punters wanting planning permission and what huv ye. The only back hander they would get fae me is across the fucking puss. And as for that fucking Lord Provost, the specky wee cunt. He would definitely get a good kicking, and any oh his off-spring before they got any ideas aboot replacing him.

I laugh to myself as I think about Gaz when he was stoned. He would be talking about something random and it would always lead to him bumping his gums about some other shit and then forgetting what he was talking about in the first place. I think this was because he knew so much about every-thing that he had too many thoughts going around in his head at once.

"Shane. What are you smiling at?"

"What? Oh I eh, was thinking about Gaz…Look I'm going to need a few weeks to get everything sorted out."

What I really mean is that I need time to get a hold of that fucking Lisa and find out what the hell is going on.

"Are you sure you want to do this?"

"Of course I'm sure. I have not stopped thinking about you since you left. Although I am still pissed off that you never called me." I make a face.

"Come on, let's go. I'll have to catch up with everyone after the funeral. I have to go and see Kate and Danny but please don't mention to anyone about what we have just talked about."

"Why? Don't you want them to know that you're running away with me?"

"No, and especially don't tell them you're pregnant."

We walk into the function suite where everyone has gathered after the funeral but I am only here to show face and make small talk. I introduce Kelly to my mother and leave them chatting as I go in search of Danny. I find him at the bar giving out some of his worldly advice.

"Hey old man" I nudge him.

"Eh'll fucking auld man ye"

"I need a word." I nod towards the front door.

"Eh, nae bather Shane" He follows me outside.

"What's up?"

"I just need a word with you on your own." I walk away from the door.

"Sounds serious"

"It's about Gaz"

"Eh'm listening"

"You know how Gaz was always up to dodgy shit."

"Sort of"

"Well for years I have been helping him put some of his money away."

"Fuck is that ah? Just keep it. He obviously trusted ye ta look eftir it. So he would have wanted ye ta keep it."

"You don't understand Danny. It's a lot of money."

"How much"

"I don't know exactly, I've never counted it. I just kept putting it away."

"Is it fae selling them fucking drugs?"

"Eh'm, Gaz never actually sold them Danny."

"What do ye mean? He always hud them on him. Eh assumed that was whar he got ah his money fae"

"Well yeah, but the stuff on him was never for sale that was just for us to take. The stuff he made money from he never really laid his hands on it."

"Eh dinna understand."

"Look no-one knew any of this except me. Gaz had a contact in Glasgow, a top guy. He also knew one of the top guys in Dundee, but he played them off each other for years. To the top guy in Glasgow, Gaz was the man and in Dundee he was just the go between. Most of the money he made he gave to me to put away for safe keeping."

"Whar is the money in some sort oh bank account?"

"Come on Danny, you knew Gaz better than that."

"Whar is it?"

"A security box, I could get it to you by tomorrow."

"Eh dinna want it."

"Then what am I going to do with it?"

"Spend it."

"Yeah right, look I will come up sometime tomorrow and I will speak to you when you're sober."

"Shane, whatever ye dae, dinna mention any oh this ta Kate."

"Don't be stupid. Why do you think I pulled you out here?"

"You're a good lad Shane." We walk back inside.

I work my way around the place and hear nearly the same sentence from everyone until I end up back to Kelly and my mother, who appears to be slightly more pissed than when I got here only twenty minutes ago. Kelly looks as though she is enjoying herself listening to embarrassing stories about me. I clock Jamie trying to work his way over to me and I can tell he is pissed but I manage to make a sharp exit with Kelly before he reaches me.

I spend the rest of the day chilling out with Kelly and we take Biscuit for a long walk, which keeps my mind off other things that are niggling away at me. This doesn't last long before I end up back at work and driving around trying to get a hold of Lisa. Late into the night as I sit in the taxi waiting on drunken customers, I end up in deep thought about everything that's happened. I start to feel sad as my thoughts move onto Gaz. This keeps me occupied as I stay on late until the shift change at the office but there is still no sign of her. I storm up to the office to make sure she's not there and I am met with a few blank faces staring up from the computer screens and phones. One guy who looks familiar to me, sits back in his chair and doesn't take his eyes off me until I walk back out of the office.

Kelly is up before me this morning and serves me coffee in bed. She's off to her friend's house to pick up her things and move them into mine. I gave her the spare key and told her to make herself at home, well for the time being anyway. At least she will be company for Biscuit so that I don't have to rush back from work to take him out.

Chapter 27

Over the last few days I have been banging in the hours to get some extra money before taking off. I have arranged a solicitor to have the flat rented out for me while I am away. I have no mortgage so at least I will have some money coming in every month.

I have checked the office everyday now and still no sign of Lisa. I am desperate to find out the truth so I drive to her flat and when I look up there is a light on. I park up and take the wheel brace out of the boot. I walk up her foul smelling stairs to her flat and put my ear to the door. I lift up the letter box but I can't hear any voices or movement. I take a few steps back and launch forward to kick the door in. It takes a few attempts but the lock eventually gives way. I am not too worried about the noise as in this block or even this whole area you can scream fire at the top of your voice and still no-one will come out. I walk in the flat and quickly scan the rooms. Nothing looks any different since I was last here. I run back down the stairs to the car and speed off feeling even more anxious to talk to her.

As I sit in the taxi on the Nethergate rank in the city center ready to move down to the next space, someone comes from behind and gets into the back of the car.

"Sorry mate, the car in front is next."

"Ah don't give a shit, ah want you tae drive me." The man says in his strong Glasgow accent. I look in my mirror to see his heavily scarred face and recognise him straight away. Screwface.

"Where do you want to go?"

"Ah don't care, just drive."

As I drive through the town he manoeuvres his position so that I can't see him in my mirror anymore. This makes me really edgy, I am ready to slam on the brakes and make a run for it.

"Ah'm an acquaintance aye your late friend" He says.

"Yeah I know."

"Look ah'm sorry tae hear about what happened, Ah know you two were really close."

"Yeah we were."

"He had a lot of respect for you. That's why ah came tae see you."

"Thanks, but I'm sure you didn't drive eighty miles just to tell me that."

"Aye your right and Gaz was right about you. No fuckin about, straight tae the point. Well first of all just so that you know, Dek worked for me."

"Murdo"

"Aye, and ah know that it was you that smashed him. Don't worry, ah know why, you think it was him that killed Gaz so ah understand. But ah'v spoke tae Dek and ah could assure ye it was nothing tae dae we him. Aye he told me he had it in for ye aboot his burd or something but that doesna interest me. Now that Gaz is gone and Dek, well Dek's fucked. Ah don't hae anybody tae dae mah drop offs. Well ah no ah can get loads ay people tae dae them but ah dinna hae anybody ah can trust."

He moves again so that I can see his scarred face in my mirror.

"No chance." I say.

"You won't even consider it? We could even negotiate a better price."

"I'm not interested."

"You would be in charge, run the whole show. Ye wouldna even hae tae touch anything as ye could pay people tae dae it for ye. You would be the man."

I think this guy has watched far too many gangster movies. If this was some punter that was into all that hard man shit they would fall for this line in a second. But I have been around long enough to know that these Weedgies talk like this all the time, I have heard their patter so much I can see right through it.

"There are plenty of people out there that would do it for you."

"Ah don't trust them, ah trusted Gaz, and he trusted you, which basically means ah'm now putting mah trust, in tae you."

"Sorry but it's just not for me."

As I reach the end of Riverside Drive, I turn around and head back towards the city centre.

"Ah'm sorry tae hear that. Ah can't say ah'm no disappointed. But if ye ever change yer mind just get in touch, ye know who ah ah'm. Oh, and you don't hae tae worry aboot Dek. He's been warned that there's tae be nae retaliation fae him, out ay respect for Gaz. No that he is capable ah doing anything now anyway."

I don't say anything as I drive back to the same rank from where this pointless journey started. As he gets out of the car he pats me on the shoulder.

"Take care."

He shuts the door and walks towards a shiny black car across the street with tinted windows. No retaliation, from Dek Murdo. I'm supposed to believe that from a jumped up drug dealing wide-o Glasgow gangster. He must think I'm zipped up the back. I'll be lucky if I don't end up with a face like his for turning down his offer.

I've been sent from Charleston to Lochee and it is a phone box job. The chances of the customer still being there are very slim. Pentland, here we are. It must be the phone box at the top of the hill. The customer is still here. I can't see his face but he signals to me that he will be out in a minute and he looks as though he's talking to someone on the phone. I lean over to change tracks on the CD player when I hear a loud crash. At first I think someone has bumped into my car but it's actually a brick that has been thrown through my back window. I see a guy running towards me from the front with a large baton. I quickly put the car in reverse and as I look back and start to move down the hill at a fast speed another car tears up the hill and into the back of me. There's no place to go, I have to get out of the car. The guy with the baton is still running towards me. I turn to run the other way but there is someone coming from each direction. They have their faces covered with scarves. As the guy running at me from down the hill gets closer his baton looks much like the others but has nails through it, these guys mean business. The guy from the phone box who now has his face covered is also running towards me with a large blade out in front of him. Before they all get too close and I am boxed in, I make a quick decision to go for the blade man. If he is swaying it out in front of him he certainly doesn't know how to use it. I run towards him and he is now holding the blade like out like it is a sword. I lunge forward with my arm reaching passed the blade. I push his wrist away from him, which exposes his whole body. I keep travelling forward smacking the palm of my hand into his face. This pushes him back onto his heals making him off balance. As I charge forward my shoulder hits him, putting him down. I turn to see the others running towards me so I stamp on the blade man's face before taking off further up the hill with the others in pursuit. After about twenty meters I hear shouting behind me and I turn to find they have given up the chase. One of them pulls out a bottle and I'm thinking, yeah right, as if they are going to reach me with that. But it's a petrol bomb. They light it and throw it in my car. I keep running up the hill which takes me to Balgay Park. I run through it until I get to the main road at the other side. I have no mobile as it was left in the car. I run until I reach the nearest shop and ask them to phone the police. Not that they will be much fucking help but I have to report it for insurance purposes otherwise I wouldn't even bother. I play the innocent victim and they tell me to stay where I am until they come for me. Give them there due, they turn up only minutes later and drive me back to my car, well what is left of it. As the flames and smoke are shooting out all around it, they tell me to wait in the back of the patrol car while they cordon off the area to keep the nosey punters at bay. The fire brigade arrives shortly after and quickly put it out. I am taken down to Bell Street station where I give a statement of what happened but I also have to endure all of the usual questions. Have you any idea who they were? Can you think of anyone who would want to do this? Blah blah blah. Just hurry up and give me a lift home you fucking tossers.

As soon as I am home I phone Kelly's mobile and she rushes back from her friend's house. I hold back the details but I do tell her that I was set up. I am more confused now as to who is behind all this. Only hours ago I had a top Glasgow gangster in the back of my car asking me to be his drug courier, I turn him down and then this happens. At the back of my mind I still think it's something to do with Murdo then I think about Lisa the psycho bitch and that maybe she is in on it too. This gives Kelly more reason for me to take off with her, as if I need any. She drives me up to the office as I explain that I will have to inform them of what's happened. I know the police will have already been up there but the real reason is that I am about to confront Lisa and find out the truth. Someone had to know where I was at that exact time and it had to have been someone at the office. If I storm in there and pull her up in front of everyone I will be able to tell by her reaction.

Kelly pulls up outside the office and I tell her I won't be long. She smiles at me as I shut the door and my mind changes so quickly it's scary. One minute I am blowing kisses to Kelly the next I am running up the stairs at the office working myself up into a rage. This is soon diminished as I reach the top of the stairs and look around to find that Lisa is not working. I was so sure that it was her who set me up. I receive a few dubious looks from the other office staff before the boss walks through from a side door.

"How are you? I have just had the police up here. They told me what happened."

"Yeah, I'm fine, just a little shaken up."

"We have checked the records on the computer and the call didn't come from the phone box, it was a mobile."

"What does that mean?"

"Well it was either random. The guys who did it were just out for anybody or someone was following you around and waited for you to enter that area before calling, in the hope that you would get the job. A car rammed into the back of you didn't it?"

"Yeah"

"Well it must have been following you."

"Or someone from this office sent me there on purpose" I say a bit louder as I look around at the faces trying to hide behind the screens.

"According to the computer your car was the second one to be sent to that phone box in the hour previous. The first was a no-job."

"A dry run for me"

The boss shrugs his shoulders "It's possible."

"What car did you send there before me? And who was it that took the call?" I say very seriously as several pairs of eyes peer at me above their screens.

"There are five people working in this office, it doesn't matter which one took the call, every computer has access to where your car is allocated. Shane I know you have been through a lot the last few weeks." He says lowering his voice.

"But you can't come up here and start pointing the finger at anyone. Come up and see me tomorrow and I will sort you out with another car to work. If you get your insurance sorted out and get another car on the road I will see about getting you another computer fitted." He says as he ushers me out of the office. I walk back down the stairs feeling very confused. I was sure that I was set up from Lisa. Kelly drives me back to the flat but I don't say much on the way as my head is going around in circles. I know some people would let something like this get to them and they would be thinking, what if those guys caught up with me? They could have killed me and they would probably be afraid to leave their house. I don't know why, I guess it's just my nature but all I want to do is find the fucker who is behind this and get them back. I feel more than ever now, that I should have finished off Murdo for good when I had the chance. Back in the flat I go to the kitchen to make a cup of tea when Kelly follows me in and hugs me really tight.

"Shane, why don't we leave now?" She has tears in her eyes.

"We will soon, I promise."

I hate seeing her upset. It makes me feel bad, and for her sake, I want to pack my bags and leave but I feel I would be running away from a problem that is going to follow me around. It doesn't matter where I go or for how long, it will always keep niggling away at me until I find out the truth.

"Let's just pack up and go."

"Kelly, I need a few more days to sort things out, is that okay."

She nods and hugs me tight again and I think to myself that this is going to be a very busy few days.

Chapter 28

I pay a visit to auld Wully that Gaz worked for and after a long discussion he agrees to give me his taxi for a few days. He told me to log on to the computer with his password. This will register that he is working and not me. That way, if it is someone at the office they will not know where I am. I also paid one of my neighbours from across the road from me to use their garage for a few days so that Kelly can hide her car. I don't actually need to work the next few days as it is not as if I need the money. The flat will pull in extra cash every month and I will now have the insurance money from my car to come as well. There is only one reason I am doing this and that is to try and find out who the hell is behind this.

Customer - # No. 1508

It is just my luck that I decide to work late and it is so fucking slow. I join the Mardi rank and no sooner have I worked my down the queue but the bouncers have thrown out a couple of drunks, who have now swaggered their way straight across to me. They are marines and are on their way back to Condor, their base in Arbroath. It is a good fare but the company is not. I have to listen to them as they rant and rave about why the bouncer threw them out of the club. The guy in the front is talking like he never did anything wrong but his friend is telling a different story. From what I have picked up it appears that the guy in the front was pestering some girl who happened to be with her boyfriend. The boyfriend apparently warned him but that wasn't a good enough rejection so he persisted until she had to physically push him away. He was not happy at this either so he decided to punch the boyfriend. The boyfriend retaliated by laying into him so his mate sitting in the back jumped in to help. Judging by the mess of their faces the boyfriend has given both of them a good go. Either that or it was the bouncer's gentle ways of persuasion to get them out of the club.

I try to make conversation as it's a long journey but it's like speaking to a brick wall. These guys don't have an opinion on anything, when I ask them a question it is like they are waiting on someone answering for them. These two guys are probably the pride of our nation, the ones who sign up willingly to fight for their country. They train all day in tactical warfare and are trusted with some of the most advanced weaponry known to man. These guys learn from day one how to follow rules and show respect. If they were ever captured they are trained to withstand brutal torture methods imposed on them. Some of them are sent into countries that they probably couldn't even spell and are ordered to kill people without even knowing why. These are brave men who are willing to go on the front line and have prepared themselves that there is a possibility they could be killed. Yet the minute they are let off their leash on the street the discipline and respect is thrown out of the window. I actually feel sorry on them. They are the type of people that the government preys on. They get them signed up when they are all young and stupid and full of life. They are so naïve that they are easily brainwashed into not asking questions. I can only imagine the conversation when they go to sign up.

'Why do you want to join the marines?'

'Eh, uh, to shoot guns.'

'Okay, you'll do.'

The ones that sign up that have any common sense are the ones who train in a certain field. They can't get an apprenticeship on the street so they do their time, learn a trade and get to fuck out. If a few years down the line, they happen to be called up to go to war such as Iraqi or Afghanistan, would they go? I highly doubt it. That is why the government preys on uneducated guys like these two numbskulls who are so gung ho they would never question orders. They would always obey and commit themselves to whatever they have been ordered to do, even if it meant taking the lives of hundreds of people. I drop off these couple of brainless twats and head back to Dundee.

***

I drive around for a while and find myself in the city centre again after dropping off a couple of fat mingers out to pull some unfortunate guy. I join the unofficial rank outside the Mardi nightclub once again. The other taxi drivers have gathered outside their cars to stand and chat. There is a car park opposite the rank which is part of a cheap supermarket. This is where a number of car enthusiasts gather every night to inspect each other's latest monstrosity that they have added to their heaps of shit. I sit in the car reading the local paper and try to comprehend the latest fuck ups Dundee Council has managed to achieve. I hear a lot of noise from the car park opposite as the young drivers wheel spin in and out of there. I watch as they lift their bonnets and rev their engines. At one point I think one of them is about to get his dick out and shoot his load as he gets a little over excited checking out someone's oversized shiny new alloys. Some of these cars have more patched up rust on them than paint and yet they spend more money on accessories than what the car is actually worth. By the sounds of it they purposefully drill holes in their exhausts to make them noisier, I guess these guys have never moved on from the lollypop stick in their bicycle wheel. The police drive past several times and appear to leave them to it. They are more interested in what the taxi drivers are doing than some fucking idiots' wheel spinning at dangerous speeds through the town. Now if I drive past them with a dodgy brake light I am stopped and put off the road for it. As the taxi driver two cars in front of me receives a fare, all the cars move up a space. The driver directly in front of me has no-one to talk to now but I see him get out of his car and hover over towards my window. What the fuck does this prick want?

"Ahright mate, how is it going?"

"Not bad." I give him my fake smile as though I feel privileged that he has come over to talk to me. I really wish he would fuck off and find someone else to listen to his shite.

"What aboot they Mercedes cars eh?"

"What about them?" I plead ignorant. I know exactly where this is going. It's all these fucking drivers ever talk about. It's a new taxi company that's started up and they're not happy about it. With their competitive prices and top of the range cars they are gaining a lot of respective customers.

"They Private Hire Cabs, they were only meant ta be opening up as executive travel for business men and the like but now they're picking up anybody. As if it's no hard enough ta earn a living withoot them."

He is obviously looking for me to be sympathetic but I really couldn't give a shit. I don't say anything and nod my head in agreement hoping he will say his piece and fuck off back to his car, but no, he continues his little rant.

"Eh'v heard that he's awa ta advertise for drivers in the paper and has put an advert up in the brew. He's actually offering ta put them through their taxi tests."

"Really, what's wrong with that? I think that's a great idea."

He looks at me like I have just called his mother a whore or something.

"Eh well you'll no be saying that when they're taking ah the work and yer no making any money."

"What is it with you cunts? You moan about people scrounging benefits and being idle but when someone comes up with a good idea to get people off their arses and back to work you're the first people to criticise it. As far as I am concerned there is enough work for everyone to go around. Your problem is that you've had it easy for too fucking long and now you have a bit of competition you have to go out and work for your money."

This new firm that's started is run by a guy named Ray. I have heard his name many times when I was growing up. He has a hard reputation and the impression I get from drivers is that it's not the new firm that is the problem but that he is behind it. The company has a large fleet of brand new Mercedes saloon cars and the drivers are kitted out in shirts, ties and waistcoats. They look really professional compared to some scruffy smelly old man who has his large gut hanging out over his trousers and his 'bricky bum' on show.

"Their drivers are ah bloody scabs, taking ah oor joabs."

This statement sounds too well rehearsed, which makes me think he has said this too many times or he has heard so many other drivers say it and has waited on his chance to use it.

"Well I'll tell you what pal, if this firm had come along a few years earlier, I would have been working for them too. I used to work in a shit hole of a factory for minimum wage where I couldn't even go for a piss without some weedy little man shouting at me for taking too long. So if you are trying to turn me against these drivers, who in my opinion saw an opportunity to better themselves by driving people around all day in a brand new Mercedes, then you have got a long way to go."

The guy storms off with his head down marching towards his car.

"Hey don't go, I'm finished yet, you fucking tosser" I shout out of the window.

I have heard so many rumours about this Ray and his new taxi firm and most of them are probably started by these stupid fucking drivers. If this Ray has any ambitions of taking over the taxi business in Dundee, good luck to him. It would definitely take someone with a lot of backing and a hell of a lot of brown envelopes placed into the pockets of the right councilors. Actually with the reputation of Dundee Council, I don't think it would take too many envelopes.

It is four in the morning and the town has cleared except from a few stragglers. I turn off the computer and head up to the office. I park in between two other cars where I have a good view of the office doors. I tilt the seat back and wait. I was at Lisa's flat several times tonight but there was still no answer. After the last time I didn't think it would be a good idea if I hung around too long. I shouted through the letter box that I only wanted to talk but she was either not in or she wasn't answering to me. I wouldn't care if Dek Murdo answered the door and he ran out and kicked the shit out of me, at least I would know he was behind it.

There is a shift change at this time and I am hoping to try and catch her if she's away to start. I have had to stay out until now because if I went home and came out again Kelly would know that I was up to something. I have only sat here for about ten minutes but it feels like an hour. Several people go in and out but still no Lisa. Another car rips past me and up to the office doors. I recognise the driver from somewhere but he was too fast and it was too dark to get a good look at him. Another guy from the office comes out. It is the same guy with the distinguished features who gave me the stare when I was up there the other day. He has a bony face and a kind of aggressive look about him that seems very familiar. He walks around to the passenger side and when he opens the door the interior light comes on, Macintosh. It's fucking Macintosh and his son. They go to drive off when another taxi comes in and blocks the road. Lisa gets out, fuck. I can't jump out with those cunts there. She passes Macintosh's car and gives him a look of disgust. Shit, what the fuck is going on? The taxi reverses, giving Macintosh room to get out. He drives off with me not far behind, my heart racing. I follow them at a distance all the way to Lochee until they turn into the Eastwell cul de sac. This leaves me no choice but to keep driving. I park up at the next lay-by and walk back up the street. I enter the cul de sac and walk through looking for the car that I saw them in. I don't have to look too far. I walk back to Wully's taxi and looking around I realise that this is a five minute walk from the phone box where I was set up, coincidence?

I drive home feeling relieved, anxious, tired and shocked all at once. I curl up in bed with Kelly who is fast asleep with Biscuit lying like lord muck at the bottom of the bed. I lie for a long time waiting on everything going around in my head to settle down. I think back to when I smashed Macintosh, it was around the same time all this started. The run in I had with Murdo must have been a coincidence, ah fuck him, he had it coming.

Kelly lets me sleep late and when I eventually surface she has been busy all morning cleaning my flat and packing some of my things. We have decided to leave tomorrow morning and she has phoned up to put me on her insurance. The plan is to take turns and drive to Dover, catch the ferry to France and then drive onto Spain. I am only taking my clothes and some personal things, I will leave the keys with my mother who will pick up the TV and stereo and stuff. The rest has to stay as it will be rented out as a furnished flat. I want to tell Kelly about last night but I think it would be best if she didn't know as it would mean having to explain that I lied to her. It's at the back of my mind that I know I can't let him get away with it but I am leaving in less than twenty four hours which means something has to be done tonight.

After a cup of coffee handed to me with a large smile from Kelly I make a mental note of the things I have to do today. Kelly makes a comment that I appear a little anxious but this is explained away that I am excited about taking off with her. I don't like keeping this from her but the less people that know the better. As I leave the flat Kelly gives me a long kiss and a squeeze of the arse. I have Biscuit with me as Kate and Danny are going to take him. I struggle down the stairs with his food bowls and his basket, not that the wee bugger used it as he was always curled up in my fucking bed. Kelly was quite sad to see him go and as much as I would love to take him with us it's just not possible. On the way I stop off at the stash to pick up Gaz's money. It's been moved around over the years to different places but it's been in here the longest. There are all different sizes of these storage containers and I drive into the yard where the smallest ones are. I park right outside leaving Biscuit sitting in the front seat. I unlock the door to the nine by five feet container to find the plastic bags still stashed in the same place as I left them. I pick them up without even looking inside. I lock the door and hand the keys back into the security office where I am given back the deposit. Before I go to Danny's I pull up into a quiet side street and start counting the money. They are wrapped in thousand pound rolls and I count one hundred and fifteen rolls. Fuck, I never knew there was that much. I put it all back into the one bag and hurry over to Danny's.

"Biscuit" Kate shouts as she opens the door.

"I have his basket and stuff in the car. I'll go and get it."

I walk into the house and see that Biscuit has settled back into his own territory in no time, with his place on the sofa next to the window. He used to sit there all the time when Gaz was not in. For the first time in days I have felt the lump in my throat again thinking about Gaz as I know Biscuit must be missing him. He will probably sit there every day now waiting on Gaz coming home. I remember Gaz used to jump the fence from around the side of the house and sneak up to the window so that Biscuit couldn't see him. When he stuck his head up to the window it was so funny watching Biscuit bolt to the door. I know he's more at home here and Danny and Kate will more than keep him occupied but it still makes me feel sad. I explain to them that I am leaving for a while and Danny takes the piss that I am running off with a burd.

"Yeah but she's loaded though."

"Ah well Eh guess that's ah that matters then."

I look at Danny and nod at the front door to signal that I need to see him on his own. He walks me out and I hand him the bags of money and tell him to put it in a safe place as this is to make sure Biscuit is taken care of. Danny looks in the bags.

"Eh telt ye we dinna want it. You'll make better use oh it than we ever will."

"What if Biscuit ever gets sick, vets bills aren't cheap. You know Gaz would want him to have the best of care."

I walk away before he has a chance to force it back on me. I head straight across the road to my mothers, who, before I even get a chance to sit down, has the kettle on and is making me a cup of tea. Jerry is not in, thank fuck because I really couldn't be doing with him just now

"Where's Jamie?"

"I don't know he said he had to nip out and that he would be back later, you know what he's like, he's always up to some-thing."

"Eh, yeah"

"I saw you over the road, I thought you were keeping Biscuit?"

"I'm leaving mum."

"What do ye mean?" She gives me an unsure smile.

"I'm leaving, I'm moving abroad."

"When"

"Tomorrow"

"What? Why?"

"A lot of reasons actually"

"It's no with that girl from the funeral is it?"

"Yeah"

"It's about time you found a nice lassie."

"Mum..." I pause

"What? What is it?

"You're eh, going to be a granny."

"She's pregnant."

"Uh huh"

She doesn't say anything as she passes me the cup of tea and sits down.

"So where is it you are actually going?"

"I can't tell you, the less people that know the better."

"What about your flat, are you selling it?"

"I'll be renting it for a while, see how it goes."

"So this is you here to say cheerio."

"Sort of, I'll pop in before I leave tomorrow. I knew you would be on your own today so that's why I came. You know I can't talk to you when he's around."

She changes the subject quickly as usual, before I start ranting about how much of a wanker Jamie's dad is.

"So am I ever going to see this grandchild?"

"Of course, I'll be back to visit now and again."

I hear the front door open and Jamie comes in.

"Ahright, how's it going?"

"No bad." I gesture for him to head upstairs. I pick up the cup of tea and follow him upstairs to his room.

"I know who stabbed you."

"So do eh" Jamie says, smiling.

"How do you know?"

"Eh hae meh contacts" He says, quite smug like he's some sort of wide-o but I let it go.

"It wasn't Dek Murdo."

"Eh ken, but that didna stop you thinking that though did it?"

"How did you know I...Kyle told you."

"What? So you told Kyle before you told me." Jamie says angrily.

"What do you mean? Kyle was with me."

"So you went eftir Dek and took a wimp like Kyle we ye an never thought aboot asking me."

"You were just out of hospital."

"So"

"Wait a minute. What are you getting worked up about?"

"Nothing" Jamie says like a spoiled child going in the huff.

"Look, it's a guy named Macintosh and I'm going to get him tonight. Do you want to help me?"

"Eh ken wah he is. He's the son oh the guy you smashed a while back."

"How long have you known it was him?"

"Oh, quite recent like" His smug look filling his face

"I don't have my car anymore and I have to drop this taxi off on the way home. Macintosh finishes his shift about four and his old man picks him up. So if you be ready about half three I will pick you up in Kelly's car."

Jamie laughs "You just make sure you're ready."

I head back downstairs to say cheerio to my mum. I fucking hate Jamie when he's being like that, all arrogant and thinking he's some sort of big man. He reminds me of his old man and if he ever tries to get wide with me like Jerry did, I won't be slow in putting him in his place. Actually that reminds me, I have still got to pull him up about what Gaz told me about the girl in the tent at T in the park. I promised Gaz I wouldn't say anything but if it needs to be said, it will. I use my mother's phone to call Kelly to meet me at Wully's when I drop off his Taxi. I say cheerio to my mother and tell her that I will see her tomorrow. She has tears in her eyes so here's to what she will be like tomorrow.

Chapter 29

Jamie

Shane didna ken what ta say when eh telt him eh kent wah stabbed is. He thinks eh found oot fae Kyle but he's surely mistaken. Speaking aboot Kyle, eh need somebody we a half decent car. That heap oh shite that Shane's burd has is nae good, there's a chance it could brake doon and thats the last thing eh need. Eh dinna ken what Shane's plans for the night were but he's gonna be well fuckin happy when eh phone him later on the night.

"Eh Kyle, is that you?"

"Yeah, who is this?"

"It's Jamie. Eh need a favour the night."

"I'm listening."

Too fuckin right you're listening, you nonce. In a wee while eh'm gonna be the fucking man and they'll ah be listening ta me.

"Eh need somebody we a car."

"Sounds familiar, what time?"

"Late, probably early hours mate."

"No problem. Just give me a phone and I'll pick you up."

"Cheers."

Too fuckin right you'll pick me up. Fae meh good source, eh ken that Macintosh is finishing an hour early on Sunday and he's no getting picked up fae his old man. He has the car because his old man goes on the piss on a Sunday. But eh'm no interested in his auld man. Eh only want him.

There's Kyle now, bang on time. He fucking kens better.

"Right what's the plan?"

"Drive me up ta the taxi office but dinna go in, just sit aroond the corner fae it."

"And then what?"

"Just fucking wait and see."

We sit for a wee while but as soon as eh see that car coming roond the corner we the flat tyre meh eyes light up.

"Right follow that car but keep yer distance cause we'll hae ta pull in quick when it stops."

The car starts ta slow doon and then pulls over ta the side oh the road.

"Right pull in now and kill the lights."

The guy gets oot and goes aroond ta the passenger side. He opens the boot and taks oot the spare. He's bending doon ta tak aff the punctured wheel. Eh ken this is meh chance ta get him, but if eh dae it now it means eh'll huv ta change the wheel, fuck that, eh'll wait.

"Clever thinking oh is daeing the passenger wheel eh Kyle."

The new wheel is on and he's tightening up the bolts so eh get oot the car and run like fuck towards him we a steel bar hanging oot ta meh side. Eh get close ta him and swing the bar oot wide. As eh run past him eh smack him in the head as hard as eh could knocking him oot. Eh signal ta Kyle and he gets oot the car and comes over.

"Come on you fucking shift. Eh dinna want anybody ta see us."

We lift the cunt and put him in the boot. Eh tighten the rest oh the bolts on the wheel and jump in ta his car.

"Follow me Kyle."

"Where are you going?"

"Just fucking follow is. You'll find oot." Eh snap at the cunt.

Eh head for Shane's and phone his hoose phone on the way, the cunt better be fuckin ready.

"Yeah what is it?"

"We're on oor way. Get yer arse doon the stairs and we'll pick ye up."

"Who is on the way...?"

Eh hang up on him before he starts ah his questions. Eh drive up his street we ah the fancy expensive hooses. It'll no be lang before eh hae ain oh them. Eh thought he made his money buying an selling hooses but eftir ah that time, him and Gaz were selling gear and never even telt is. Eh always thought that Gaz was up ta no good but eh never thought in a million years that Shane was at it. Eh guess Shane was the main man as he's the ain we the expensive flat and the fancy car. But Gaz, well Gaz was always pleading poverty. Well eh'll show the cunt eh'm gonna be the man. That Glesgay cunt telt is how much money eh could be making. If eh get myself started up they'll see that eh'm no a cunt ta be fucked we. Shane is waiting at the corner oh his block and eh drive up beside him.

"What's going on?"

Eh get oot the car and open the boot just as Kyle pulls up behind is.

"Is that Macintosh?"

"Eh." Eh say we a big grin.

"How did you..."

"His old man wasna picking him up the night, he had the car at the office."

"I'll explain it ta ye on the way. Come on."

"Where are we going?"

"You'll find oot."

Eh close the boot and drive aff heading for Tempy Woods we Kyle still following us. Eh only need him so that eh could get a lift hame. Eh drive in as far as eh could so that naebody fae the main road could see us. As soon as Kyle parks and turns aff his lights, eh open the boot. But ta meh surprise Macintosh launches oot and takes aff. Shane sprints eftir him and punches him ta the groond. Eh catch up we them and Shane is on top oh him throwing punch eftir punch. He gets up and then eh start kicking him in the puss as he tries ta cover up. Eh look aroond ta see Kyle standing over him we the steel bar that eh used earlier. Eh'm quite shocked as eh didna think Kyle had it in him. Macintosh is screaming and yelping like a wounded animal until Kyle hits him in the head we the bar and he goes quiet.

"That's fir Gaz" He says as he turns and walks back towards the car. Eh gee him another kick in the puss but he doesna make a noise, no even a whimper.

"Is he dead?" Eh ask

"Don't think so."

Eh pull oot meh blade and walk towards him.

"What are you doing?"

"Awa ta finish him aff."

"Oh no you're not"

"Well here ye go. You dae it"

"Nobody's fucking doing it."

"What? So you're gonna let him aff we a hiding eftir stabbing me and killing Gaz, Yer best mate."

"We're not killing him and that's it Jamie."

"That fucking burd oh yours is making ye saft"

What is we him. Eh canna believe what eh'm hearing. For years when eh was growing up, ah eh ever heard was 'You're brother is fuckin mental' 'Naebody messes we your brother'. Eftir smashing Murdo eh thought he really is the fuckin man but now he canna even finish aff some piece oh shit that killed his best mate.

"Some fuckin mate your turning oot ta be."

Shane takes a couple oh steps towards is and smacks is in the mooth. Eh put the blade oot in front oh is and he steps back.

"What are you going to do? Stab me now, are you? Well...What are you waiting on?"

Kyle walks over fae the car we the bar still in his hand, looking like he's ready ta use it. Well if he wants some he'll fucking get it tae.

"Dae ye no realise that piece oh shit lying there tried ta kill you. It was you that he went ta stab, no Gaz and you're just gonna let him go."

"Jamie his time will come, believe me...But not like this."

Eh drap meh hand ta meh side we the blade in it and Shane walks towards the car. Fuck him. Eh dive forward and plunge Macintosh in the stomach. Eh pull oot the blade and plunge him again...and again...and again...and again, until eh feel myself being thrown onto meh back we the knife still in meh hand.

"What's wrong with you?"

Shane stands over me.

"Gaz always warned me about you, for years he said there was something not right about you. I always thought he was taking the piss, I always took your side and made excuses saying you were just young. We thought that letting you hang out with us that maybe you would change but after what he told me about you starting on that girl in the tent, I guess he was right all along."

"Fuck you. Ah they hidings you have given people over the years, you've got a fuckin hard neck."

"You just don't get it do you?"

"Get what?" He doesna answer. He walks over ta Macintosh and drags him towards his car.

"Help is then" He shouts.

Kyle walks towards him.

"Not you Kyle. I don't want you to get any blood on you."

"What are ye dein?" Eh ask.

"Cleaning up your fucking mess"

Chapter 30

I know I came out tonight to get Macintosh but I never intended on killing him. I know he killed Gaz and that he actually intended on killing me. Jamie is right about that but I just think this is all wrong. My plan was to give him a hiding and set him up to suffer for the rest of his life. If we leave him here there will be a massive murder enquiry and no doubt they will find some sort of evidence relating us to his murder so I will have to make this look like an accident. I get Jamie to help me put Macintosh into the back seat and I open the boot, shit no petrol can.

"Kyle you wouldn't happen to have a petrol can in your car would you?"

"Yeah why, what are you away to do Shane?"

"I told you, clean up his mess. Kyle, I need you to drive to the petrol station just outside Dundee, the one at the start of Invergowrie."

"Yeah, I know where it is."

"Fill up your petrol can and meet me and psycho-boy here at Emmock road."

"Where is that?"

"Trottick, the hill as you head up to the old Bentleys farm."

"Eh'll go we Kyle."

"Will you fuck, this is your mess. You're fucking driving this car."

Kyle takes off sharpish and Jamie drives us to Trottick with Macintosh lying curled up in the back seat. I didn't even check to see if he was still alive, I wouldn't think so after Jamie's onslaught. Jamie tries to speak on the way but he is told to shut his fucking trap and drive. I had it all planned out. Wait until Macintosh gets home, kick his door in and set about him and his old man. No sneaking about and jumping him on his own when his back is turned. Just a toe to toe in his own house and break their legs to make sure they can't walk for a while. Just as they get their plaster off I would arrange to do it again and again. Now due to this fucking idiot of a half-brother of mine I am now travelling in a car covered in blood with a suspected dead body in the back. Now I am on my way to try and make this all look like an accident. We arrive at Emmock road and Jamie pulls into the side with the lights off. We sit in silence but we don't have to wait long as Kyle's car pulls up behind us. I drive up the hill and Kyle follows behind me until I reach a place where there is a good stretch of straight road before it turns on a bend. We park up and I instruct Jamie to turn the car so that it faces back down the hill. Jamie helps me put Macintosh into the driver's seat while Kyle starts splashing the petrol all over the front and back seats. I strap Macintosh in with the seat belt and roll down the driver's window so that I can steer it from the outside. I turn the key to start the engine but leave it out of gear.

"Right start pushing"

We slowly push the car until it is in the middle of the road and the wheels are straightened up. As I jog along the side of the car I pull out Kyle's lighter and ignite a piece of paper that was lying around in the car, I throw it onto the back seat and within seconds the inside of the car is ablaze. The three of us push hard from the back and run as fast as we can until the car picks up speed down the hill. The car pulls away from us in a blaze as it heads towards the first bend. It veers off the road and into a tree with a loud crashing sound. We hurry back towards Kyle's car and I think to myself that I am glad I strapped Macintosh in because if his body came out during that crash and police saw the stab wounds, then all this would be for nothing.

We get in Kyle's car and I look back before we take off up the hill to see the smoke rising above the tall trees. We travel through several tight country roads that eventually lead us back into Dundee and to my mother's house. Kyle waits in the car while Jamie and I go in to change our clothes.

"Right Jamie, give me something to wear and put all your clothes into a plastic bag, the blade as well."

As we are getting changed Jerry comes barging into the bedroom clocking the blood stained clothes.

"What the fuck is going on? What the fuck have you done now? Where the fuck has all that blood came from?" He shouts in his English accent while looking at me in his menacing stare, a stare I have encountered many times over the years.

"I've been cleaning up your fucking sons mess. So if you don't want him ending up in jail I suggest you shut your puss and fuck off back to your bed."

And he does just that, he lowers his head and walks out without saying a word.

"Your boots as well"

"What?"

"Put your boots in the bag as well."

"But eh'v just bought them."

"I don't give a shit, they have blood on them."

"But they're meh brand new timberlands."

"Well you should have thought about that before you decided to turn into an evil bastard with that blade."

I put my trainers in the bag and borrow a pair of Jamie's, which are two sizes too big.

"I'll bring these back later"

I head out the door with the carrier bag over my shoulder to Kyle who is waiting impatiently in the car.

"Come on, what took ye?"

"Settle down mate, I had to get everything we had on."

"What aboot mine?"

"You weren't near him or touched him so you should be okay. Do you have any petrol left in that can?"

"A wee bit"

"Good, go back to the woods."

Kyle drives us back into Templeton woods. I get out and take off Kyle's car seat covers as they will also be covered in blood. I walk on my own, deep into the darkness to the same spot on the track that Jamie stabbed him. I dump the bag and the seat covers in the middle of the dirt track and pour what was left in the petrol can onto the clothes inside the bag. I light it up and watch it burst into flames. Walking back to the car I turn several times to see the flames settling down. All that will be left is the blade, but there will be no trace of anything on it. Kyle drops me off and I apologise for him being dragged into all this.

"It's no your fault. It's that fucking brother oh yours."

"Hey, half-brother, don't you forget...Half-brother."

"It doesna matter, he's still a fucking spacer and if it wasna for you eh would hate to see what he would turn oot like."

"I know. Kyle if he ever calls asking you to do anything for him again, do me a favour and tell him to fuck off. Even if it's only to give him a lift some place, just make your excuses."

"Don't worry."

"Listen Kyle you had probably be best giving the inside of this car a wipe down"

"I'll do it when I get home"

"Take care Kyle, I'll be in touch."

"Good luck mate."

I creep quietly back into the flat and have a quick shower before climbing into bed as I try hard not to wake up Kelly. I see the sun creeping through the curtains so I get my head down and try to get a few hours' sleep as it is going to be a long day tomorrow.

***

"Hey babe, time to get up." I hear Kelly say loudly and sounding quite excited.

"What time is it?"

"Nine o clock baby" She says as she climbs on top of me.

"I thought you wanted to leave earlier."

"I was but after you disappearing during the night I thought you needed a few extra hours sleep."

I look at her and feel quite guilty as I didn't think she heard me leave.

"I don't know what you were up to and I don't want to know, but I do want you to move your ass as I need some breakfast."

"Yes sir" I shout.

"It's yes mam" She says smiling.

I pack my bags into Kelly's car and lock up the flat. We head into the town and I pick up a newspaper before going to a café for a large greasy breakfast and some strong coffee. I scan the paper thinking that I will see news about Macintosh but as it only happened several hours ago I know I am being stupid. I drive to my mother's but tell Kelly to wait in the car.

"I will just be a minute" I say as I pick up a bag with Jamie's clothes and trainers.

Kelly blows me a kiss as I walk away.

I enter the kitchen.

"Mum"

"Shane, I thought ye hud left withoot saying cheerio."

"Don't be daft. Here, these are the keys to my flat. This is the list of things that has to stay, so you are welcome to the rest. This is the name of the solicitors to hand the keys into."

"So whar's Kelly?"

"She's out in the car."

"Why didn't you bring her in?"

"It was just a flying visit, we can't stay. Is Jamie in? I have some of his things here."

"He has his new girlfriend with him."

"What girlfriend?"

"I don't know. He's been seeing her for a few weeks now. She turns up here at the early hours of the morning."

"Oh well, I won't bother him then."

What a relief I don't have to go and talk to him. If I see him it will just bring back all the bad feeling of last night. My mother walks back out with me to the car. Kate and Danny are out in their garden with Biscuit and they let him out the gate when they see me, he pounds over with his tail whizzing around.

"You'd better look after my boy" My mother says to Kelly.

"Oh I'm sure I will manage."

I say my goodbyes and just as I am about to drive off Jamie comes out of the house in his boxer shorts.

"Shane." He signals me to come over.

I get out the car and walk to the gate. He puts his hand out for me to shake it.

"Good luck."

"Cheers."

"Whar is it yer going?"

"Just for a drive"

"Whar"

"Nowhere" I smirk. He is the last fucking person I want to know.

As I go to drive off for the second time I look back to give them a wave and see that Jamie is now joined by his new girlfriend...Lisa.

"Shit...You stupid bastard."

"What?" Kelly says.

"Oh no sorry, I'm speaking to Jamie."

"Somehow I don't think he heard you."

"Fuck it, it's his problem now. We're out of here" I smile.

About a mile down the road Kelly pulls out a carrier bag from under the seat and opens it.

"Wow. What's all this?" She pulls out some rolls of money.

"Where did you get that?"

"Danny gave it to me when you were in seeing your mum. He told me to hide it from you until we were on our way. He said it's your half and told me to buy the baby something nice."

"I can't believe him."

"Where is it from?"

"Gaz"

I smile fondly as we hit the main road on our journey to a new life and leave behind the memories of good friends, happy times and one loyal dog.

Printed in Great Britain
by Amazon

58826747R00129